John Mortimer is a playwright, novelist and former practising barrister. During the war he worked with the Crown Film Unit and published a number of novels before turning to the theatre with such plays as *The Dock Brief*, *The Wrong Side of the Park* and *A Voyage Round My Father*. He has written many film scripts, radio and television plays, including six plays on the life of Shakespeare, the Rumpole plays, which won him the British Academy Writer of the Year Award, and the adaptation of Evelyn Waugh's *Brideshead Revisited*. His translations of Feydeau have been performed at the National Theatre and are published in Penguin as *Three Boulevard Farces*.

Penguin publish his collections of stories: *Rumpole of the Bailey*, *The Trials of Rumpole*, *Rumpole's Return*, *Rumpole for the Defence*, *Rumpole and the Golden Thread*, *Rumpole's Last Case*, *Rumpole and the Age of Miracles*, *Rumpole à la Carte* and *Rumpole on Trial*, as well as *The First Rumpole Omnibus*, *The Second Rumpole Omnibus* and *The Best of Rumpole*. Penguin also publish two volumes of John Mortimer's plays, his acclaimed autobiography *Clinging to the Wreckage*, which won the *Yorkshire Post* Book of the Year Award, *In Character* and *Character Parts*, which contain interviews with some of the most famous men and women of our time, and his bestselling novels, *Charade*, *Like Men Betrayed*, *The Narrowing Stream*, *Paradise Postponed* and its sequel *Titmuss Regained* (which together have been published as *The Rapstone Chronicles*), *Summer's Lease* and *Dunster*. *Paradise Postponed*, *Summer's Lease*, *Titmuss Regained* and all the Rumpole books have been made into successful television series. John Mortimer lives with his wife and their two daughters in what was once his father's house in the Chilterns.

JOHN MORTIMER

UNDER THE HAMMER

PENGUIN BOOKS

PENGUIN BOOKS

Published by the Penguin Group
Penguin Books Ltd, 27 Wrights Lane, London w8 5tz, England
Penguin Books USA Inc., 375 Hudson Street, New York, New York 10014, USA
Penguin Books Australia Ltd, Ringwood, Victoria, Australia
Penguin Books Canada Ltd, 10 Alcorn Avenue, Toronto, Ontario, Canada m4v 3b2
Penguin Books (NZ) Ltd, 182–190 Wairau Road, Auckland 10, New Zealand

Penguin Books Ltd, Registered Offices: Harmondsworth, Middlesex, England

First published 1994
3 5 7 9 10 8 6 4 2

The moral right of the author has been asserted

Filmset by Datix International Limited, Bungay, Suffolk
Printed in England by Clays Ltd, St Ives plc
Set in 10/12 pt Monophoto Sabon

For Jacquie Davis

Contents

The Fatal Attribution

I could have painted pictures like that youth's
Ye praise so.

Robert Browning, 'Pictor Ignotus'

'Time's certainly kissed you, hasn't it, Sarah? About the only kisses you get nowadays. The cold lips of an old man, eh?'

The man who spoke was himself old, with a grey beard and a falling lock of grey hair. He might once have been handsome. He might have looked like everyone's romantic idea of an artist, although Peter Pomfret was never anything but a moderately successful picture restorer, living above his shop in a turning off Portobello Road. Now his cheeks were sunk, his eyes feverish; the bones of his naked arms, as he lay in bed yellowing with age like an old newspaper, seemed in danger of pushing through and breaking the skin. His voice, once resonantly seductive, was high and querulous. The woman he was insulting was thirty years younger, but she seemed also touched with age. Her hair, once blonde, was greying; she wore a longish skirt of some ethnic material, pink ankle socks and trainers. She stared at Peter Pomfret without emotion through small, round glasses.

Although he was speaking to her, he was looking at a picture propped up against the end of his bed, at an intricate pattern of white, marmoreal flesh against a rich blue background. In the centre of the composition a naked Venus knelt, a crown set back on her head, her delicate fingers holding an arrow. Behind her stood Father Time, also naked; one old hand was on her small, white breast, another held an hour-glass. There was also a weeping cherub and a monk praying, his eyes turned up to heaven. Peter Pomfret was looking at neither of these figures. He was staring at the figure of the beautiful young girl with the old man's hand on her breast. Then he winced and gave a cry as he felt the pain in his own chest.

'I thought you were dead, or at least fallen off that damn bicycle of yours!' He spoke to Sarah again without looking at her. 'It didn't occur to me that you'd met a lover. There's not too many men about with a thing about ankle socks worn with gym shoes. Well, where are they?'

'Your pills? I didn't get them.' Sarah Napper was unperturbed. 'It was closed. The chemist was closed.'

'For God's sake!' Pomfret turned and stared at her, a look full of contempt. 'There are hundreds of chemists.'

'Dr Hanley told you to go into hospital when the attack started. You know he did.' Sarah didn't move.

'Can't stand that fellow Hanley,' Pomfret grumbled. 'He asked me to call him Kevin. Furthermore, he carries an umbrella while wearing jeans. Can't be ordered around by that type of vulgarian.'

'He told you to go into hospital,' Sarah repeated.

'To be called Honeychile and blanket-bathed by some huge nurse named Lillybelle. What the hell do you take me for?'

'You'd be properly looked after.'

'Why should I be humiliated? When I've got you to humiliate?' But then he felt another stab of pain and called out, 'For God's sake! The chemist in Portobello

Road. Get on that bloody machine of yours and pedal for dear life.' And then, more faintly, he was pleading, 'Please, old girl. Shouldn't have said all that to you. Words run away with me. Shouldn't have said any of that. It was just my little joke.' Sarah Napper left him then. She went down to the shop below, to the back room which smelled of paint and linseed oil. She didn't look at the family portrait she had been cleaning. She went to a paint table and picked up the full bottle of pills she had collected from the chemist that morning. She put it carefully away, in the back of a drawer, and did her best to forget about it.

'And I have laboured somewhat in my time, And not been paid profusely,' says Andrea del Sarto, the contemporary of Michelangelo and Raphael, in Browning's poem about him. Some artists not only laboured greatly but weren't paid at all. At any rate, Van Gogh and Gauguin and del Sarto got no share of the huge prices eagerly given and taken for their works in Klinsky's, that world-famous auction house, where not only paintings and sculpture go under the hammer, but manuscripts, vintage cars, the contents of stately homes and antique golf-clubs. The little shop in which the first Emmanuel Klinsky used to sell dubious Italian masterpieces to the aristocracy, in the days of that well-known connoisseur and rake King George IV, has grown into a handsome pillared building conveniently near the Ritz. Long banners hang outside it, as they hung from the walls of medieval castles, and the name of Klinsky's, written in gold, flutters above the traffic. Similar banners, emblazoned with the same name, hang over buildings in New York, Paris, Rome and Tokyo. Art, created in poverty, is held in all these places to be a sign of wealth.

On the morning when the picture restorer, Peter Pomfret, desperate for his pills, was humiliating Sarah Napper whom he had once loved, a figure in black leathers came thundering up to Klinsky's on a Harley-Davidson and parked the machine in a small courtyard under a sign which read NO PUBLIC ACCESS. PARKING PLACE FOR THE CHAIRMAN OF KLINSKY'S ONLY. He parked broad side on, in a careless and daring manner. Then as his machine juddered to silence, he raised his helmet to reveal to the world the grizzled head and the usually sceptical features of Ben Glazier. Despite his casual parking he was not the Chairman; he was an expert who knew little about money but a great deal about painting. He was, as the Chairman often said with considerable irritation, 'far too old to behave like a Hell's Angel'. Such criticism didn't concern Ben at all. He started to unzip his leather jacket and, carrying his helmet under his arm like an old warrior, walked into Klinsky's auction house which, over the years, had become his home.

Inside Klinsky's marble entrance hall Lucy Starr, the young, resting actress who tended the reception counter, looked up from her copy of the *Stage* and said good morning. Ben smiled at her, as he did at young women, apart from the particular young woman for whom his feelings were too deep, and perhaps too complicated, to be frittered away in smiles. He didn't smile at Keith Shrimsley, the office manager, who was on his way to Accounts and asked, in the flat tones of an Estuary man, if Klinsky's was about to make a fortune out of the Raphael on sale that morning. 'It's a pity,' Ben told him, 'that old Raphael isn't around to take his cut.' Halfway up the stairs he stood, squashed against the wall, making way for another Venus, this time a statue modestly draped from the waist downwards, who was being carried by two sweating, blaspheming porters in green baize aprons. At the top of the stairs he turned towards a big doorway, from which he could hear chatter in various languages and the sounds of suppressed excitement, which meant that a sale was about to start. This was Ben's world and he went in to give a casual welcome to it.

It hadn't always been his world. Ben wasn't born into a house of great art; his mother liked pictures of weeping clowns and Asian beauties. Ben's father lost his job in Glasgow and came down to London to join the Police. He used to take the small Ben and his mother out for a walk every Sunday afternoon, down from the Police House in North London to Trafalgar Square, so the boy could feed the pigeons. Then they'd have tea at Lyons Corner House. One Sunday there was a thunderstorm, so they dived into the National Gallery for shelter. So far as Ben knew, his mother and father had never been in there before; but there he was, aged twelve, face to face with a serene, secretive, shy goddess who'd just exhausted Mars with love-making. It was a vision he never forgot.

It led him to get a job as an office boy in the National Gallery when he left school, to pick up knowledge whenever he could find it, until, more years ago than he cared to remember, he ended up at Klinsky's. In his day Ben had found a number of girls who looked as though they might have been painted by Botticelli and loved them, but they were inclined to leave him for men with far sexier bank accounts. Perhaps, after all, he didn't care enough for them. He certainly cared enough, probably too much for a man bumping his head against sixty to care for a woman only just thirty, for Maggie Perowne, head of Old Master Paintings, in charge of that day's auction and, incidentally, his boss. He saw her and worked with her every day, but as he came into the sale room, and she stood in her pulpit ready to start, he looked at her with some of the wonder of a boy of twelve suddenly confronted with the post-coital calm of Mars and the Goddess of Love. Then he pulled himself together and went to make sure that the Raphael portrait had been brought down safely.

Maggie Perowne may have looked calm but her mouth was dry and there was a gaping, breathless space where her stomach ought to have been. What if the punters sat in solemn silence, treating the treasures, as they were put on the easel, with complete contempt? It didn't happen, of course. The bids came swiftly and business was brisk enough – until she got to the Raphael.

It was a portrait of a young man, a wide-eyed, hopeful youth with a soft beard and a velvet cap. From the start, the bidding was sluggish. The line of glossy-haired, bright-eyed girls, the underpaid, flat-sharing daughters of well-off daddys in the City, who sat at the rank of telephones, tapping their white teeth with their pencils, found a strange lack of interest from Switzerland, Paris and Bonn. Roy Deracott, art dealer of Deracott's in Bond Street, a square, gravelly-voiced man whose head looked as though it had been subjected to some sort of compression, so that his mouth was extra wide and his forehead surprisingly low, saw all this and gave a low growl of contentment. He had started certain rumours, had a few discreet words in certain ears. 'Was the Raphael right?' he had been asked and answered that it was a fine piece of work certainly, an excellent nineteenth-century imitation; he'd heard there were signs of Prussian blue in the shadows, a colour not yet invented when Raphael was alive. The picture had been expected to make five million. It climbed painfully to one. At that point it stuck and, although Maggie played desperately for time by repeating, 'One million, I'm bid. One million pounds for it. One million pounds. Last warning,' as often as possible, she had no option but to knock it down to an elegant Nigerian at the back of the room who was buying, if the truth be told, on behalf of Roy Deracott.

At the end of that day Sarah Napper stood in the bedroom over the picture restorer's shop with Dr Hanley, who did, in fact, wear jeans while carrying a rolled umbrella that contracted like a telescope. The bed was empty and stripped of sheets and blankets. Peter Pomfret wasn't there, or indeed anywhere in this world; his soured, disappointed and cantankerous soul having been released from his body on the way to St Mary's Hospital, Paddington. Dr Hanley had found Sarah upstairs when he had called in to break the news to her. He saw that she had tidied the room, but there was still a half-empty bottle of whisky on the bedside table and an open bottle of pills which had spilled its contents on to the floor.

'I left them by his bed, Doctor. He must have forgotten to take them,' Sarah said, not for the first time.

'You told me that before. He either forgot or decided to rely on the whisky instead.'

'I was always afraid of this happening,' Sarah told him again. 'I shouldn't have left him alone up here. He promised me he'd take the pills. Didn't want me to fuss over him. You know what he was like.'

Dr Hanley spoke from bitter experience. 'I know very well. He was an old man who refused to be treated in hospital.'

'He was difficult in so many ways, but I did love him I suppose.'

'I'm sure you did all you could. You mustn't blame yourself for anything.' He spoke in the bright, matter-of-fact tones he always used to the bereaved, but Sarah didn't seem to be listening. She was looking at the end of the bed. There was nothing there now, but she was thinking of what she had, carefully wrapped up, in a cupboard in her workroom, and she thought of the kneeling, naked woman in the cold embraces of old Father Time.

'Only one million. For a Raphael? What did we do? Have it on special offer' Lord Holloway, Chairman of Klinsky's, still angry the day after the sale, presented an alarming colour scheme. His bald head turned a deeper shade of pink, his ginger moustache bristled, his blue eyes became watery, his voice rose plaintively so that he seemed more childish or much older than his middle age. He looked round his office, furnished with interesting antiques, at Ben Glazier, Maggie Perowne and Keith Shrimsley as though they were, jointly and severally, plotting against him. 'When I was in super-markets,' he told them, 'we prided ourselves on accurate pricing.'

It was a time in the free market economy when it was the fashion to put great organizations into the hands of those who had succeeded in quite other fields. So the head of prisons had been put in charge of a chain of hotels, and a successful man from computer games was in charge of prisons. A former editor of women's magazines administered the Health Service and Bernard Holloway, from Come Into The Garden Foods, had been thought to be the very chap to slim down Klinsky's and make sure that the pictures sold like oven-ready lasagne dinners. He came, sacked a number of the older retainers, and caused a good deal of fear and unhappiness without having much effect on the company's finances. However, he still boasted that he was going to drive Klinsky's to increase its market share. The presence on the staff of so many young women who had been to the best girls' schools seemed to cause him a mixture of confusion and delight, and compensation for his nagging anxiety in the treacherous and enigmatic world of high art.

'It reached its reserve – just,' Maggie said. 'The owner asked us to put a low reserve on it. When we got there, the bidding died. Nobody's fault.'

'If we can't sell a Raphael portrait properly, what can we sell?' Holloway was not to be comforted.

'Kylie Minogue's sequinned hot pants, apparently.' Ben diverted the Chairman's outrage. 'Aren't they going under the hammer next week?'

'Don't you knock that, Glazier. The pop department's showing us some remarkable figures. Aren't they, Shrimsley?'

'Basically they certainly are, Lord Chairman.' The toneless accountant's voice was properly servile. His Lordship rewarded him with a tight little smile and turned on Maggie again.

'Just remember in future, Klinsky's is not in the business of selling fakes.'

'Fakes?' Ben repeated the word in a voice of surprise and wonder. 'What's a fake exactly?'

'Your precious Raphael, perhaps?' Holloway persisted.

'In my opinion' – Ben did his best to sound judicious – 'it was either by Raphael or someone else with exactly the same name.'

'I take an extremely serious view . . .'

'That picture gave me a great deal of pleasure.'

'That's not the point.' Holloway feared that the grounds

for his protest were shifting dangerously beneath his feet.

'Pleasure's not the point?' Ben smiled tolerantly at the Chairman. 'My dear old chap, have you never got pleasure from a girlfriend faking her delight? Until you found out, that is?'

Lord Holloway considered this remark, decided his safest course was to ignore it and retreated to his old profession. 'At Come Into The Garden Foods we had a reputation for quality!'

'But you've got to understand' – Ben's patience was also wearing thin – 'we're not selling eggs. We're dealing in dreams, legends, carnal knowledge and religious aspirations. The beauty of youth and the sadness of old age. You can't price those things. The value of the work of art is just an idea in someone's head. Some people got a different idea. That was what Maggie was trying to tell you.'

'We're under considerable pressure to reduce staff,' Holloway said, doing his best to sound as though he regretted it. 'Isn't that the view of the accounts department, Shrimsley?'

'Basically, Lord Chairman,' Shrimsley was delighted to say, 'and, at the end of the day, it is.'

'So all jobs here are on trial, in a manner of speaking.' On which note the Chairman decided to close the meeting. 'Thank you both for coming. no doubt we've all got work to do.'

Ben got up with relief. He wanted to look at something real, like a picture, but at the door he turned to ask in all innocence, 'By the way, are you sure the Kylie Minogue item has been properly authenticated? Anyone can run up a pair of hot pants, you know. The point is, was Kylie ever *in* them?'

*

After her escape from the Lord Chairman's office, Maggie Perowne went for comfort to the wine department of Klinsky's to be cheered up by the man she had to admit, often with a sigh of despair, she loved. Or was it love? Did she only lust after Nick Roper whom Ben called a Hooray Henry, a public school playboy, an old Etonian champagne lout? Nick Roper was younger than Maggie, much taller, broader, a young man who was good at shooting things and wore outrageous braces to keep up his Savile Row trousers. Had the sexes been reversed he would have been, she thought, despite his size, her dolly bird, her little bit of fluff, her piece of crumpet, something to boast about to the chaps in the golf club.

She shuddered when she thought like that and was grateful she belonged to a more grown-up, a discreeter, sex. And yet she wondered why it was that she loved Ben Glazier, in her way, and had never been to bed with him. She wasn't sure she loved Nick, but often went to bed with him. As soon as she saw him, dark-haired, dark-eyed, standing in his shirt-sleeves sniffing a glass of the wine someone wanted to sell by auction, she knew exactly why that was.

'It's not been exactly the best morning of my life, Nick,' she told him. He smiled, looking at her with his head tilted back, as always.

'It's those pictures of yours. Bloody unreliable things. I don't honestly know what you see in them. Now, with a decent bottle of Latour '62, you know exactly where you are. This is a nose no one could possibly fake. You lose your job, Maggie, and you can come and help out in the wine department.'

'Take me to lunch, Nick.' She laid her hand flat on the chest of his striped shirt, looking up at the stiff white collar and his face smiling down at her. 'Can't do it!' he said.

'Somewhere quiet. You can cheer me up.'

'Sorry, darling. Lunch with Andrew at Brummel's. He's heard of some '48 clarets.' Nick put a small quantity of wine in his mouth and swirled it around.

'Couldn't I come?'

He moved away from her, spat out his taste of wine and said patiently, as though repeating some truth she should have learnt long ago, 'Not to Brummel's, darling. Girls not allowed.'

'I'm not a girl, for God's sake. I'm a woman!'

'We don't have them in Brummel's either,' Nick assured her and went to take the phone his secretary was holding out to him, among the bottle racks and maps of wine districts.

'Have a marvellously romantic lunch with Andrew in your club.'

'I'll try. Oh, and I do hope you solve your problems.'

'I'll never solve the biggest one.' Maggie picked up the bottle and poured herself a full glass of vintage Latour.

'What's that?' Without waiting for her answer, he started to talk into the telephone. All the same, she told him quietly, 'Fancying you. Cheers!'

She drained the glass at a gulp and moved to the door and left him, although he called after her in distress, 'Maggie . . . ! You've *drunk* the '62!'

Next door to Peter Pomfret's picture restorer's in the narrow street off the Portobello Road were unclean windows behind which piles of chairs, tables, birdcages, chipped jugs, damaged busts and grimy chandeliers with a few drops missing were piled unsteadily under a sign which read O.W.L. JOHNSON. HIGH-CLASS ANTIQUES AND BRIC-À-BRAC. COME AND TAKE A LOOK. BROWS-ERS WELCOME. In the doorway stood Owly Johnson in person, peering anxiously at the world through bottle-thick glasses and complaining in a worried whine to anyone who would bother to stop and listen. Around lunchtime he saw Sarah Napper push her bicycle out of Pomfret's and noticed that on the carrier she had tied a flat object, wrapped in brown paper. He didn't ask her what it was, being concerned with his own troubles.

'Had them in again last night, Sarah. Another break-in!'

Sarah reacted to this news not at all. She was busy bumping her bicycle off the pavement and mounting.

'Got my cow creamer and a couple of lovely decanters.' Owly's whine was lowered in volume. 'You hear anything in the night, did you?'

'No, nothing,' she called over her shoulder as she bicycled away, as fast as she could, in the direction of Ladbroke Grove. From there she turned up to Notting Hill Gate, along Bayswater Road, and came down Park Lane with her trainers and ankle socks circling wildly. She sped through the lights to find Piccadilly and a part of London where the bric-à-brac was cleaner, a great deal costlier, but not necessarily more valuable than it was round at Owly's.

Lucy Starr was once more reading the *Stage* when she looked up to see a flushed woman, out of breath, with wisps of hair straying from the comb at the back of her head, holding up a battered portfolio and saying, 'I brought these in because there's been a death in the family.'

'Oh, yes?' Lucy left the *Stage* reluctantly. 'Can I help?'

'I got left all these various bits and pieces in somebody's will.' Sarah was giggling nervously as she undid the bows on the portfolio. 'I just wondered if there was anything which might be of the slightest interest to Klinsky's?'

*

Ben Glazier came down the big staircase with his hackles still risen over an encounter with Shrimsley. He had been sitting in his office making notes on a possible Pontormo and listening to an Ella Fitzgerald tape. He was singing along with 'Every time we say goodbye, I seem to die a little', when Shrimsley burst in on him to remind him that his 'contraption' had reappeared, despite numerous warnings, in the Chairman's parking place, which, in Ben's view, was about the size of Fulham football ground and had ample room for a genuine Old Master motor bike as well as his Lordship's ostentatious white Roller. When the office manager said it must be removed immediately, Ben told him that was quite impossible as he was going out to lunch.

He was crossing the hallway and Lucy, who had been unable to find anyone in Old Master Paintings, was filling in time by telling Sarah Napper about the part she was up for at the Baptist's Head pub in Dalston. 'Interesting new writer. I play a social worker driven to madness by sexual harassment.' She spotted Ben and asked him to have a glance at the portfolio the lady had just brought in on her bike.

'How many strokes?' Ben showed an immediate interest. Sarah was puzzled and silent. 'Your bike?' Ben had the portfolio open and was leafing through pale representations of wild flowers, grazing sheep and sunsets. 'What stroke engine?'

'On my bike?' Sarah laughed in case he might have been joking. 'No, only pedals, I'm afraid. These little Victorian flower paintings are rather pretty, aren't they? Would they be of any interest to you?'

'I suppose they might be. If we happened to run a tea-shop. Go well with the scones and Dundee cake. Good grief!' He had just turned over a particularly unpleasant watercolour featuring a malevolent child, a kitten and a baby lamb, and there she was: Venus naked and kneeling with an old man's hand on her breast, and the sands of time running out.

'Where did this come from?'

'A very dear relative who died,' she answered. 'Do you like it at all? I've always found it rather creepy.'

'Would you let us keep it for a day or two? There are some other people I'd like to see it. Would you mind?'

'Why should I mind? You might find *someone* who likes it, I suppose. I mean it's not worth anything, is it?'

This was a question Ben wasn't prepared, at the moment, to answer. He asked Lucy Starr to get Sarah's address, give her a receipt and, entirely forgetting lunch, he picked up the unframed panel and felt the weight of it. The picture had been painted on slate, only one of the many unusual facts about it he would have to consider. Now, as he carried it carefully, almost reverently up to the main office of Old Master Paintings, he tried to suppress his excitement.

Maggie Perowne, Camilla Mounsey her personal assistant, and the secretaries were out at lunch. Ben was alone with Sarah Napper's offering. He leant it against a table leg with its back towards him. Then he ran his finger along a shelf of art books and pulled one out. It didn't take him long to find the colour reproduction he was looking for among the works of Agnolo di Cosimo known as Bronzino, the sixteenth-century Tuscan Mannerist. It was a picture Ben had admired almost as long as that of the goddess with exhausted Mars. It hangs in the National Gallery and is known simply but mysteriously as an allegory. The work seemed to be the same in both pictures: what the book called 'a cold, smooth quality in the painting of the flesh that makes it appear to have been carved from some precious stone' was also noticeable in Sarah Napper's offering. But there were important differences. In the National Gallery picture it was a curly redhead, an adolescent cupid, who caressed Venus's small and perfect breast. She had his arrow poised to stab his wing and so, perhaps, prevent his flight. Envy tore at his own hair, infuriated by the sight of young love. Pleasure had a honeycomb in one hand and the stinging end of its long tail in the other. Folly was a laughing child with a thorn in its foot, about to throw rose petals. Time's part in the proceedings was to hold back the dark cloak of night so Venus, Cupid and Folly could enjoy their brief hour in the sunlight. There were two masks in the corner of the National Gallery picture, but no hour-glass and no praying monk.

Ben was busy re-reading all he could find about Bronzino when Maggie, not in the best of tempers, came back from the lunch she hadn't enjoyed, alone with the *Evening Standard*, in the Italian café round the corner. 'What've you got there?' she asked when she saw the back of the picture propped up against the table leg. 'Not another of your great discoveries?'

'Or it could be something the Lord Chairman's auntie painted by numbers during a wet weekend in Weston-super-Mare,' Ben suggested and discovered how quickly Maggie's beguiling looks could become withering.

'To be honest I've had it up to here with your jokes.' she said. 'All that chatter about faked orgasms in the Chairman's office. Charming, that was!'

'The whole conversation was entirely pointless. What does my Lord Come-Into-The-Garden-Foods know about art?'

'He knows a good deal about paying our salaries.'

'He probably thinks Tintoretto is a colourful brand of Italian ice-cream.'

'He doesn't pretend to know much about art. He's a business man.'

'Botticelli biscuits. Michelangelo cupcakes. Chocolate-filled Leonardos. Slices of honey-cured Rembrandt. Masaccio with Come-Into-The-Garden Bolognese.' Ben was enjoying himself before he sprung the great surprise.

'Camilla thinks he's rather sexy.'

'Good grief! You don't, do you?'

'I can't see it myself.'

'I thought you might. You have such obscure objects of desire. That Hooray Henry in the booze department, for instance. How can you possibly explain that?'

'I sometimes wonder.' That was an answer for which he felt unreasonably grateful. He put the book of reproductions open on the table in front of her. 'Now here's a girl with an older man in the background.'

'The Bronzino Allegory, "Venus, Cupid, Folly and Time". It's in the National Gallery.'

'"A work of rebarbatively frigid eroticism",' Ben quoted the disapproving text. 'I've always liked it.'

'It's bloody marvellous. What about it?'

Ben picked up Sarah Napper's picture and put it on the table beside the book. 'Another version.'

Maggie couldn't help a quick intake of breath, but she was sceptical. 'The one Bronzino never painted?'

'I can't be quite sure he didn't.'

'We've got to be careful.' She picked up the picture and felt its weight. She seemed half afraid as she took it to the window, looking at it more closely. 'We can't take any more risks.'

'Of course not. Anyway, I know I was right about Raphael. Nothing wrong with it.'

Camilla Mounsey came back from lunch at that point, but they were too busy to notice her as she sat at her desk and summoned artistic information on to her screen.

'When did this come in?'

'Just now. It was brought to reception by a woman on a bicycle. I happened to be passing.'

'And you think you picked up a Bronzino?'

'What do you think? You see, Time's moved even nearer to Venus.' He looked at her, but couldn't be sure of her reaction.

'Did this woman on the bike make any claims for it?'

'None at all. She thought her tea-shop flower pieces far more attractive.'

'And you didn't tell her what you felt?'

'Astonishment, actually. Painted on slate, but the painting seems right. Flesh that looks as though it were carved out of jewels. No hesitation. Nothing fumbled. I felt astonished, also a bit alarmed.'

'Alarmed?'

'Yes, the fear of falling in love with something that might turn out to be a fake.'

'Falling in love?' Maggie frowned.

'With the picture, I mean,' he hastened to assure her.

'If it's right, it's enormously important. The Lord Chairman's going to be worried to death!'

'That's always a plus.'

'We'll have to tell this woman . . . I suppose she had a name?'

'And an address. She left it with Lucy.'

'Tell her we'll have to investigate everything. Extremely carefully.'

'Including her,' Ben agreed.

Some days after an unexpected and doubtful version of the Bronzino allegory was brought into Klinsky's by

Sarah Napper, a very elderly and rich Japanese buyer was helped out of his car and into a wheelchair to be transported into Deracott's Fine Art and upstairs into Roy Deracott's office. There he was pushed slowly and reverently up to a young man with a soft beard, a velvet cap on the back of his head, who was looking hopeful against a blue Italian sky. He also met an elegant Nigerian who smiled complacently. 'Let me introduce you to your Raphael, sir,' the gravel voice of Roy Deracott came from behind his chair. 'I'm afraid we had to pay a fair old price for it, but it's the genuine article. You have my word for it.'

The man who had felt most keenly the loss of the Raphael for what he regarded as a snip, the Lord Chairman, was watching anxiously as his chauffeur manoeuvred the milk-white Rolls out from the danger threatened by an antique Harley-Davidson, negligently parked. Beside him sat Camilla Mounsey, Maggie Perowne's PA, or Number Two as she liked to call herself, the product of Wycombe Abbey School and the British Institute in Florence, with a mummy who had studied graphic design and worked briefly in an advertising agency, and a daddy who was a name at Lloyd's. Camilla was determined to rise in the business, not least because, since the disasters at Lloyd's, the family had gone about in grim despair and her allowance had shrunk to mere pocket-money. In these times of difficulty she had become a close and, she fondly imagined, a secret personal friend of Bernard Holloway. She had the sort of fondness for him she had felt for an aged and permanently worried sheepdog of her father's which, as a child, she frequently embraced.

Embracing Bernard Holloway, she had decided some time ago, would have the added advantage of furthering her career at Klinsky's. She did this, thinking of the old family pet who smelled quite bearable when brought in from the rain.

'I've told Shrimsley to give Glazier a final warning. I shall not tolerate his arrogant parking habits much longer,' the Chairman said when his car had been extricated from the courtyard.

'That's the trouble with Ben and Maggie. You can tell they've been brought up without a good nanny to teach them manners,' Camilla told him.

'Is that right?' Holloway looked at her, deeply impressed, imagining the infant Camilla having her blonde hair brushed by a devoted woman in uniform.

'You can tell by the way Maggie behaves, she wasn't brought up with beautiful things. Her father was a commercial traveller, you know. He travelled in toiletries.' Camilla said the last word in an assumed cockney accent and between inverted commas.

'I never knew *that*.' Holloway, who had started life in food-packaging, managed to look shocked.

'Did her art history at Manchester,' Camilla went on remorselessly. 'You can say what you like about Manchester, but it certainly isn't Florence.'

'Of course not, Camilla. No one could say it was,' Bernard Holloway agreed. 'They both made a bad mistake over the Raphael affair.'

'Now they reckon they've got hold of a Bronzino,' Camilla told him, wide-eyed with astonishment. 'Some strange woman brought it on a bicycle. Of course, it's not for me to voice an opinion.'

'I'm always glad of your opinion, Camilla. You're my eyes and ears at Klinsky's.'

'So glad that we're going to lunch at the Ritz?' She was delighted. 'Oh, Bernard. Thank you!'

'Well, perhaps not the Ritz.' The Chairman looked nervous.

'All the years we've known each other, Bernard, and you've never sat me down to lunch at the Ritz. You've even given up promising!'

'I thought it might be more fun to go somewhere where they know us well.'

'And keep their mouths shut?' she was unkind enough to add.

'Exactly!' He was pleased that she had showed such delicate understanding of the situation. 'Somewhere discreet.'

'Like that poky little restaurant behind Victoria Station?' Camilla pursed her lips in distaste.

'It's good home-cooking. And we don't want a lot of people eyeing us up, do we?'

'Don't we? I know *you* don't.'

'Nothing wrong with O'Finnegan's is there?' he asked, almost threateningly.

'I suppose not.' Camilla thought about her career and forced a smile. 'So long as it's with *you*, Bernard.'

'Oh, I'll be there,' Lord Holloway promised her.

Along Piccadilly, up Park Lane and down the Bayswater Road to Notting Hill Gate, Ben rode his Harley-Davidson back the way Sarah had approached Klinsky's on her bike, happy in the knowledge that Maggie was behind him on the pillion, her hands on his waist, her protests at his playing the traffic lanes, and his speed when the road was clear, safely retained inside her helmet.

The address Sarah Napper had left with Lucy Starr turned out to be a newspaper shop with many mid-Eastern and far-Eastern newspapers in racks under the high shelf for *Busts and Bottoms*, *Vixen* and *Asian Babes*.

The soft-eyed Indian woman at the cigarette counter was anxious to help. Yes, Miss Napper sometimes had letters sent there. 'Accommodation address. We provide a service. May I ask why you want to know?'

'We're from Klinsky's football pools. She might have won something,' Ben told her.

'Do you happen to know Miss Napper?' Maggie was still recovering from the way they had zipped through the junk stalls and fruit barrows in the Portobello Road.

'Very nice lady who rides a bicycle. I often see her go into the old picture shop across the road. Had a good bit of luck, has she?'

If Sarah had been trying to conceal her address, it was a fairly ineffectual attempt. They were soon outside the late Peter Pomfret's shop which Ben viewed with some gloom, saying that picture restorers had been known to knock off the occasional Old Master when there was a lull in business. They were staring, discouraged, at the 'closed' notice hanging behind the glass door when Owly Johnson, who had been watching their arrival with considerable interest, darted out of his doorway and said that if they were looking for Sarah she was in there to his certain knowledge. 'It's unlocked. She's often unlocked when it says 'closed'. Foolish of her, really, with all the crime that we've got about.' So they pushed open the door which pinged as they went into the empty shop.

Sarah emerged from her workroom, peering at them through her small, round glasses and seeming annoyed by the interruption. They had come, Maggie said after she had made the introduction, about the picture Miss Napper brought in.

'It's not that naked woman being fondled by an old man, is it?' Sarah hunched her shoulders with a small shiver. 'I always thought that was rather spooky, although he liked it very much.'

'*He* liked it? Who was he, Miss Napper?' Ben was curious to know.

'My, my relative. Who left everything to me in his will.'

'Did he possess a name, this relative?'

'I don't think I should say at the moment.' Sarah seemed taken aback by the question. 'I'll ask my solicitor.'

'You told me your relative kept it in the back of a cupboard. Where was the cupboard?' Ben pursued his inquiries.

'Well, in his home. That's where it was.'

'And his home was where?'

'I don't know if I'm allowed to say.' Sarah smiled helplessly. 'You have to be so careful of the law, don't you?'

'Yes, Miss Napper,' Ben told her seriously. 'You have to be very careful indeed.'

'Do you honestly think it might be something really exciting?' Sarah turned to Maggie, as a way of escape from Ben's questions.

'I expect you know Bronzino's Allegory with Venus and Cupid. It's in the National Gallery?' Maggie asked her.

'Not particularly. I hardly get to galleries. We've been so busy here.'

'The picture you brought us bears a remarkable re-semblance –' Ben started off but Sarah interrupted him, suddenly breathless with excitement. 'To the Bronzino? *His* old picture? It couldn't possibly be . . . I mean, you think it might be' – by now she was gasping – 'by *Bronzino*?'

'We haven't made up our minds at all yet, Miss

Napper.' Maggie was cautious. 'We're going to think about it hard and get some more people's opinions.'

'And we'll need full details of its history,' Ben warned her. 'Its provenance. I'm sure you know the word. From you – or your solicitor, of course.'

'Oh, never mind about all that. Never mind about all these words. Can't you just look at it and decide what you feel?' Sarah came out from behind her counter then and went to Maggie, smiling and effusive. 'Thank you! Thank you so much for coming with this wonderful news! I really am most grateful. In fact . . . In fact, I'd like to give you something.' Now she was searching among the dusty pictures in the shop window and brought out a small canvas, an oil painting of a windmill against fleecy clouds in a blue sky. 'A little token of thanks for all your interest. It's not a Bronzino, I'm afraid. But it is an oil and a genuine Sarah Napper. I'll be very hurt indeed if you don't take it. Here. I'll put it in a bag for you.'

She found an old plastic bag from Tesco's. When it was wrapped up, Maggie took the picture and forced a smile. When she and Ben were mounting the motor bike, she asked him what he had made of Miss Sarah Napper. 'Why did she give us an accommodation address?' Ben asked. 'Because she didn't want us to know she was a picture restorer? Also she knows damn well where it came from. All that nonsense about the solicitor! Is she a restorer or a forger?'

'So far as I'm concerned she's only done one crime we can prove.'

'What?'

'Given me her ghastly picture. All right, back to the Wall of Death!' And Maggie put on her helmet.

Sarah Napper's discovery was propped on a chair in the main office of the Old Masters department. Ben Glazier sat opposite it, staring at it hard and dictating notes into a small machine. 'Painting on slate,' he said, 'is unusual for Bronzino. However, slate *was* used by Florentine painters of this period. Vasari deals with this method in his book on technique and recommends sliced Genoese paving-stones.' This was the scene which met Camilla's eyes as she came in from another lunch date, her make-up a little smudged and her balance on her high heels less certain than usual. She called across to Maggie, who was busy with a catalogue, in challenging tones, 'I know what you're going to say to me. You're going to say, "Had a good day at lunch, Camilla?"'

'Actually, I wasn't going to say anything of the sort.'

'We went to a rather dear little place behind Victoria Station,' Camilla told her. 'You should try it, Maggie. They specialize in Irish stew. As served to the genuine Irish.'

'I suppose if I wanted to forge a Bronzino, I'd paint it on slate . . . No need to fake wormholes in a wooden panel with a dentist's drill.' Ben stopped dictating and used a small magnifying glass to look carefully at the back of the slate.

'Is that your great find of the century?' Camilla tottered towards him, looking amused and unconvinced.

'There's something rather encouraging on the back here,' Ben called across to Maggie.

'A fossilized lump of Florentine sixteenth-century chewing-gum?' Camilla found her joke hilarious. Ben took a thin sheet of paper and a soft pencil and started to make a rubbing of the mark on the back of the slate. As he was doing this, Camilla was saying that she knew Maggie didn't approve of her coming back from lunch at three in the afternoon.

'I really didn't notice,' Maggie was rude enough to say.

'But I was doing important business for Klinsky's.' Camilla sounded very grand indeed. 'I'm not at liberty to tell you more about it, just at present.' With which Camilla wandered away to the Old Masters lavatory.

'It's here.' Ben looked at the pattern that now showed white against the black pencil marks. 'Something that'll give Miss Napper's picture an air of authenticity at least.'

'Don't tell Camilla,' Maggie warned him. 'She'll be terribly disappointed.'

Alone at last, Camilla wiped the tarnished mirror, pursed her lips and whispered seductively, 'Bernard! Why don't you ever show me off in public?'

Maggie's father had travelled in soap. He also sang ballads, accompanied himself on the piano and took her, from the age of five, once a week to the cinema. She drew well at school, decorated her bedroom with posters of exhibitions and got a scholarship to Manchester University. When she got a first in art history and wrote to Klinsky's, her mother looked at her sadly and asked why she didn't go for a job at the Nat West Bank and make something of herself. Now she was head of Old Master Paintings, and her mother, now widowed, would shake her head sadly and say that if only Maggie had found a nice niche at the bank she might have been married by now, like her sister.

Maggie's flat in Belsize Park showed what she sometimes regretted, that she had visual taste in the way that some people are born with perfect pitch, or a talent for higher mathematics. At times she longed to introduce a real piece of kitsch: a pink glass bowl full of plastic fruit, gilded cherubs to hold back the curtains, a pair of red-faced cardinals drinking port, a cigarette box decorated with nuns, which played 'The Sound of Music' when you opened it. But she was physically incapable of living with such things. In her living-room there was a big white sofa and chairs, a dining-table set for two with art nouveau candlesticks, bookshelves and a disc-player now discoursing a Haydn quartet. She couldn't, of course, afford any of the Old Masters she dealt in, but she'd saved much of her Klinsky's salary, and a few lucky commissions, and bought her own treasures: a Léger lithograph, some Henry Moore prints signed by the artist, a John drawing of a long-legged, standing nude, a small, much-prized Bonnard etching and a small bronze of a horse and rider by Liz Frink. Over the fireplace hung her prized possession, a glowing painting of a naked girl curled upon a sofa by Matthew Smith. Among these possessions, Maggie, wearing a silk shirt and black trousers, called to the man in the kitchen who was opening and banging doors. 'Nick, darling, what the hell are you doing?'

'Just getting the Bolly out of the fridge. Andrew gave me a couple of cases. Tickled pink by the price I got for his slightly iffy Pichon-Longueville.'

When he had found two tall thin glasses, Nick Roper threw the wire and gold paper of the bottle at the tidy-bin, which was being held open by a small oil painting. He pulled it out and saw a recognizable windmill against fleecy clouds. He brushed off a few tea leaves and a couple of potato peelings, and put it on the drinks tray which he carried into the living-room.

'What's that?' He asked for Maggie's expertise. 'I found it in the rubbish bin.'

'It's a picture someone gave me. And,' she had to admit, 'I couldn't think of anywhere else to put it.' Nick was laughing at her as he propped the picture up on the mantelpiece, stood back and asked what was so terrible about it.

'It just doesn't go with anything else I've got,' she told him.

'It looks all right to me.'

'It's well drawn. It's accurate. It looks like what it's meant to look like.'

'That's more than you can say for some of the stuff you've got plastering your walls. These women, for instance.' (Léger's solid girls were linked closely to wheels and girders.) 'They look like pieces of machinery.'

'I thought that would rather appeal to you.' Maggie was angrily protective of her Léger.

'Oh, God!' Nick passed her a glass of champagne. 'We're going to have all this female stuff again, are we? We're not going to quarrel?'

'No. No, of course not. We're going to have a wonderful dinner.' She raised her glass to Nick. 'Cheers, darling.'

'What's wrong with that picture?' He had wandered to the mantelpiece and was making a close study of Sarah Napper's windmill.

'I'll tell you.' She stood with an arm round his shoulder. 'It's got no life. It's got no energy. It's got no opinion of its own. It's got absolutely no personality. Anyone could have done it.'

'It's signed Sarah Napper.' He examined the canvas as though it were an Old Master.

'Oh, yes. It's authentic. I can't think why anyone should bother to forge a Sarah Napper.'

'I just think a lot of people would like it.' He broke away from her, his voice rising in protest. 'You're so bloody *patronizing*, Maggie. You think the only thing that's any good is what *you* like.'

'It's because I like what's original. What's done with passion. What has something to say. What's done as well as it can be done. On top of that I like what's *true*!'

He looked at her and smiled. 'Didn't you sell a phoney Raphael? That's what they're saying.'

'The Raphael was good!' Maggie protested. 'It was right! I swear to God it was right. I had no doubts about it. Not like this perhaps Bronzino.'

'Another iffy picture.' Nick's temper was restored and he was back in control, having, he thought, caught her out. He sat at the table, where the avocados were already halved and laid out on small, green plates. She sat opposite him, the candles flickered between them. 'Tell me all about it,' he said.

'It might be another version of the Bronzino Allegory in the National Gallery. And if it were . . .'

'Klinsky's would make a great load of dosh?' Nick got the point at once.

'And that extraordinary woman would be worth a fortune,' Maggie said.

'Which extraordinary woman?' He filled his mouth with avocado.

'The one who painted that windmill you're so fond of. That uninteresting artist, Miss Sarah Napper.'

'Oh, her. What does Ben think about this Bronzino business?'

'Secretly, I think he wants it to be right.'

There was a pause while Nick spooned out more fruit and swigged champagne. Then he said, more amused, 'Secretly, Ben wants a lot of things.'

'What's that meant to mean?' Maggie asked, although she knew the answer perfectly well.

'You, for instance. Not so secretly, he wants you. Poor old Ben, I do believe he's jealous of me.'

'That sounds appallingly self-satisfied, even for you.'

'Why? You don't mean I ought to be jealous of him?'

'I didn't say that.'

'You don't mean he's in with a chance? He doesn't think he might actually notch you up on his braces?'

'Your dinner-time chat, Nick! It's about as subtle as Sarah Napper's painting.'

'But tell me!' Everything she said seemed to make him more confident.

She thought about Ben and knew she would rather be talking to him. They would have been easier together, more alike. But then when dinner was over, she said, 'My feelings about Ben are something you couldn't possibly understand. So don't try. Change the subject.'

'God, you look sexy when you're cross!' He looked at her with admiration and she felt, as she saw his smile of triumph, near to despair about him.

> I could cry salty tears;
> Where have I been all these years?
> Little wow,
> Tell me now:
> How long has this been going on?

Ella on compact disc sang to Ben Glazier, alone in his flat, overlooking Bloomsbury Square, where he lived in a state of total muddle. Bits of statues, paintings, drawings, etchings and prints he'd picked up in the course of a lifetime were perched on unsteady towers of books erected on his table among half-empty coffee cups, a bottle of wine and a glass. The Bronzino book open at the Allegory was propped in front of him. Beside it was his tracing, the pale image of a stag over the letter S, scratched on the back of Sarah Napper's slate. Also open was another reference book, a work on collectors' marks, the signs and seals of ownership the old aristocratic punters used to stamp their titles on works of art. Ben was singing along with Ella as he turned the pages, looking for a stag mounted above an S. And then he was silent, and turned his attention once again to the naked, white Venus, fondled by a young lover, oblivious of time.

Maggie was completely happy. In bed Nick was silent, purposeful, pleased with his own performance, often unexpectedly thoughtful. Without his clothes on he seemed years younger, almost a boy who smelt of soap and the heat of a summer day. She was on top of him, melting into a state of unknowing, with pictures and the price of pictures quite forgotten, when the telephone rang and wouldn't stop ringing. 'If that's my mother ...' She dismounted reluctantly, rolled over on to her stomach, picked up the troublesome little instrument, gritted her teeth and muttered, 'Yes?'

'"Little wow, Tell me now:",' Ben started to sing down the phone.

'Oh, for God's sake, Ben. Do you know what time it is?'

'What the hell does time matter? I've been looking back down the centuries. Let me tell you, there's a collector's mark on the Napper Bronzino and I've identified it.'

'All right, tell me.' Maggie's world had come back to her. Nick sighed and lit a cigarette. Later she put down the telephone, rested her head on his chest and told him that the collector's mark seemed to be that of the Marquis of Saltery, whose descendant was alive and living in Saltery Hall, somewhere in Dorset. Ben wanted her to zip down there on the back of the dreaded Harley-Davidson.

'Do you smoke after sex?' Nick seemed to be totally uninterested in Ben's discovery.

'You know I've given it up.'

'No! What you're meant to say is, "I don't know. I've

never looked."' He laughed. She didn't, but moved even closer, her leg burrowing between his.

'You know what, Nick?' she told him. 'You're the only thing in this damned flat that isn't a result of my ghastly good taste.'

The door of Pomfret's shop pinged and Sarah came out of her workroom to meet Nick Roper, who leaned on her counter, exuding charm. He introduced himself and said that he had been deeply impressed by a painting she had done. 'A really smashing landscape with a windmill in it.'

'You saw my windmill picture?' Sarah's eyes, behind her round glasses, were startled.

'It was quite wonderful, Miss Napper. I'm a great admirer of your work.'

'I gave it to the head of Old Masters at Klinsky's.' Sarah was proud of the fact.

'A girlfriend of mine, as a matter of fact,' Nick confided in her. 'She didn't appreciate it, I'm afraid to say.'

'She didn't?' Sarah was amazed.

'Oh, she finds fault with everything,' he smiled, disarming her completely, 'particularly with me. Miss Napper, I'd like to talk to you about something.'

'Oh, yes?' She looked nervous, but Nick leaned even further over the counter in the most reassuring manner. 'I'd love you to paint another one. Specially for me. But not a word to Maggie Perowne. As I say, I don't think she understands your work.'

While Sarah was being expertly charmed by Nick Roper, the picture she'd brought into Klinsky's was being studied by an even greater expert than Ben on the later painters of the Italian Renaissance. Sir Hugo Mint, author, among other works, of *Bronzino and the Mannerist Tradition*, was white-haired, ramrod straight, pink-faced and could have been a retired general but for his fluttering fingers and caressing voice. He fitted an eyeglass carefully into his right eye and brought it very close to the slate. 'My dear Ben, where did this emerge from? This extraordinary catch?'

'A Miss Napper brought it in. Her solicitor told us it was left to her by a picture restorer called Peter Pomfret. She worked in his shop. I don't know what else she did for him.'

'Where did *he* get it?'

'Found it in the back of a junk shop in Rome. That's the story. Well, Hugo, what do you reckon?'

'In his *Lives of the Painters* Vasari wrote that the Allegory with Venus and Cupid was painted by Bronzino for the King of France ...' Hugo started as though giving a lecture and, when Ben told him that even he knew that, produced a note he'd made on a card pinched from the Garrick Club. 'But do you know that in a copy of the 1550 edition of Vasari, the one in the Vatican Library, there's a handwritten note in the margin, possibly by Monsignor Giorgio, which says ... Let me read it to you: "Some say Bronzino executed another, similar, allegory in which Venus is depicted in the embrace of Time. This second picture, however, cannot be found." So that's your picture, Ben. Turned up after all these years. Couldn't you manage a smile?'

But Ben still looked doubtful. 'I suppose if you wanted to forge a picture it might be sensible to try one that's been recorded as lost.'

'How many forgers know about that note in Vasari?'

'*You* know it.'

'You're not suggesting I'd be party to any sort of dishonesty?'

'Well,' Ben considered the matter carefully, 'you tell the customer exactly what he wants to hear. And all the auction houses love an expert who'll say the picture's right, so they keep on paying you profusely.'

Sir Hugo looked shocked, but then quite tenderly forgiving. 'You do say the most terrible things, don't you? Rough trade! That's what's always made you so attractive.'

As they walked out of Klinsky's, through galleries packed with the stuff of future sales, Sir Hugo took a trip down memory lane. 'I remember so well, Ben, when you had your first job at the National Gallery. Office boy, tea-maker, general dogsbody. But such a charmer. Such a little Glasgow *ragazzo*!'

Ben also remembered when the far younger Hugo Mint took him on a trip to Italy to meet the great Bernard Berenson, king of all the art experts. Ben had resisted Hugo's advances in every *albergo* and *pensione* on the way.

'So sad!' Hugo lifted a fluttering hand and touched Ben's cheek, 'You've lost all those ravishing looks.'

'At moments like this' – Ben said as he moved briskly out of reach – 'I'm profoundly grateful that I have.'

'That's the old Ben!' Hugo wasn't in the least offended. 'You always come out with such delectably *wicked* remarks. What on *earth* is that?' Hugo's roving eye lit on a glass case containing a very small pair of sequinned shorts.

'Kylie Minogue's hot pants,' Ben said mournfully. 'It's our latest art treasure. Forget the Tuscan Mannerists, Hugo. You'd better become the world's greatest living authority on Tom Jones's Y-fronts.'

'Oh, golly!' Sir Hugo looked severely shaken. 'Whatever would Berenson have said about that?'

*

34

Maggie Perowne drew the line at two hours of clinging to Ben's back, so they travelled to the West Country in her small white Opel, which Ben said was like a slow death in a sardine tin. At last they drove past the ivory-covered lodge and up the long, winding drive to Saltery Hall. Despite various notices announcing that it was open to the public, the porticoed house had a neglected look, the terraces were unweeded and the grey stone of the building had a greenish tinge, as though it had been sunk, for a century or two, beneath the sea. There were a few cars, and no coaches, on the gravel sweep round a waterless fountain, and no one answered the door when they pulled a creaking bell. They pushed their way in and found an elderly gentleman in a tweed suit, with thin grey hair brushed over a pink skull, and watching eyes. He didn't so much bark at them as yap, like a small and angry dog. 'Who are you? Are you members of the public?' He moved closer to them, as though he might give them an angry nip. Maggie explained they were from Klinsky's auction house and had an appointment with Lord Saltery.

'Have you, by God? Then you're in luck. I'm Saltery. Now state your business.'

'We asked if we might look through your picture records. Would that be all right?'

'All right if you're prepared to pay.'

'Oh, yes. We'll pay.'

'To root about in my house? All right, then. I took you for members of the public. You've no idea the amount of lavatories the public require – and teas. That's what they come for it seems. To drink tea and go to the lavatory.'

'I suppose the records might be in the library?'

'Oh, you think so, do you? This way then.'

He led them slowly across the hall and up a broad staircase, talking all the way. 'And the public comes in here to notice my things. Damn cheek, really! I remember my grandfather had some fellow to stay, probably one who wrote books, and this fellow said, "That's a very fine Chippendale whatsit you've got, Saltery." And my grandfather said – it was only Saturday morning and this fellow had come for the weekend – "I see that you and I are never going to agree. There's an 11.15 train back to London and I'll thank you to be on it." Damned cheek of a fellow to notice another fellow's things!' He paused for breath. 'Just as bad as noticing the food when you get asked out to dinner!'

Now they were walking down a long gallery, past a number of routine family portraits and what Ben thought to be a distinctly dubious Constable. Lord Saltery's high-pitched, staccato commentary continued uninterrupted. 'Not too many things to notice nowadays, though. Terrible gamblers, the Salterys. My old father gambled away a lot of the pictures. My brother and I tried to gamble them back. Not much luck, I'm afraid. There used to be a man looked after the books and pictures. My brother had to get rid of him when he got into Queer Street. All the papers are in a bit of a mess now, I'm afraid you'll find.'

Ben felt unaccountably happy. He and Maggie were together, far from London, far from that old Etonian yahoo on whom Maggie seemed determined to waste so much of her young life. It was already late in the afternoon. They could stop for dinner at some quiet hotel, with a fire in the dining-room and only two other guests, perhaps two other lovers. After the claret and the brandy, Maggie wouldn't want to drive back to London. This dream of the future, in which he already half believed, was shattered when old Saltery pulled open a door and announced, 'This is the library. Root about in here if you want to.' Ben looked into a long room at the end of which a shaft of late sunlight, heavy with dust, lit up a young man working at a desk who stood up and turned round smiling – and Ben saw the very old-Etonian yahoo he hoped they had left behind.

'I thought,' Ben said to Lord Saltery, 'you tried to keep day-trippers away from here.' And, to Maggie who was silent, 'You might have warned me about the rendezvous at Saltery.'

'I had no idea,' Maggie said, and the owner of Saltery Hall started a laborious explanation, 'This is not a day-tripper. This is my cousin Sylvia Roper's boy. Been here to help sort things out. Do you know each other? Nick Roper . . .' But when he saw Nick kiss Maggie, he ended lamely, 'I see you know each other.'

'When you said it'd been in the family, I thought I'd come down and help you out,' Nick explained to Maggie when she released herself from him. 'No luck, I'm afraid.'

'You've been doing our job for us?' Ben was puzzled. 'Gone through the accounts, list of pictures, all that sort of thing?'

'There are a lot of missing papers,' Nick explained. 'Distinct lack of order and method at Saltery Hall. And, I'm afraid, no mention of a Bronzino. But if you two think the picture's right, I'm sure you can convince the world of it.'

'Darling Nick' – Maggie was looking at Nick in a way which made Ben feel distinctly queasy – 'you're such a wonderful optimist!'

Maggie and Ben didn't have dinner alone together in front of a fire in a small country hotel. Maggie drove him into Blandford and they said goodbye in the station car park. Maggie said, 'you know, I've never met Nick's mother. You don't mind going back on the train?'

'Probably less of an ordeal than meeting Nick's mother.' Ben minded very much, but he could find nothing to talk about except business. 'If the Salterys ever had a Bronzino, there must be some record.'

'Perhaps someone didn't like it?' Maggie suggested.

'Some wife? It's not everyone what wants to see an old man with his hands on a young woman's breast,' Ben agreed.

'I bet old Father Time enjoyed it, though. It made him feel young.'

They heard a train approaching. Ben opened the car door. He turned to her for a last word. 'He might have enjoyed it. But it didn't turn back the clock.'

He went. They hadn't even kissed.

Sarah Napper, hard at work on restoring a Victorian seascape, heard the shop door ping and didn't get up to answer its summons. Moments later, her workroom door opened and Ben Glazier came in. 'I'm sorry,' he said, 'to interrupt your work.'

'You didn't bring that Miss Perowne with you this time, did you? You didn't bring that Miss Perowne who doesn't think I can paint? At least, not to her satisfaction.'

Ben was looking round the room. Pinned on the top of Sarah's easel was a postcard of the Allegory with Venus and Cupid. He said, 'I thought you didn't know that picture?'

'I went to see it at the National after you talked about it. And I spent out on a postcard. Anything wrong with that?'

'Of course not. No law against buying a postcard.

Your solicitor told us Peter Pomfret left you the picture. He was a restorer.' He moved to the paint table and, finding a bottle that interested him, picked it up.

'Peter Pomfret didn't restore pictures! I did all the work that came in. He understood how much he owed me.'

'I'm sure he did.' Ben took the cork out of the bottle and smelt it. 'Walnut oil! Were you thinking of making a salad?'

'Of course not.'

'Didn't Bronzino use walnut oil for mixing his colours?'

'I don't know. You're the great art expert.'

He had crossed to a bookshelf and looked at the titles of some paint-stained art books lying on their sides. 'You've got quite a library.' He pulled a big book out, turned the pages. 'Were you married to Mr Pomfret?'

'Do you always ask all these questions when anyone wants you to sell a picture?'

'That depends on the picture.'

'We were married,' she told him, 'as much as anyone can be.'

'I'm afraid I don't know much about that.' He looked down at the book in his hands. 'Van Meegeren. You've got a book on the great faker of Vermeers. Are you interested in forgery?'

'I don't know why you call them forgeries. They're just beautiful pictures. That's what they are. They give pleasure. Like the one I brought you gave pleasure to Peter.'

'Really? I thought you found it at the back of an old cupboard. Hadn't he hidden it away?'

Sarah ignored his question and said as though to herself, 'Sometimes I thought he loved that picture more than he loved me.' Then she looked at him and protested,

'No one realizes the work that goes into these things. Your Miss Perowne doesn't know what a marvel it is to paint like an Old Master.' Her voice rose in anger, 'Could Miss Maggie Perowne do that? Could she?'

Ben shut the book, put it back on the shelf and said quietly, 'You mean, *you* can paint an alleged Bronzino?'

'Alleged Bronzino.' She laughed. 'I never said anything about Bronzino. I never even mentioned the name! It was you people that said that. You and that girl I gave my picture to. Did I ever say anything about Bronzino? Did I ever say a word about him?'

'Come to think of it, Mrs Pomfret . . .'

'You don't have to call me that.'

'Come to think of it, I don't believe you ever did,' Ben had to admit.

'So what did you come here for?'

'We'll need your permission to have it examined scientifically.' It was time, he thought, to give up speculating and get down to business.

'Examined? Why? Is it ill or something?'

'Possibly. We want to take X-rays. Infra-red. Ultraviolet light. We want to test the paint. Try and date the slate. Can we?'

'I'm sorry, no.' Sarah was determined.

'What?'

'No! You can't do all that to my picture. If you think it's a Bronzino, sell it as one. That's up to you. If you don't – if you think it's a forgery, as you call it, – it's still a beautiful picture. Isn't it?'

'Yes, it's beautiful,' Ben had to admit. 'But is it good, as well? Isn't that the point?'

'I don't think that's the point at all. The point is, was it painted by a very clever person and does it give you pleasure?' She picked up her brush, a gesture of dismissal. 'Now, I'd better get on with my work. In case I'm not going to be rich after all.'

Whether or not she was going to be rich, Sarah Napper told herself, she had certainly become popular. Half an hour after Ben had left her, she got her bicycle out and pedalled off to a lunch date. It was only a short journey to the Bistro Lautrec in Kensington Park Road with its blown-up posters of La Goulue and Aristide Bruant, its parrot, its snooty French waiters and canned Edith Piaf regretting nothing. And there, Nick Roper, who was usually late for everything, was waiting for her with an eager smile and a bottle of champagne. When they had ordered, steak tartare and chips for him and a salade Niçoise for her, Nick raised his glass to her and said, 'Here's to the great new picture you're painting for me.'

'I hardly ever had this before.' Sarah drank and screwed up her nose. 'It sort of tickles, doesn't it?'

'Oh, and to all the great pictures you've already painted!' Nick drank the toast.

'Peter Pomfret gave me champagne once, when we first met. That was yonks ago, and not at our wedding.' She laughed a little. 'In fact, we never had one.'

'Oh, talking about Peter Pomfret.'

'We don't have to,' Sarah assured him.

'And the Bronzino you put into Klinsky's.'

'I've never said it was a Bronzino! Never, at all!' Sarah was determined to make herself clear. 'That's just what your girlfriend thinks it is.'

'She has her doubts,' Nick admitted. 'And she slipped up rather badly lately over a Raphael. But I went down to the house of an old relative of mine called Spoofy Saltery. Lucky enough to find a record in the library.'

Now he had his wallet on the table and was taking a carefully folded sheet of paper out of it. He started to read: '8th January 1756. Bought by Selway (the then Marquis's agent in Rome). Painting of Venus naked with Time. Work of a Florentine, Agnolo di Cosimo, known as Bronzino.'

Sarah looked at him for a long time before she asked, 'Are you sure it was *that* picture?'

'I found something else.' Now another, smaller, whiter paper came out of his wallet. 'I brought it with me. A loose page in the library account book, 1963. The Bronzino Allegory was sent to Peter Pomfret for cleaning. I couldn't find a trace of it having been sent back.'

'I don't know anything about that.'

'The picture was sent to Pomfret by an efficient fellow called Gilkes, who worked at Saltery. Then Gilkes lost his job and I guess Pomfret hung on to the picture,' Nick explained as though to a child. 'I suppose they simply didn't notice it was gone in the chaos of Saltery Hall. I'm afraid to say, this little bit of paper makes your legal claim to a Bronzino decidedly iffy.'

Sarah emptied her glass and asked, 'What are you suggesting?'

'That you stick to your story,' Nick told her. 'You say that Pomfret picked the picture up in Rome, where it might have been sold any time since 1756! And I say nothing at all about this little bit of paper. Provided . . .'

'Provided what?'

'You and I come to some reasonable agreement about the proceeds of the sale.' Nick smiled charmingly and Sarah seemed to think it over. Then she shook her head. 'It's no good, I'm afraid. No good at all.'

'Why not, Sarah? By the way, your glass looks depressingly empty.'

He lifted the bottle but she put her hand over her glass.

'Because I know exactly who painted that picture your girlfriend's so worried about.'

'Who?'

She was almost laughing again, but there was no mistaking her answer which came clearly and proud, 'Me!'

After what he felt justified in regarding as a successful bit of business over the Raphael portrait, Roy Deracott gave a party by courtesy of his ancient Japanese customer. The walls of his gallery were glowing with Pre-Raphaelites, some of which were indisputably right. The space between them was filled with critics, dealers, punters and very few painters. They were eating mini samosas and drinking a fizzy liquid which Nick Roper called, with considerable distaste, 'in the manner of *méthode champenoise* or school or Spanish-style fizz'. Under a pale Sir Lancelot and a consumptive Guinevere kissing in a wood beside his tethered horse, Ben told Maggie about his conversation with Sarah Napper.

'Every word I used to tease the Lord Chairman! She said it all to me!'

'She said "lie back and enjoy a faked orgasm"?'

'Not exactly that. Although perhaps she faked one or two for the benefit of old Pomfret. But she said, "The point is, was it painted by a very clever person and does it give you pleasure?" She wanted me to admire her for being such a beautiful forger!'

'Then we can't sell it!' Maggie was determined. 'Once we start flogging off fakes . . .'

'We might lose our jobs?'

'I love you, Ben. You've got such a practical approach to art.'

43

'That's not true.'

'Not true that you've got a practical approach?'

'Not true that you love me.' Ben tried to comfort himself on the *méthode champenoise* and decided that it tasted like vanilla-flavoured Alka-Seltzer.

On the other side of the room, under a painting of the Lily Maid unwinding her auburn tresses, Nick was assuring Roy Deracott that the Bronzino brought into Klinsky's was dead right. 'Of course, I'm only a humble wine-o, but Spoofy Saltery is my second cousin. We've got indisputable proof of provenance.'

If it is right, Roy Deracott thought, there might be no harm and many advantages in spreading some healthy doubts about it. Such tactics had worked extremely well with the Raphael portrait.

The Pater Institute in Oxford is a kind of artistic hospital, filled with the latest technology, where paintings may be examined, scrutinized and submitted to exhaustive tests so that all diseases, faults and weaknesses are exposed and lies detected. The world of high-art trading is often reluctant to use the Institute. Like patients who would rather not know about their fatal diseases, dealers prefer to rely on optimistic art experts rather than on machines that tell uncomfortable truths. The Institute's report on a picture is only seen by a potential buyer who, not liking to admit that he was nearly taken in, often keeps quiet about it. The faulty picture then goes on its merry way to exhibitions, galleries and museums and keeps its shameful secret. Maggie wasn't content to leave Sarah Napper's picture untested. She drove over Magdalen Bridge with it in the back of her Opel, knowing that she had no right to do what she fully intended to do.

'You got a note from the owner saying we can do this?'

Walter Starkie, the wispy man in a white coat, asked as he took careful possession of the slate. 'Of course!' Maggie started to search her handbag, said she couldn't find it, offered to ring and have it sent over, but Walter, who had conceived the idea of asking Maggie to lunch at Browns, shrugged his shoulders and carried the perhaps Bronzino into the operating theatre. There it was to undergo ultra-violet light and the infra-red Vidicon system, have radiographs and an X-ray print taken and submit to examination through a binocular microscope. The pigment was analysed and the backing compared with a sample of Genoese slate borrowed from the Geological Institute. Maggie and Walter Starkie stood in a queue in Browns and had lunch together as this process started. Then she drove back to London to wait for the results of the chemical tests and the final report. Walter had spent lunchtime telling her stories of outrageous forgeries and trying to hold her hand. She felt no particular hope for the perhaps Bronzino.

Matters of human medicine were being discussed in Pomfret's picture restorer's, where Dr Hanley, still wearing jeans and carrying his telescopic umbrella, had, as he said, just dropped in to Sarah. 'I was passing. I thought I'd see how you were.'

'I'm all right. Perfectly all right, thank you.' She seemed in no mood to chat.

'I was thinking about Mr Pomfret.' The doctor sounded only moderately anxious.

'Were you? I don't think of him, very often.'

'He was impossible, of course. One of my most difficult patients. But he shouldn't have died like that.'

'Why shouldn't he have died? He was old, wasn't he?' Sarah's voice rose irritably. 'Why shouldn't he have died like that?'

'Well, not as quickly, perhaps. He was taking the GNT tablets regularly, wasn't he?'

'You saw what he did. Spilled them all over everywhere. What should I have done? Watched him take them?'

'You didn't do that?' Dr Hanley frowned.

'Of course I didn't. I've got this shop to look after, and all the restoration work. I didn't have time to stand by and see he took his medicine like a child. I have better things to do.'

'I see . . .' He looked at her doubtfully.

'Well, other things, anyway. Did I have to see he took his pills? Is that the law? Is it?'

'No. No, it isn't. I was just worrying in case there was anything more we should have done.'

'I'm not worrying. Thank you very much.' She opened the shop door so that there was nothing to stop him leaving.

'No. No, I can see you're not. Well. I'm glad you're all right.' And, because he could think of nothing else to say, the doctor went.

In the Old Masters Department, Maggie was reading out the Pater Institute report to Ben. It was long, thorough, extremely methodical and started: ' "The base appears to be Genoese slate and has passed all the geological tests. The ground and pigments have all the characteristics of mid sixteenth-century material. Radiographs and X-ray prints showed under modelling and sure handling of the drawing. The infra-red Vidicon system showed details which appeared spontaneous. The binocular microscope showed up coarse pigment particles consistent with grinding colours." ' When she had finished reading, Ben gave a long, low whistle. Maggie folded the report neatly and went to pay another visit to the much-visited Miss Sarah Napper.

*

They were alone together in Pomfret's workroom. Sarah was pale, with a smudge on her forehead because she had pushed back her hair with paint-stained fingers. She looked with considerable hostility at Maggie Perowne who stood with her feet apart, a white raincoat swung open, a silk scarf at her neck, her hair wet from the rain which drummed against the shop windows, looking like a young soldier in some distant war, ready to attack. And then Sarah was half laughing at her, as she said again loudly and triumphantly exactly what she had told Nick Roper.

'I painted it, I tell you. Can't you understand that? I did it! Sarah Napper painted your so-called Bronzino. Here. Here in this little prison. All alone. *He* didn't do it. *He* didn't even help. I painted the Allegory. The master-piece. The picture *he* loved to look at. Sarah Napper is the great artist who did that!'

'I don't think you're a great artist, Miss Napper,' Maggie told her quietly.

'Oh, no! I know you don't. You didn't like my picture, did you? My windmill against a cloudy sky. You despised it! You thought I had nothing to say. You were going to throw it out with the rubbish. But when you thought what I painted was Bronzino ... Well, then you were all falling over yourselves to say how brilliant I was. What a marvellous, gifted artist!'

'How did you know I didn't like your picture?'

'Because *I* painted it. It's not a Bronzino. It's a Napper. Can't you understand what I'm telling you?'

'How did you know I wanted to throw your picture away?'

'Because *he* told me.'

'*Who* told you?'

'Your boyfriend. Your precious Nick Roper.'

'Nick told you!' Maggie couldn't bear to believe it.

'Oh, yes. Very nice to me he was too. Bought me champagne! A great admirer of my work. But he didn't want me to tell the truth about my great masterpiece. "Let them sell it as a Bronzino!" That's what he said to me, smiling and pouring out the bubbly. "Keep quiet," he said, "and we'll go halves, won't we, old girl?"'

'You're not telling the truth!' But Maggie, sickened, suspected that she was.

'Oh, yes, I am. Can't you take it? Is the truth too strong for you?'

'You're not telling the truth about the Bronzino. We've had a report. Listen . . . No, just listen to this.' Maggie began to read: '"This is, indeed, the work of Bronzino. No forgery could come through our tests unless it had been done in the 1550s and left for some four and a half centuries." That's the result of the scientific examination.'

'Scientific examination! I didn't give permission for that. They asked me. I refused permission.'

'All the same, we did it. Stop lying, Miss Napper. To me and to yourself. You can't even paint a picture of your own, and you can't paint a Bronzino. I understand how much you want to be a painter. We all did, perhaps. All of us fluttering round the fringes of the art world. You wanted it so much that you were prepared to tell a lie that might have landed you in prison!'

'You don't understand.'

'I'm afraid I do.'

But Sarah sat at her easel and said, with complete conviction, 'You don't understand anything at all.'

Maggie put the copy of the report on the paint table. 'I'll leave this for you to read. Think about it and then ring me. I propose to attribute your picture to Agnolo di Cosimo, known as Bronzino.

*

48

The Jewellery department at Klinsky's was closely guarded by a number of electronic devices which only opened doors to those who knew the code numbers and pressed buttons in the right order. At that time it contained a collection of precious gems, in ornate settings, which had been smuggled out of Russia before the Great War, sold and re-sold, became the property of a Middle-Eastern ruler, and were now to be auctioned on behalf of his widow who didn't think she would have much use for a tiara when she returned, as she had always planned, to Godalming, her place of birth.

Lord Holloway had promised Camilla a view of these glittering objects. They both appeared in the outer office when an efficient girl called Caroline, who carried all the code numbers in her head, led them through doors which opened at the touch of her finger, and into the inner cavern which housed the most precious property. There, she thought it more tactful to leave them to browse.

'One thing about my work at Come Into The Garden Foods,' the Chairman said, when they were alone, 'we didn't often get to see diamond tiaras, once the property of a Russian Royal. It's a bit more glamorous than inspecting the cold meat counter.'

'I meant to tell you' – Camilla never missed a golden opportunity – 'Maggie's going to give the iffy Bronzino a full attribution. It'll be the story of the Raphael all over again.'

'I gave her fair warning.' Holloway looked anxious. 'We can't afford any more mistakes.'

'I told you, Bernard. It comes from doing art history at Manchester. And not growing up with beautiful things. In Florence you learn to be so very sensitive to what's right.'

'That's the first thing I noticed about you, Camilla. Your sensitivity.'

'Was it, Bernard?' Camilla purred.

'I've been thinking of a shake up in Modern British Paintings. It needs new leadership.'

'Really? Who were you thinking of?'

'Perhaps someone who's grown up with beautiful things ...' Bernard Holloway had in some ways a romantic nature which had often led to embarrassing situations. Now he unwrapped, with trembling fingers, the principal tiara which was, in size and shape, like a coronet. He turned to Camilla and placed it in a ceremonial manner on her bright, recently restyled hairdo. 'I crown you, Camilla,' he told her, 'head of Modern British Paintings.'

'Head of a department?' Camilla was smiling with delight. 'You know I never dreamt of anything like that. But, thank God, Mummy persuaded me to do the History of Art.' She smiled at him and said, 'Shall I wear it to work?'

Ben Glazier came to the conclusion that it was about time that the Chairman saw the Pater Institute report and took it down to the third floor only to be told that Lord Holloway had just popped up to Jewellery. So Ben followed the Holloway trail and found that Caroline had gone off to do a lengthy job on her make-up, leaving the lists of code numbers on her desk with a delightful disregard for security. Less happily, the Lord Chairman hadn't remembered the magic formula needed to release him and his friend from the inner chamber. When Ben came down the passage he saw a face peering, like an angry and confused fish lately added to the aquarium, through the glass panel of the door. Once released, the red-faced Chairman came stamping out, telling Ben that it was an unsafe system of working, and furthermore, he was nearly suffocated, and as for the Pater report he would study it at his leisure. When he looked into the strongroom, Ben saw Camilla topped with diamonds and apologized for interrupting her coronation.

Owly Johnson's beleaguered shop had been attacked again, and this time he had called in the law. Detective-Sergeant Strachan and Detective-Constable Lacey were on his premises and a plaintive Owly was telling them his woes. 'And they pinched a *super* Edwardian epergne and the most delicious little chocolatière,' he told them. 'And that's the third break-in in the last two months. What are you going to *do*?'

'Well insured was they, Owly?' Detective-Sergeant Strachan wasn't over-sympathetic.

'That's not the point. There's been a break-in! Don't you believe me?'

'Until we find out different,' the Detective-Sergeant allowed.

'I'm not always here at night,' Owly told them. 'That's the problem. Sarah Napper, the lady who works at Pomfret's next door, she's always here at night. I wonder if she heard anything.'

'We can ask her.' Detective-Sergeant Strachan was prepared to go through the motions.

'That would be something, I suppose.' Owly didn't sound hopeful.

Sarah was sitting in her workroom, but not working. For a long time she hadn't liked to touch the report Maggie had brought her. Then she tore it into small pieces and dropped it into the waste-paper basket. Now she sat and thought about many things, including the visit of the doctor and the bottle of pills she had bought and hidden at the back of a drawer when old Peter Pomfret cried out for them. She heard the street door and walked into the shop to be faced by two large men and Owly Johnson.

'Miss Sarah Napper?'

'That's her,' Owly said and Sarah stood staring and terrified.

'We're from the Notting Hill police station.' Detective-Sergeant Strachan held up his card. 'Miss Napper, we're investigating . . .'

'There was nothing illegal in what I did!' Sarah interrupted him, terrified. 'Nothing wrong at all. I didn't have to watch over him. He wasn't a child. He was an old man. Very old and he was drunk. He'd drunk the whisky. If he wanted to spill his pills all over the floor, was that my fault? Was it?'

'I don't think you quite understand, Miss Napper. We only want to ask a few questions. It's about a crime.'

'Excuse me. You'll have to excuse me' – Sarah was retreating – 'just for a minute. I'll be back. Only be gone . . . a minute.' She went rapidly through the door into the back room and closed it. The police officers looked at each other in some surprise and Owly tapped his forehead.

Sarah's bicycle was in the passage that led to the kitchen. She pushed it out of the back door and across the blackened piece of earth, muddy from the rain, the store place for rotting frames and useless furniture, an old bath, a broken washstand and other abandoned aids to life at Pomfret's. She pushed her bike through the gate in the garden wall and mounted it on the pavement outside. She began to pedal fast and then faster. She had no idea where she wanted to go. Her only thought was to put as much distance as possible between herself and the policemen from Notting Hill who wanted to question her about crime, the crime which had allowed Peter Pomfret to die, her crime. That was all it could be. She was entirely sure of that.

She was riding in the middle of Westbourne Park Road, with cars hooting and swerving to avoid her. The lights at the intersection with Chepstow Road glared red in the rain. Sarah pedalled faster, straight across. The lorry, coming down from Notting Hill Gate, braked and skidded, but couldn't avoid Sarah. The quickly growing band of onlookers saw a smashed bicycle under its wheels, and a foot wearing a pink ankle sock and a grubby trainer.

'Another version of his famous Allegory "Venus, Cupid, Folly and Time", painted in the year 1555. This important work is fully authenticated by a note in the Vatican Library. The re-emergence of this Bronzino is one of the most important artistic events of recent years. Estimate, six to eight million pounds.' Maggie was alone in her flat, working on the catalogue for the great evening sale in which the Bronzino would star. There was a ring at the doorbell and, when she opened it, she had a view of a smiling Nick Roper, a bottle of Bollinger in each hand, demanding admittance.

'Hallo, Nick.' She sounded very tired. 'You'd better take your champagne somewhere else.'

'Why on earth?'

'Because, my darling, you're enormously beautiful, but the truth of the matter is you're a fake.' She shut the door on him then and leant with her back against it, staring at nothing but emptiness.

On the night of the sale the Bentleys and Rollers, the Daimlers and the Jaguars, purred up to Klinsky's entrance and disgorged punters in evening dress, most of whom had come to watch other people spend money. A little cluster of reporters appeared round the Lord Chairman and some cameras flashed to cries of 'This way, Lord Holloway' and 'One for the *Daily Telegraph*.'

'The Bronzino is a marvellous discovery,' Bernard Holloway told them. 'We're very proud of it.'

'Who identified the picture?' The girl from *The Times* was challenging.

'We have a superb team in Old Master Paintings. Magnificently led by Maggie Perowne and our old stalwart, Ben Glazier. I'm enormously proud of them both,' Holloway told her in his most avuncular manner.

'So you're doing pretty well in your new job at Klinsky's?' the man from the *Telegraph* was asking.

'It's been hard work, of course. But I've never been afraid of hard work. And then I have one great advantage, haven't I? The security of a happy family life and the constant support of my wife.'

'Stop talking about yourself, Bernard,' Lady Holloway, Muriel to the Lord Chairman, a large and fearless woman in a fur cape, gripped her husband's arm. 'These people have come to see the pictures and not to listen to you.' So, protesting not at all, his Lordship allowed himself to be led away.

'If it goes over ten million, I'll give you a treat,' Ben told Maggie as she was waiting, as usual in terror, to mount the pulpit.

'What sort of treat?'

'Have you ever been to a tea dance at the Galactica Hotel, Bayswater?'

'Never.'

'Neither have I. It seems they play my kind of music.'

It wasn't, Maggie thought, the most tempting offer

she'd ever had. But like practically everything else in the world, she forgot it as the bidding rose rapidly from five million, one hundred thousand to five million, six. The telephone girls raised their pencils and the dollar, franc, mark, lire and yen sign above Maggie's head translated the rising bids. Roy Deracott, sitting next to Elsie Campanile, an Italian agent with a face like a parrot, who was waving scarlet-framed spectacles to increase her bid, whispered that the picture was, in fact, done by some old restorer's girlfriend. 'Be quiet,' Roy said. 'Haven't you read the Pater report?' At long last, Maggie sold the Bronzino to an unnamed client at fifteen million pounds, and Lord Saltery, sitting in the audience, planned to install ten bathrooms and no longer offer teas to the public.

The Galactica Hotel tea dance wasn't, perhaps, in the top ten of such events. The room smelt faintly of antiseptic and the décor, sparkling no doubt in the thirties, was in some need of repair and renovation. The enthusiastic female singer was shaky on the top notes and the trio provided a plodding backing. But Ben was holding Maggie in his arms, he was dancing with her, he was singing in her ear, he was enjoying a rare moment of total happiness because she had, she just told him, ditched the Hooray Henry from the wine department.

'They all laughed at Christopher Columbus
When he said the world was round;
They all laughed when Edison discovered sound.'

The singer told them.

'*Recorded* sound,' Ben corrected her, fairly loudly, and then sang along with the band:

'They all laughed at Wilbur and his brother
When they said that man could fly;
They told Marconi
Wireless was a phoney –
It's the same old cry!
They laughed at me wanting you,
Said I was reaching for the moon;
But you came through –
Now they'll have to change their tune'

And then, in a moment of doubt, Ben asked his partner, 'You really *have* given Master Nick the order of the Imperial Elbow?'

'I told you.'

'Given him his cards?'

'I said he was a beautiful fake.'

'Beautiful? Did you say that?'

'But a fake. It's all over. Let's not talk about it.'

'No. No, why should we? *If* it's all over.'

He looked at her then. There were tears in her eyes as she danced. She lowered her head against his arm. 'Let's sit down,' he said, resigned. 'The tea may be better than the singer.'

But the singer was singing, very cheerfully:

'Ho, ho, ho –
Who's got the last laugh –
He, he, he –
Let's at the past laugh –
Ha, ha, ha –
Who's got the last laugh now?'

The Jolly Joker

I am not I: thou art not her or she:
They are not they.

Evelyn Waugh, Author's Note, *Brideshead Revisited*

In the large and comfortable office of Lord Holloway, Chairman of Klinsky's auction house, a curious exhibition had been arranged. They were a number of grainy, blown-up photographs of a small, distant and chaotic African country of which few people had heard until similarly harrowing pictures turned up on television. Between each image of human suffering – huge-headed, swollen-bellied children with matchstick limbs, covered in flies, and hopeless mothers with flat, empty breasts – there was a work of affluent European art, an Italian statuette of a nude goddess some way after Canova, a gilt French eighteenth-century clock, a Dutch still life of hares and pheasants on a kitchen table, a painting of aristocratic, bewigged, nymphs and shepherds in a pastoral landscape. Somewhere, among these treasures, there was an accurate, academic and almost disturbingly realist painting by the English artist Edward Hardcastle. The picture showed the back view of a woman, seated, looking out of a window. Beside her, on a table, were a half-peeled lemon, a glass, a knife, and a bowl in which orange and purple pansies were planted.

Lord Holloway, standing in front of his desk, was introducing a tall, eager young man with ginger hair and strangely hawklike features who had a stoop, a smart Italian suit and, Ben thought, the pale and deeply serious look of a religious maniac, a young Savonarola dressed by Armani.

'I've arranged this little gathering' – the Chairman opened the proceedings – 'so you can meet Piers Frobisher who has tremendous fundraising experience. Am I right, Frobisher?'

'In all modesty, Lord Chairman,' the young hawk said, quite seriously, 'I must admit you are.'

'Klinsky's should play its part in the common good,' the Chairman went on, encouraged. 'And Frobisher tells me that a charity auction will do no harm at all to our image.'

They had assembled obediently: Maggie Perowne, head of Old Masters, and Camilla Mounsey, promoted to Modern British Paintings, a department Ben Glazier now referred to as Old Mistresses. Other heads of departments were there, including Nick Roper from Wines who tried several smiles across a crowded room at Maggie and got no reaction from her whatsoever.

'Are we going to save the starving on Dutch paintings of dead game-birds and French clocks?' Ben asked from the back of the room as Maggie whispered to him to shut up. 'Or shall we drop old English watercolours on them by parachute?'

'We are going to save them,' the Chairman answered with dignity, 'on the proceeds of art, which is a perfectly saleable commodity. Now Piers Frobisher runs Feeding the Multitude, the registered charity working very closely with us on this one.' He then started to introduce the staff to the charity gatherer who stopped him after the first dozen names to say, 'I think I've met everyone else at the Sheridan Club at one time or another. The Sheridan's a great place for making contacts.'

'Of course,' said Ben in spite of Maggie's mutterings, 'charity suffereth long and hath to make contacts.'

'It's not what you know. It's always *who* you know,' Frobisher said with great solemnity, as though it were an article of faith.

'Charity doth pretty well now, doth it?' Ben could be heard to ask, but Lord Holloway decided to sum up firmly, 'I'm sure we're all grateful to Piers Frobisher, who has agreed to give his help and advice for a very reasonable remuneration. I hope we're all going to work together on what Frobisher agrees we call the great Klinsky's Cash and Carry. In all modesty, I may say that I was able to suggest the title from my long experience of the catering trade.' Lord Holloway stopped then, as though expecting a laugh. There was a polite giggle from Harry Lomax in Antique Herbals and Garden Books, but the rest was silence. 'We shall, of course,' the Chairman went on, 'be able to provide substantial and, I'm sure, welcome aid for the people of . . .' Here he looked to Camilla for help, which she readily supplied, 'Neranga.' 'Yes, indeed. Now, if there are no questions . . .'

But Ben had one. 'We've always found the trouble with these charity dos has been people dumping the most ghastly objects on the poor and starving. Things they've kept in the attic and couldn't stand the sight of anyway. Dubious family portraits, reproduction Chippendale, schools after the schools of imitators of forgotten painters. How can we avoid getting the most terrible rubbish?'

'That'll be your job, Glazier,' the Lord Chairman told him firmly. 'And the heads of all departments. Check all the entries with the greatest care. We're not having any rubbish in our charity event! Now, as we are launching a new initiative, I'm inviting you all to take wine.'

The girls who cooked the directors' lunches, closely

related, some of them, to those who helped write the catalogues and took telephone bids, handed out glasses of a modestly priced Rioja. Piers Frobisher was admiring the painting of the woman seated by a bowl of pansies and Camilla agreed that the work was, indeed, exquisite. She also told the Chairman, who was at her side, that it was by Edward Hardcastle, and Holloway wanted to know more about this painter. Ben, uninvited, provided the information. 'I remember Hardcastle. He went to the Royal Academy Schools. Pestered me with questions when I went to lecture there. Boring little man who painted boring little pictures. I mean, those lemons look far too like lemons to be in the least convincing.'

'He was a wonderful artist, with a great following.' Camilla was pained. 'That'll go for at least thirty thousand at a charity auction.'

'He's always been strangely fashionable,' Ben agreed 'with people who think they ought to have pictures but don't really like them very much.'

'It appeals to me, at any rate,' the Lord Chairman said, taking the picture from Frobisher. 'Did you say he *was* a wonderful artist, Camilla?'

'Tragic. He died about ten years ago. I don't think he was much over forty.'

'Tell you what' – Holloway was prepared to plunge – 'I'll buy it. Personally. Just before the sale. I'll pay the owner a fair price and I'll put it in our Cash and Carry, all profits to feed the starving. What do you think of that, Camilla?'

'I think it's extraordinarily generous and quite typical of you, Bernard.'

'That's your first PR job, Piers: KLINSKY'S CHAIRMAN PLANS CONTRIBUTION TO CHARITY BY BUYING AN ENGLISH MASTERPIECE WITH HIS OWN MONEY.'

Holloway put the painting reverently back, beside the photographs of the starving. 'Get reproductions of this in the supplements. Work out how much porridge it's going to pay for, or whatever they eat out there in Neranga.'

'Charity,' Ben said, not quite under his breath, 'raiseth the company's image.'

Paint. Paint of different colours. Ordinary house paint, diluted, was poured, apparently at random, on an end of a large canvas lying flat on the floor of Ned Nunnelly's chaotic studio somewhere near the World's End. Then Ned lifted an end of the canvas, slowly, gently, and the paint dribbled downhill. As it dribbled, he blew at it with an electric hair-dryer, causing it to splatter widely and ar random.

Ned Nunnelly was in his fifties, going fat, and balding on the top of his head. Otherwise he was a hirsute man with long hair at the sides and a generous, nearly black beard and moustache. He wore paint-stained jeans and a lumber-jack shirt, together with steel-rimmed, tinted spectacles. He seemed entirely happy in his work and even happier when a young American girl, dark-haired and pale-faced, came out of the bathroom in a white towelling dressing-gown to inspect his achievement. 'Mm,' she said, 'yes,' crossing her arms and standing in front of the paint that had now finished dribbling. Her name was Patti Duprey and she had been an art student in New York.

'You really think so?' Ned was gratified.

'It's a great image, Ned! One of your most significant images, I'd say. That was a great technique you discovered.'

'At least it feels free. To me, at any rate.'

'Putting the air in it, the way you did, kind of freed it,' Patti agreed.

'I watched you drying your hair. I watched the way it moved when you dried it. That's how the idea came.'

'So I participated?' Patti was extremely proud of herself. 'Very good.'

Not long after the creation of this image, which he named Pandora, Ned Nunnelly saw the heart-breaking pictures of Neranga once again on the television, and read that Klinsky's was inviting great and valuable works of art for an auction to relieve the famine.

In a moment of generosity he decided to sacrifice Pandora to this cause, a move which Patti said only proved he was the genuine and caring person she had always known him to be. Accordingly he fitted the canvas into a taxi and took it to the auction house, outside which hung a huge banner bearing the legend:

CASH AND CARRY

KLINSKY'S GREAT CHARITY SALE APRIL 10TH AND 11TH

IN ASSOCIATION WITH FEEDING THE MULTITUDE

'The greatest of these is Charity' I Corinthians
Admission by ticket only £50.00

Ned paid off the taxi and lugged Pandora past a sympathetic Lucy Starr to the big gallery on the first floor where the staff of various departments were sorting out what Ben had unkindly called the rubbish. He was put in touch with the head of Modern British Paintings and stood before her, holding what he was inclined to think was one of his finest works.

'It's rather large.' Camilla looked at the work doubtfully.

'I found a new way of working,' Ned began to explain with mounting excitement. 'Pandora, that's what I call this image. She kept the winds in a box. With air.

Remember? I mean, do you realize what's the biggest creative power in the universe? What carved out mountains? What puts up those great sculptures, sand dunes in the desert? The winds, for God's sake!'

'Terribly *interesting*, of course.'

'Interesting? You think it's as bad as *that*?' Ned was easily deflated.

'Of course it's not *bad*.' Camilla always tried to be polite. 'It's probably terribly good. Of its kind. It just might not be exactly what the big givers are looking for when we ask them to dig deep into their pockets. Besides which, people have such small walls nowadays.'

'I thought you lot all had Georgian mansions.' Ned was starting to get angry, a process which put fresh wind in his sails.

'But would it quite *go* in a Georgian mansion?' Camilla asked.

'Listen. I want to do something for those kids I saw on television. Bloody hell!'

'I'm sure we'd welcome a donation on your way out.'

'Thanks very much! Come on, Pandora, out of this frigging mausoleum. Into the fresh air where you belong.' By now, a furious Ned started to drag Pandora, the first mortal woman painted with a hair-dryer, down the gallery and out of Camilla's unsympathetic presence.

The charitable gifts were piled on tables. Harry Lomax, a small, tweedy, rabbit-faced man, was looking at the Edward Hardcastle painting with an interest which surprised Ben Glazier, standing beside him.

'There is something extraordinary about that picture,' Lomax said.

'The dead hand of art history.' Ned, having travelled so far, decided to put Pandora down, give her a rest and join in the conversation.

'You don't like it?' Ben looked at him with some sympathy.

'Royal Academy chocolate box. Needs to be flushed down the toilet, together with all the bloody Gainsboroughs and Canalettos taking up space on your walls.'

'You'd have a bit of a job flushing a Canaletto down the toilet,' Ben warned him. 'I don't know if it's ever been tried.'

'Look at it, though. Just look at it! A dead picture, painted by a dead hand.'

'Well, that makes sense. The artist's dead.'

'Bit of luck, that,' Ned thought. 'He won't be doing any more of those. Well, I'd better get Pandora home.'

'Pandora?' Ben looked at the paint-strewn canvas.

'Of course. The girl who had a box full of winds. Too much fresh air in her, for you lot.'

So Ned left them and Ben, looking after him thoughtfully, recited a poem he often remembered when he saw pictures like Ned Nunnelly's. It went:

> 'The artist and the artist's wife,
> they led a horrid, haunted life,
> surrounded by the things he'd made
> which are not wanted by the trade.'

And then he asked Harry Lomax, 'Just why did you find that picture so interesting, Harry?'

'Didn't Camilla say the artist died about ten years ago?'

'So far as I can remember.'

'Then, you see, it's the "Jolly Joker".'

'It doesn't look a load of laughs to me.' Ben wondered if Harry had gone slightly insane, all alone up in old Herbals.

'No, the "Jolly Joker",' Harry explained patiently, 'that's the name of the pansy growing in the pot. One of the order of the *violaceae*, but a new one. You see, it's got two lower petals and three upper petals.'

'What's so hilarious about that?'

'Nothing. That's just like all other pansies.'

'So it's normal?'

'Not really. The bottom petals are bright orange and the upper three bright purple. I suppose this makes it look like a jester. Wonderful things they do with plants nowadays.'

'Nowadays?'

'Well, I know I deal in Antique Herbals and Garden Books, but I do keep up with the times. They only bred the "Jolly Joker" about four years ago.'

'It didn't exist before then? You're sure of that?'

'Quite sure!' Harry Lomax was never in any doubt when it came to flowers.

Camilla, when Ben found her, was engaged with a youngish black African who was carrying a carving of a pregnant woman. She was looking at this smooth, swollen-bellied, ebony goddess with no more enthusiasm than she'd shown for Pandora. 'The primitive stuff goes on the table at the other end, Mr McKenzie,' she said and got an angry answer, 'This is not primitive!'

'No.' Ben took the small wood-carving and admired it. 'I'd say it was very beautiful. And quite sophisticated.'

'Good. You understand. You a person in charge?'

'One of many.'

'I am Winston McKenzie. Your name, please.'

'Glazier. Ben Glazier.'

'Thank you, Mr Glazier. I'll remember to ask for you when I call again.' Winston McKenzie left them then, carrying the wood-carving with extreme care, and Ben told Camilla that he wanted to ask her about Hardcastle. With considerable pride she showed him the front of *The*

Times Arts section. A reproduction of the Hardcastle picture nestled under the headline: KLINSKY'S CHAIRMAN PLANS TO START CHARITY BALL ROLLING BY BUYING BRITISH.

'Amazing!' Ben was filled with wonder. 'The art market's just a little whore. Bestows her favours on the most unlikely people. But about that picture . . .'

'I hope you can see how sensitive it is.'

'Yes, all that . . . But, just remind me, when did you say Hardcastle died exactly?'

'Ten years ago. I've checked it for the catalogue. At a place called Shenstone-on-Sea. He left a widow and no children. Terrible loss.'

'Yes, I'm sure. Thanks.'

'Going well, is it?' Camilla asked him, as he started to move away.

'Let's say, it's interesting,' Ben called back to her.

While Ben was in conference with Harry Lomax, Ned Nunnelly was carrying Pandora out of Klinsky's. He got some sympathy from Lucy Starr, the ever-hopeful resting actress at the reception counter. He told her he couldn't give his picture away and she told him that she knew how he felt because she was often rejected. When he added that the Philistines upstairs had no understanding of work painted by the elements – by Boreas, the north wind, for instance – she told him that there was not much charity in the acting business either. She also told him about going up for parts. 'Your face aches from all that smiling. Smiling when you come in. Smile when they look you up and down. Smile when they ask you to read some load of rubbish. Smile when they say they'll let you know but never do.'

Ned clearly felt he'd met a friend. 'What do I care?' he said. 'I've got a show coming on soon.'

Lucy announced joyfully, 'And I've got a part at the Baptist's Head in Dalston. Not, actually, a part with lines or anything. I'm on the stage most of the time, though. Not that there is a stage, as such. I've got a leaflet – if you're ever in Dalston – tells you about the first night. My name's Lucy Starr and I'm going to live up to it!'

'And I'm Ned Nunnelly. Best of luck!' And so they exchanged leaflets.

At the end of the day Ben told Maggie Perowne all about the 'Jolly Joker'. Lord Holloway, she predicted, would have a fit when he found out. 'Klinsky's buys British,' she said. 'You mean, Klinsky's buys a British fake?'

'Perhaps there's no need to tell him? I mean, he's paid good money for it. That'll go to the starving in Neranga. If we tell him, he'd only take the bread out of their mouths.'

'Ben! What are you saying? We're going to have a charity auction full of forgeries?'

'Not full of them. Just one little fake, perhaps. I mean, Hardcastle was a bit of a faker even when he painted his own pictures.'

'If it's a fake, we've got to withdraw it from the sale. For God's sake, Ben! It's only right.'

'You have such an overdeveloped sense of morality.' He looked at her with great affection.

'I do, when it comes to pictures.'

'Not when it comes to young men. I hope to God your bent old Etonian hasn't been up to his tricks again.'

'If he has, they're confined to the Wine department. That's all over! Completely.'

'So what do we do about this possibly phoney picture?'

'We've got to be sure about it.'

'What do you suggest?'

'We investigate. For God's sake, Ben, we've done it before! Then, if it's really a fake, we'll have to tell Holloway.'

'*You'll* have to tell Holloway. You're the one with the overdeveloped sense of morality. I can find out who put it in here for sale. Anyway, I can try.'

So Maggie left it, a little doubtfully, to Ben. On her way out, Lucy Starr made her promise to go to the play at the Baptist's Head, Dalston, and told her that tickets, though greatly in demand, could easily be arranged for any friend of hers. While Maggie was being talked into attending this entertainment, Nick Roper appeared from nowhere in particular and asked how long she was going to go on treating him like a fake Rembrandt etching. 'Or some such bloody thing. Forgive and forget. Come out to dinner. San Lorenzo, like we used to.'

'Once. On your birthday. It was my treat, if I remember.'

'Mine this time. What do you say?'

'Impossible. My mother's coming to stay.'

'Bring Mum!'

But Maggie wasn't having it. 'Mum's at the flat doing home-cooking. When I was a child, we ended every meal by beating our breasts. It was our nightly sign of indigestion. Besides which, you've behaved like a complete bastard. And, what's more, I'm not having her meet you, Nick. She disapproves of my London life quite enough already. If she met you, she'd have me taken into care!'

Mrs Perowne, as a young woman, had something of Maggie's beauty and had appealed greatly to her film fan, piano-playing, commercial traveller of a husband. Her features remained clear, but seemed to have been pressed

together by the spreading plumpness of her face so that
her lips were pursed and her eyes half-closed in a mistrust-
ful manner. On her visits south she found much to object
to in Maggie's flat, and with her work which, having to
do with art, she felt wasn't a real job in any proper sense
of the word.

'However much did *that* cost?' she said, standing in
front of Maggie's much-prized lithograph.

'The Léger? It's only one of fifty, signed. I honestly
can't remember how much it cost.'

'Modern art, I suppose. The things they think look
pretty nowadays!'

'It's not all that modern, Mum. 1920. Before you were
born.'

'Before I was born, I doubt if women looked all flat-
tened out. I'm sure your gran didn't.'

'What about a glass of white wine? I'm going to have
one.' Maggie's mother made her feel like a confirmed
alcoholic as she looked disapproving and said, 'No thank
you, dear. I don't want to be drinking at all hours.
Anyway, the meal will be ready directly. Do you know
how much I had to pay for that little bit of beef, do you?
Can you guess?'

'No, Mum. Go on, astonish me.'

'Twelve pounds! I don't know how they have the nerve
to do it. I told the young man in that butcher's you think
so highly of – the one that wears that white trilby hat
arrangement and seems to think such a lot of himself – "That
little bit of beef'd go for half the price in Salford!" You
know what he had the cheek to tell me? "This isn't Salford,
Madam." "You're too right, it isn't." That's what I said.
And more's the pity, I was tempted to add. I'll just take the
weight off my feet for a moment. Then I'll go and pay my
respects to that little scrap of beef that cost a fortune.'

Mrs Perowne sighed deeply and sat down, contemplating the rapaciousness of southern butchers while her daughter began to search cupboards and drawers for the remains of a packet of cigarettes.

'Funny thing' – Mrs Perowne looked about her – 'you've never got it really cosy in here, have you, dear?'

Maggie had found one dried-up Silk Cut, shedding tobacco and entombed in an alabaster box. She resurrected it eagerly. 'I think it's nice that splash of colour I miss in your furnishings,' her mother went on remorselessly. 'Now, Linda and her Barry!' Maggie knew it wouldn't be long before her sister, a particularly perfect person, entered the conversation. 'Well, Barry's gone up to area manager. And, as I say, they just got this lovely red velvet three-piece suite with gold trimming, which was quite a bargain. And, as Barry says, it's warming up the room. Gives it a real homey appearance.' At this point she looked at Maggie in some horror and began to cough extravagantly, 'Put that out, please. I don't want to have to sue you for passive smoking, do I? That really would get our name in the papers.'

There was a ring at the doorbell and Maggie escaped to answer it. She opened the front door and before she could slam it again, or interpose her body against a most unwelcome visitor, Nick had invaded her hall. As usual, he was carrying champagne. 'Who is it, dear?' Mrs Perowne called from her seat on the sofa. Nick shouted, 'You must be Mum!' and surged into the sitting-room. So Maggie followed with a sickening heart to where he was flattering her mother outrageously. '*Now* I can see where Maggie gets her good looks. Maggie! Why didn't you tell me your mum was such a stunner?'

'I can't believe this is happening!' Maggie's desperate mutter to her former lover.

'I brought a bit of Bolly to wash down the home-cooking.' Nick plonked the gold-topped bottles on the table like flags of conquest.

'That's very nice. Very nice indeed.' To Maggie's horror, her mother was purring. 'I don't believe we've had that since Linda's wedding. That's very kind of you, Mr ... Oh, I don't believe we've been formally introduced.'

'I'm Nick. Nick Roper. One of Maggie's *closest* friends. You mean, she never told you she'd asked me to dinner?'

'I haven't, for God's sake! What do you think you're doing?' Maggie was beginning to panic. 'There's not enough beef, is there, Mother?'

'Oh, I'm sure we can eke it out,' Mrs Perowne was delighted to say. 'FHB, as Maggie's father always used to say. Family hold back!'

In time – it seemed to Maggie that it was a long, long time – dinner was over, most of the champagne had been drunk and Mrs Perowne was showing Nick the family snaps which he was looking at as though they were the rarest and most fascinating works of art.

'That's Karen, is it? What a beautiful baby!' Nick showed enormous interest.

'The first grandchild. I've been waiting for Maggie to contribute.' Maggie took a quick, pain-killing gulp of champagne.

'Don't tell me! That's Linda.' Nick held up a blurred picture in triumph. 'Your looks again, Mum. Who's the little fellow in the suit?'

'That's Linda's Barry. He's done very well for himself. Not tall like you, of course.' And then Mrs Perowne had a terrible moment of doubt. 'Not married yourself, are you?'

'Oh, not at all. I'm free as the wind.'

'Well! I'm very glad to hear it. I wouldn't want our Maggie mixed up with anyone married. That happens far too often with young girls nowadays. You remember the Winthrop girl, Elsie, don't you, Maggie? Used to go to school with our Linda.'

'A married man?' Nick was deeply sympathetic. 'I'm sorry to hear it.'

'So was Mrs Winthrop,' Mrs Perowne told him. 'Especially when his wife tried to set fire to the Winthrops' front door.'

'Look, I hate to break up the party.' Maggie was desperate and, although Nick protested, she insisted. 'Mum's exhausted. I mean, she came down all the way from Salford. You *are* exhausted, aren't you, Mum?'

'Not really.' Mrs Perowne betrayed her. 'The wine's perked me up, nicely.'

'Well, *I* am.' Maggie gave an exaggerated yawn. 'I'm going to bed. We've got another hard day tomorrow on this charity sale.'

'Awful party pooper, your daughter. But, all right.' Nick stood up and Maggie was thankful. 'Good-night Mum. Get your beauty sleep.' And then he kissed Maggie's mother.

'Delighted to meet you, Nick.' Mrs Perowne emerged from the kiss best pleased. 'Oh, and Nick, look after our Maggie, won't you?'

'I'll try.'

In the hall, as she let him out of the front door, Maggie at last spoke her mind. 'I told you once, I'll tell you again. Get out of my life!'

'Why?' Nick was a picture of injured innocence. 'I thought I did rather well. Weren't you pleased?'

'Pleased? You're a liar, Nick, a con artist and a cheat. And the absolutely unforgivable thing about you is my mother likes you!'

*

While Maggie was enduring the blossoming of friendship between her rejected lover and her mother, Ben Glazier was at another party at Deracott's, drinking the iffy champagne in the gallery. He started his inquiries into the works of Edward Hardcastle. 'His pictures are quite a cult nowadays,' Roy Deracott growled. 'We had an exhibition last year.'

'And you put one in for the charity auction?'

'The one Klinsky's paid for with *its own money*?' A gravelly laugh from Roy. 'What's happened, Ben? Has your Chairman undergone some sort of religious conversion?'

'To charity? Yes, he has. Watch out, he'll be sending you food parcels. Can you tell me, Roy? Who brought the picture to you? A friend of the dead artist's? A relative, perhaps?'

'I don't know,' Roy shrugged. 'Did he have relatives? I think there might be a wife. Didn't she figure in some of the paintings?'

'Is that her in the one we bought? "Woman with a Bowl of Flowers"?'

'Don't ask me, Ben.' Roy still seemed gently amused. 'From now on, my lips are sealed.'

As Ben was making his way out through the crowd, someone called his name and he saw the hawklike Piers Frobisher stooping over a drink. He asked, 'I don't know if you've ever met? Christopher M'tatu, Foreign Secretary of the country you're helping so much.'

He introduced a large African in a shining silk suit who was engaged in sampling a tray of little vol-au-vents and sausages on sticks. 'You're in the government there, are you?' Ben asked. 'And you're not particularly hungry?'

*

Shenstone-on-Sea, in the county of Sussex, was once, in distant, happier days, a small fishing village. Now it was part of the urban sprawl which stretched along the South Coast. The fishermen pushing the boats out for a catch had been replaced by crowds of boat people, weekending mariners in yellow anoraks and wellies, bobble hats and nautical caps, who raced out of the small harbour, now known as the marina. They did this to show their boats off to each other and impress their female crew, some of whom wore T-shirts with 'Galley Slave' written upon them.

When Ben approached Shenstone it was, as usual, covered in cloud, and a brisk wind was chopping white scars on the grey sea. Ben asked for directions and found his way to a half-timbered cottage on the outskirts of the town; surrounded by a small but glowing garden, it seemed an oasis away from the supermarkets, garages and flats for holiday lets. A woman was clipping the hedge. She was wearing jeans and a fisherman's sweater, her hair was grey and blown by the wind, her face was tanned in a way which came not from sunshine holidays but from sailing and gardening in all seasons. Her eyes were very blue and had wrinkles of laughter around them. She might have been fifty years old and Ben thought that she was beautiful. He switched off the engine of his Harley-Davidson and asked if she were Mrs Hardcastle. She admitted it and he told her he was Ben Glazier who'd rung her from Klinsky's.

'Good God! I never thought a man from Klinsky's travelled around like that. I expected a Roller, at least. Anyway, you'd better come in.'

The cottage had a living-room with a log fire, a sofa and armchairs whose chintz had been gnawed by two spaniels. They leapt up, barked at Ben, went for his groin and then, quickly bored with him, went back to sleep on the hearthrug. There was also an easel and a paint table which was clean, with the tubes of paint neatly set out, the brushes in a jar, and no sign of any of them having been used recently. There were Hardcastle pictures on the walls: accurate, pleasant, characterless paintings and drawings of Liz (she had asked Ben to call her Liz) as a younger and much younger woman. Liz made coffee, poured it into thick china mugs, and they sat in front of the fire and he showed her a photograph of 'Woman with a Bowl of Flowers'.

'That's Ted's,' she said without hesitation. 'No doubt about it. That's the way Ted painted. He took trouble, you see, like an Old Master. He'd got no patience with people who splash paint around, or bicycle across puddles of Crimson Lake.'

'That "Woman with a Bowl of Flowers", is she you?'

'Well, you can only see the back of her head, can't you?' Liz picked up the photograph and looked at it again.

'The back of a head of dark hair.'

'Ted died ten years ago. It's grey now.'

'You remember sitting for it?' Ben asked her.

'Not for that picture, no. I can't say I remember that particular one.'

'Are you sure? If it's you, you must've been there when he painted it.'

'Not necessarily. Ted painted me so often, he always said he could do me by heart. There're lots of pictures of me I didn't sit for.'

'So he might have painted this when you weren't there?'

'Quite easily.'

'But not after he was dead?'

'Is that meant to be a joke?' Liz was suddenly serious.

'I'm sorry. I have this complaint. Inappropriate joke syndrome. But Klinsky's bought that picture with its own money, something quite unheard of. Naturally we want to find out all we can about it. Its date, for instance.'

'I honestly can't remember. It was so long ago.'

'I understand, but perhaps you could help us about this. You sent a lot of your husband's pictures to Deracott?'

'Oh, yes. He had an exhibition.'

'Including this one?'

'Not as far as I can remember . . .' Liz hesitated. 'I don't go to London anymore.'

'In fact, you really can't remember this picture at all?' He got up and wandered round the room, the dogs stirred, growled and then went back to sleep.

'Not exactly.' She smiled, a small apology for her vagueness. 'Do you paint yourself?' he asked her.

'Oh, no! I'd be hopeless!'

'You didn't meet your husband at art school?'

'Oh, no. I was studying music. And I wasn't marvellous at that. My mother and father lived in Shenstone. We met when our boats collided in the harbour. I wasn't much of a sailor either.'

'But your husband was?'

'Oh, yes. He loved it. Loved it too much, as it turned out. Ted was a wonderful sailor. I mean, he'd done it since he was a boy. He could sort of sniff at the wind and discover exactly what it had in mind. He knew there was going to be a bit of a wind that afternoon, but not a gale. I suppose he'd got it wrong, for once. They sent out a helicopter and it found the boat turned over. That's all.'

'That's how he died?' Ben moved away from the paint table and looked at the pictures. There was no self-portrait.

'There's a hell of a current out there,' Liz explained. 'Ted was carried off, God knows where. They showed me a body that'd been washed up, months later. Unrecognizable. The sea does strange things. I grieved for Ted and that object seemed . . . irrelevant somehow. Is that all you want to know?'

'Thank you. I can't think of anything else.' He sat down by the fire again, but said reluctantly, 'Well, I suppose I ought to get back on the infernal machine.'

'Do you have to? Come on. It's too late for work. I thought I might lure you down to the pub.'

'Why not?' Ben looked at her, feeling, for some reason, that they had known each other a long time.

The Sailors' Rest was a small, cluttered pub with a bar decorated with nets, lobster pots, ships in bottles and brass lanterns. There was a piano, but no Space Invaders. The clientele seemed to consist of boat people whose discussions of accidents and near death by drowning were punctuated by much happy laughter. Ben and Liz sat on a high-backed bench in a corner, faced with two pints of best bitter.

'I used to come in here with Ted,' Liz remembered. 'He liked to hear me play that dreadful, tinny old piano.'

'You were happy?' Ben looked at her and thought it was a silly question. There was something about Liz that encouraged happiness.

'Oh, yes. We were very happy. Before he went off to Canada.'

'Canada?' Had Hardcastle left her, and why?

'He had a visiting fellowship at the Ryerson Institute in Toronto. When he got back he seemed, well, worried. He stopped painting, for months.'

'That was unusual.'

'I've got a feeling – he didn't say much – but I got the

distinct feeling something had gone wrong in Canada. Whatever happened, he didn't lift a brush in the six months before he . . . well, before he died.'

There was a silent, a peaceful, not unhappy tribute to a dead husband.

'You used to play the piano for him. What sort of music?'

'Oh, the old ones. Gershwin, Cole Porter, Julie Styne.'

'My sort of music.' Ben was delighted. 'Songs where the words mattered.'

A large, baldheaded man, who Ben suspected was another yachtsman, came up to them and asked if they could steal Liz to put a bit of music in their souls. She went to the piano then and Ben put her pint on top of it. Then she started to play and he noticed how quickly the bar became silent when she sang, a little huskily:

> 'Our romance won't end on a sorrowful note,
> Though by tomorrow you're gone;
> The song is ended, but as the songwriter wrote,
> "The melody lingers on".
> They may take you from me,
> I'll miss your fond caress.
> But though they take you from me,
> I'll still possess: . . .'

Liz at the piano was obviously one of the regular attractions. The audience, who'd frequently heard her sing this before, joined in raggedly, knowing only some of the words.

Ben helped them out with:

> 'The way you wear your hat,
> The way you sip your tea,
> The mem'ry of all that –
> No, no! They can't take that away from me!'

Two hours and several pints of best bitter later, Ben and Liz arrived, a little unsteadily, in front of the cottage, singing in fairly loose harmony:

> 'We may never, never meet again
> On the bumpy road to love,
> Still I'll always, always keep
> The mem'ry of – '

'Good-night.' Ben raised his hand in a sort of salute.

'Where do you think you're going now?' Liz wanted to know.

'Back home, I suppose. Back to the smoke.'

'On that killer vehicle? Full to the gills with Shenstone's best bitter? Do you think I want another sudden death? Why don't you come in and sleep it off?'

'Into your delightful cottage?'

'What about it?'

'If I can find the way.' He fumbled with the gate.

'Hang on to me.'

'Delighted. "The way you hold your knife",' he sang as they wandered arm in arm up the garden path. '"The way we danced till three".'

'"The way you changed my life . . ."'

Liz didn't change his life. There was only one great change he wanted, and he would still be wanting it as much the next morning. But he got between the cool, linen sheets under the patchwork quilt in her bedroom. He felt her body, still firm and slender beside him, and was sober enough to wonder why Edward Hardcastle hadn't been happy when he came back to this woman from Canada.

The next day, the wind had dropped and the sun was shining. Ben felt the country air getting to his chest. He wasn't used to bacon and eggs and so much loving attention in the mornings. He thought he'd better get back to his lonely life in the city. He had time, however, to look at the garden and at the pansies growing at the side of the path, unusual pansies with orange and purple petals. 'That's an interesting pansy,' he asked her. 'Isn't it the "Jolly Joker"?'

'Do you know absolutely everything?'

'Most things, yes. Where did you get it?'

'Shenstone Garden Centre, I think. I'd no idea what its name was. Ted loved flowers.'

'He must have.' They kissed goodbye and he roared his bike engine, feeling younger than he had the day before.

The pictures chosen for the auction were being hung in the big gallery. Ben and Maggie were taking another look at the 'Woman with a Bowl of Flowers'. They talked quietly and there was no one about except a couple of porters chatting up a secretary who was listing the pictures at the far end of the room.

'As a matter of fact,' Ben was saying, 'Mrs Hardcastle was extremely nice.'

'You mean, she was an extremely nice faker.'

'Not necessarily. Thousands of people might have the "Jolly Joker" in their gardens. That's not conclusive. Anyway, she loved her husband. It was very touching the way she talked about him. I don't think she's been a party to anything. Well, not to a forgery.'

'She obviously charmed the pants off you.' Maggie looked at him with deep disapproval.

'She sang the sort of songs I like.'

'She *sang* to you?' Maggie was incredulous.

'We sang to each other.'

'You go off to catch a thief, to trick a trickster, to expose a forger, and there you are, *singing* together!'

'We had to go through quite a quantity of best bitter.'

'It's a miracle you didn't break your neck. Biking home in the dark.'

'She was very considerate about that,' he said quietly and Maggie looked at him with a wild surmise. 'Ben! Where *did* you spend the night?' It was a question he didn't answer.

'Not in the late, great Edward Hardcastle's bed?' He still didn't answer and she turned away from him, only half joking. 'God, I'm furious! I thought you were yearning for me.'

'There's not a lot of future in yearning for someone who yearns for Hooray Henrys and con artists,' he tried to explain. But Maggie didn't intend to dwell on the subject of Nick's character, or what, in a strange moment, seemed to her Ben's infidelity. She simply told him that his precious Mrs Hardcastle was clearly the number one suspect.

'She can't paint.' He thought that concluded the matter.

'She must know painters. She could find someone who'd do it for her. She has a connection with Deracott. We've got to find out if she brought him that picture.'

'Or whoever did. There's one other thought.'

'What?'

'We might try and get hold of someone who was at the Ryerson Institute in Toronto about ten years ago. What are you doing this evening?'

'I'm afraid exactly what you are.' For Ben had also been rash enough to agree to swell the audience at Lucy Starr's first night in the Baptist's Head, Dalston.

*

The room over the Baptist's Head was cold and bleak in the day time, with a few black drapes, a dusty central space and a bank of mercilessly hard benches for the spectators. At night it was only a little more cheerful. Lights created a pool of interest and the sound of canned music, pinging machines and shouted orders floated up from the pub below. Ben, sitting next to Maggie on one of the benches, with a stout girl reclining against his knees, thought it a pity that actors were so dedicated to the idea that 'the show must go on'. The present show, for instance, could have stopped at any moment without any damage to its entertainment value. He sighed, tried to shift his knees, gave up the attempt, and looked at Maggie giving an excellent impression of enthralled delight. Then he turned his attention, reluctantly, to the actors. There were only two of them, and they wore identical black T-shirts and jeans, accentuating their pallor. One was Lucy Starr, who sat mute in a chair; another was a young man who berated her. Around them large plastic bricks of various colours were built into a wall.

'Chatterbox! That's all you are!' the actor told the silent Lucy. 'A natural chatterbox! Questions and answers. All day and most of the night. What're you doing with those bricks? What's the point of building? Robbing me of my confidence, that's what you're doing. Washing it away, on a flood of questions. Words. Drip. Drip. Drip. Like a Chinese water torture. I tell you. I build because I have to. I don't build with words. I build with bricks.' He stood very close to Lucy and shouted, 'Bricks are words. Do you understand? Stop challenging me. Stop undermining me. Stop talking!'

Looking round the room, Ben was surprised to see the bearded painter who'd brought an abstract into Klinsky's with a dark-haired girl. They were sitting forward, listening intently as the actor continued his tirade.

'All right, I'll ignore it. It's just a noise off. Like the sound of the distant motorway traffic. Or the wind. Is it meaningless? Is it a siren in the night? A police siren? Does it mean an accident? Or a murder? I won't listen, I won't!' He put his hands over his ears. 'Your voice. Eternal chattering. I can't get away from it. No escape. Nowhere.' And then, after what seemed to Ben like an endless pause, he shouted, 'All right. I surrender! You can stop it now. You've won. Understand that. You won the argument! Nothing means anything! Anymore!' At which he kicked over the wall of bricks, the house lights came up and Lucy and the actor bowed to a smattering of applause. When Maggie asked Ben what he thought, he said he thought they needed a drink.

In the pub downstairs, Ned Nunnelly recognized the man from Klinsky's and introduced himself and his partner Patti. 'You hated my painting done by the wind,' he shouted over the music. 'You were all over that glossy bit of kitsch done by the horrible Hardcastle.'

'You seem to have a particular hatred of Hardcastle?' Ben was restoring his circulation with a large brandy.

'God, what a bore! I was at the Academy Schools with him.'

'Really? I don't remember you?' Ben was puzzled.

'As a matter of fact I avoided your lectures on dead painters. I had enough of them watching Hardcastle produce his ghastly little imitations.'

'Did you see much of him?'

'Little as I could. He was always asking me to go boating with him. Can you believe it? Christ! With all the girls there were to chase at art school. Can you imagine why I'd want to go out boating with Hardcastle?' Before the question could be answered, Lucy appeared with the actor. Ben, his spirits now recovered, bought them all drinks, while Lucy made up for her long stage silence. 'You were a super audience! Weren't they an absolutely *super* audience, Lester? Lester played my husband. These are all the top people from Klinsky's. Ben Glazier and Maggie Perowne and . . .' 'Ned Nunnelly,' he told them. 'I'm not from Klinsky's. God forbid. I'm an artist like you. This is Patti.'

'Patti Duprey. Say, you guys, what a great piece of theatre!'

'We love it. We think it says everything there is to say about male impotence,' Lester told them. 'Of course, Lucy had a terrific responsibility. No lines.'

'Don't worry, Lucy. You were great!' Patti congratulated her. 'It must be so difficult not saying anything.'

'That's what Lester says.' Lucy told them. 'Anyone can say lines. But if you can do it without them, well, it's like swinging on a trapeze without a safety net.'

'Or riding a motor bike without an engine,' Ben murmured.

'Don't you pay any attention to him, Lucy.' Patti gave Ben a look of deep disapproval. 'You were just great. You know where I'd like to see that piece of theatre? I'd like to see it off Broadway. That's what I'd like to see.'

'That's really terribly kind of you. I don't know what to say, really. Are you an actress?'

'No. I'm, well, I'm a painter's friend.'

'I just thought you might be an actress. I mean, you're so beautiful and . . .'

'And what?'

'Oh, nothing.' Lucy couldn't think of what to add. Then she looked at Patti and had an inspiration. 'I mean, what terribly pretty earrings!'

And Patti smiled and said thank you, and held back her hair. Ben and Maggie joined in the admiration of the earrings, two glittering goldfishes with ruby eyes.

A week later more facts emerged about the sadly short-ened life of Edward Hardcastle. Ben remembered another lecturer he'd met at the Academy Schools, a Canadian called Gary Fanner whom he'd seen off and on over the years, and who had gone to teach for a spell at the Ryerson in Toronto. He called a number he'd kept in his book for years, found Fanner was back in England and would be delighted to meet Ben and Maggie Perowne for lunch in the Caprice. There he told them he remembered Hardcastle teaching in Canada and having, it seemed, a fairly unhappy time. 'Well. Students, ten years ago. Their ideas came from New York, I suppose. They just began to find Hardcastle's paintings so old fashioned, so it was a big mistake to bring him over. Some people began to laugh at his work, quite openly. Girl students laughed and that was what hurt him most of all. My then girl-friend and I, we took him out a few times. We got the idea he was very much married in England. He lived in some quiet little village by the sea somewhere.'

'Shenstone,' Ben told him.

'Wherever it was. I suppose he thought visiting English teachers were jumped on by beautiful, ravenous North American girls. He was going to live like a student.'

'Like the sort of student he never was?' Maggie was kind.

'Anyway, he was going to lay them end to end. That was his dream. But when he got there, well, they just laughed at him, and he never got a glimpse of a pair of student panties. I believe he went back to England an unhappy man.

And never touched a paintbrush again, Ben thought, and six months later he was drowned in a boating accident.

Back at Klinsky's Ben met the tall African, who had brought the polished carving of a pregnant woman into the sale, waiting for him by Lucy's desk. Winston McKenzie had taken a careful note of Mr Glazier's name and, as he was clearly a person of authority, he had much to tell him about the politics in Neranga and the work of Feeding the Multitude. He had been, he said, a journalist on the *Sentinel* of Neranga, and would speak nothing but the truth. Ben took Mr McKenzie into an empty office and listened to him carefully, and for a long time.

Maggie walked through the long gallery on her way back to Old Masters, and took another look at the 'Woman with a Bowl of Flowers'. It was then she noticed something that Ben and she had missed. The woman with her back towards her had her hair held by a comb. One ear was visible, and from it dangled a goldfish with a ruby eye.

'Visitors from Klinsky's? You've had second thoughts and you want to buy Pandora? I can't let her go.' Indeed the lady was neatly framed on to an easel, as Ned Nunnelly let Maggie and Ben into his studio. 'Deracott's giving me an exhibition.'

'Is he now? I wouldn't have thought you were Roy Deracott's type of artist,' Ben suggested.

Maggie, looking at Pandora, said, 'Perhaps he owes you a favour.'

'A favour. Whatever for?'

'Perhaps because you've been supplying him with Edward Hardcastles, ever since that unfortunate boating accident?' Ben spoke quietly and Ned Nunnelly laughed.

'You think I'd waste my talent painting Hardcastles? Whatever for?'

'Money,' Maggie gave him the answer. 'You haven't made much out of your own work in the last ten years.'

'What's Roy Deracott been telling you?' Ned looked anxious.

'He's told us nothing,' Ben admitted. 'He's very protective of his sources of income.'

'All right then, you've no bloody evidence!'

Ben put the photograph of 'Woman with a Bowl of Flowers' on the paint table. 'You remember doing this one, I'm sure. Only you were getting careless. You painted a plant that didn't exist when Hardcastle was alive – a brand-new pansy called the "Jolly Joker". The joke, you hoped, was going to be on Klinsky's.'

Ned moved to look at the picture. 'I don't know anything about plants,' he said.

'But you know about earrings.' Maggie was sure of that. 'Or did you forget you were painting the back of Patti's head? Couldn't you resist doing the earring? Are you such a careful, academic painter? Little goldfish with ruby eyes? Lucy admired them that night at the theatre.'

'Hardcastle always painted his wife.' Ned was defensive.

'Do you know that much about him?' Ben affected surprise.

'Perhaps she had those earrings?' Ned looked at the photograph again.

'We've asked her. She never wore earrings.' Ben had made the telephone call and had been pleased to.

'Well, somebody else then.'

'Nobody else.' Ben was sure of it. 'You painted Patti.

Not from life, of course. She never knew you were painting Hardcastles. She'd have left you, if she did. But you were thinking about her, her hair, her ear, her goldfish earring.'

'That's totally ridiculous! I'm not a *forger*.'

There was silence then. Ben looked at him and said, 'You're quite right. You're not a forger.'

'Ben! What do you mean? I thought we agreed.' Maggie felt lost.

'We agreed Hardcastle didn't paint that picture when he was alive. He couldn't have. But we can't rule out the possibility that he painted it after he was dead.'

'What do we do now?' Ned laughed at them again. 'Hold a seance and ask him?'

'I think we should ask him.' Ben was quite serious. 'Yes.'

'Ben! For heaven's sake!' Maggie suspected another joke, but Ben wasn't smiling when he said, 'Wait a minute. Let's just think about Edward Hardcastle. An academic painter, married to a very nice wife, lived at the seaside, sold well. Then he goes off to Toronto in search of adventure. Mainly in search of girls. Girl students, he believes, are going to be swept off their feet by his great talent. And what do they do? They reject him. They laugh at him and his whole way of painting. So he goes home and he can't lift a brush. He's bored with his work, bored with himself, bored with his life too, I suspect. So he decides to commit a murder.'

'Murder?' He'd gone too far, Maggie thought. Now he really *is* joking.

'Oh, yes. He decided to murder Edward Hardcastle. He arranged to do him in. A death at sea, with the body lost somewhere in the deep. He'd been sailing small yachts since he was a child. Do we really believe he turned his boat over and drowned in a gust of wind? He turned the boat over, yes, somewhere where he could get to the shore and get away to America and become someone else entirely. A different sort of painter who blew paint across the canvas with a hair-dryer. The sort of artist the beautiful young students in Chicago and Los Angeles and Greenwich Village would be likely to fall for. He grew a beard. He wore tinted spectacles. He put on weight over the years. Edward Hardcastle was dead. Long live Ned Nunnelly!'

'Of course you're bloody joking!' But Ned Nunnelly wasn't laughing.

'No, Ned. You're the jolly joker. It worked out rather well: your wife got the life insurance and you got a new life. The only trouble was that Ned Nunnellys didn't sell. So you had to keep on painting Hardcastles. All alone. Certainly not in this studio. It was your secret vice. You painted Hardcastles because you *are* Hardcastle. I don't suppose that's any sort of crime at all.'

There was a longer silence. Ned Nunnelly seemed to shrink. He took off his glasses to wipe his eyes. Then he had one urgent request. 'For God's sake, don't tell Patti!'

'I don't think I'm bound to tell anyone. Even Liz.' Ben had made his mind up. 'I don't suppose she'd want to live with Ned Nunnelly.'

The door opened and Patti came in wearing her white bathrobe.

'Hallo. Good to see you. Can I make you some coffee?' She smiled at the unexpected guests.

'No, really. We just called to congratulate Ned on his exhibition.'

'Isn't it great?' Patti was clearly delighted. 'Pandora's going to be thrown open to the public!'

'Oh, yes' – Ben started to move towards the door – 'just one thing. You got it wrong about Pandora, Ned. You know what she really had in her little box? All the evils and illnesses that afflict the world. The chap who kept the winds in a bag was Aeolus. He invented sailing ships and could always work up a convenient storm at sea. I just thought you'd like to know.'

Ben was surprised to find that the charitable organization Feeding the Multitude was lavishly housed in a tower block on the South Bank. Piers Frobisher welcomed him with enthusiasm and took him up to the roof garden from which he pointed out the beauties of Somerset House and the dome of St Paul's. He invited Ben to lunch, an invitation he seemed to forget when Ben told him that he had been visited by a native of that country Klinsky's wished to benefit. He'd had a disturbing story to tell which Ben had no hesitation in repeating.

'Who was this visitor?' Frobisher asked. 'Someone who doesn't like the government of Neranga?'

'I don't think the government of Neranga likes him. And he certainly doesn't like your charity. Don't you remember the old text: "Charity doth not behave itself unseemly. Rejoiceth not in iniquity. Charity puffeth not itself up." Haven't you done just that?'

'Have you talked to anyone else?'

'Not yet.'

The tall, stooping man crossed his arms, lowered his birdlike head and appeared lost in thought. When he looked up again, he was smiling in a friendly fashion which Ben found distinctly unnerving. 'Of course you understand,' he said, 'you can't get anything done in those sort of countries without greasing a few palms.'

'Including the palm of the Foreign Secretary?' Ben suggested.

'Christopher M'tatu? I believe he has a terribly expensive tailor. Look here, Ben . . .'

'Oh, please, do call me Mr Glazier.'

'I know you've put in an enormous amount of work on this charity sale. No doubt Feeding the Multitude would think it right to make you a special payment, in recognition of your services.'

'Can I have that in writing?'

'Perhaps better not. We'll just shake hands on it.' Piers Frobisher held out his hand.

'I don't think so.'

'Why not?'

'I really don't want to get grease all over my palm.' Ben left them thinking, for one uneasy moment, that he didn't want his life to end by toppling off a roof garden before he'd managed to consummate his long-lasting love for Maggie Perowne.

The Lord Chairman was quite easily persuaded. Ben told him that there was some doubt about the authenticity of the 'Woman with a Bowl of Flowers', which caused his Lordship a few days of sustained panic, but when Ben said he had now proved beyond doubt that the Hardcastle was genuine, he agreed to dispense with the services of Feeding the Multitude and hand the whole shooting-match over to Oxfam.

Ben only saw Liz once again. He got an invitation to her wedding and took Maggie down on the back of the Harley-Davidson to Shenstone-on-Sea. He recognized the bridegroom as the boat person who had invited Liz to the piano, and he did it again at the wedding-party which was held in a packed Sailors' Rest. Liz obliged:

'The way your smile just beams,
The way you sing off-key,
The way you haunt my dreams –
No, No! They can't take that away from me!'

Liz was smiling at Ben as he joined in the chorus. Then
Maggie murmured in his ear, 'You don't suppose we
should drop the slightest hint that she's committing
bigamy?'

'Absolutely not,' Ben told her, and took a deep breath
to join in 'Long ago and far away I dreamed a dream one
day' – He sang directly at Maggie Perowne.

The Virgin of Vitebsk

This will last out a night in Russia
When nights are longest there.

William Shakespeare, *Measure for Measure*

'We're not going to like it, you know.'

'Like what?'

'Russia.' Ben Glazier knew he should have felt more cheerful. He was sitting next to Maggie Perowne on the BA flight. Admittedly they were in the steerage, surrounded by a noisy party of teenaged girls, apparently released from their studies at some posh school to sample the cultural delights of Moscow; but they were escaping together from Klinsky's auction house and the fatal charm of the head of the Wine department.

'You mean *you're* not going to like it?' Maggie was wearing a raincoat with a fur collar and a round hat which made her look, Ben thought, not much older than the A-level students around them.

'Neither of us,' he told her. 'We come from the workers, you and I, Maggie. My dad was a copper and yours travelled in paper cups.'

'He didn't! He travelled in frightfully nice soap.'

'All the same. We come from the world of cold frontrooms you never went into, strong tea and ducks on the wall, net curtains over the window, and people having a "blessed release" instead of dying and not wanting to trouble the doctor. We don't want to go back to that, do

93

we? Not to our roots. Not back to the workers. I bet you that's what Russia's like. Only posh people like that sort of thing, only people like Camilla, because it's all such fun and so different from Daddy's place in Virginia Water.'

'You know what, Ben?' Maggie looked at him with a new understanding.

'What?'

'You're a terrible old snob.'

'I'm not a snob! I'm an escapologist. All my life I've been struggling to get away from strong tea and net curtains and now I'm sailing back to my appalling youth!'

It had started weeks before when Lord Holloway, Klinsky's Chairman, summoned them to a meeting in the Epicure Hotel in Piccadilly. Both his wife and his cook were away on holiday, and long service in the food trade had not taught him how to cook his own breakfast, for which meal, he told them, he always took a softly boiled egg, wholewheat toast and a decent quantity of roughage in the form of bran. Ben told him that they got enough roughage as it was in Klinsky's and ordered a kipper, which he dissected carefully as the Chairman told them that the world had undergone a considerable change. 'The Russian bear has embraced the free market economy. Now that the Cold War has ended, we're seriously thinking of opening Klinsky's in Moscow.'

'To do a roaring trade in wooden dolls and fur hats?'

'"You're a cynic, Ben.' The Lord Chairman smiled tolerantly. 'That's just as well. You're not gullible. Either of you. You've got your heads screwed on. You've done Klinsky's good service and I'm very well aware of that. So that's why I'm sending you to sniff out the possibilities of our Moscow opening. Just a toe in the water at first. A small organization. A retail outlet. And a point of sale for Russian lines in art output.'

'I'm an art expert, not a supermarket manager. Why send me?' Ben wondered.

'You've grown accustomed to working with Maggie.'

'Working, yes. That's all I've grown accustomed to.' Ben regretted it.

'Oughtn't you to send Meredith Bland from Icons?' Maggie asked the Chairman, who shook his head sadly. 'I'm afraid our man in Icons has been refused a visa by the Russian Embassy.'

'Was Merry caught *in flagrante* with an Orthodox monk behind Lenin's tomb?' Ben asked in all innocence.

'I believe it's some sort of misunderstanding. However, Meredith will give you all his Russian contacts, and Klinsky's has put its trust in you.'

'And we're off to Siberia.' Ben sounded gloomy. 'Maggie, would you mind passing the roughage? We'd better get used to it.'

'I'm afraid I've got another breakfast meeting.' Holloway was looking at his watch. 'Work never stops, does it? Well, good luck to both of you!'

On their way out, Maggie stopped at the newsstand. Gazing round the lobby Ben saw a bright-haired girl, just identifiable as Maggie's new Number Two, Miss Annabelle Straddling-Smith, get out of the lift and disappear in the general direction of the dining-room. 'The next business meeting,' he said, and asked, 'Wouldn't you say I had at least as much sexual allure as the Lord Chairman?'

'Considerably more,' Maggie assured him.

'Then why aren't I bonking in the Epicure Hotel?'

*

Meredith Bland was a ginger-headed man with a swelling stomach and a high, precise voice. He sat in his office among the darkly glowing icons of the Old Russia, and gave Ben and Maggie tips on the Moscow of today. 'Most important contact is Olga Krupenska, General Krupenski's widow. She still has an office in the Voynitsky Gallery. Knows everybody. And Ivan Grekov, at the Ministry of Culture. An absolute charmer.'

'Is he a monk, by any chance?' Ben asked.

'Ivan Grekov, a monk? Quite the reverse! Did a spell at Harvard Business School. Goes on holiday with the Club Med.'

'Are you telling us, Merry, that these people are going to help us to open Klinsky's, Moscow?'

'They'll say they will. Perhaps they can. It's so hard to tell where the power lies. Don't let it get you down. I'd advise you to take advantage of any incidental pleasures.'

'And is that why *you* can't get a visa?' Ben speculated. 'Too many incidental pleasures?'

'Oh, that was some bureaucratic nonsense!'

'Secretive sort of people,' Maggie was looking at the icons. 'They all have those beautiful almond eyes and you have no idea what they're thinking.'

'Possibly that they're worth a hell of a lot of money nowadays. Particularly if they're by Rublev.' Meredith Bland was leafing through a book of reproductions. 'When you're there, you might find out if anyone's had any news of "The Virgin of Vitebsk". This one. Painted around 1425.' He pushed the open book towards Maggie. She saw a young girl kneeling, holding a flower, before the angel who announced her pregnancy, simple and graceful figures against a gold background. 'Rublev's masterpiece,' Meredith Bland told them, 'lost before the war. I've heard rumours that it's about to surface. The tragedy for the art world is that even if it does, it can't be got out of Russia. Export of old icons is absolutely forbidden. They search cars and lorries, X-ray your luggage to make sure. But the law's not necessarily the most important thing in Moscow.'

'What is?' Maggie was still looking at the photograph.

'Money. And what money can buy. Now, I faxed Intourist to get you my favourite interpreter–guide, Alyosha. An absolute charmer. But devoutly heterosexual, and I'm afraid it shows.'

As they waited in the departure lounge and Ben checked, once again, that he'd got his passport, boarding-pass and traveller's cheques, he watched the schoolgirls being marshalled by a plump and anxious mistress, a woman made stouter by layers of warm clothing. She seemed to be in a mild panic at the responsibilities she had taken on and looked, Ben was surprised to notice, with some interest in his direction.

'Schoolgirls going to Russia,' Ben said. 'And they don't seem in the least scared. I feel extremely apprehensive and they look as though they were off on an exciting trip to the Natural History Museum.'

'I think someone else is going to Russia.' Maggie was staring with dismay at the new arrivals in the departure lounge.

'It can't be Shrimsley from Accounts!'

'Do you mind!' Maggie corrected him, 'Shrimsley, our office manager.'

'He probably set out for Lanzarote and lost his way.'

'Somehow I don't think he'd set out for Lanzarote wearing a fur hat.'

'Quick! Evasive action!'

Ben put his head down and led Maggie quickly to the

back of the queue, afraid to look when they heard Shrimsley behind them, 'Welcome, comrades!'

'Oh, Shrimsley,' Ben asked, 'going for a sunshine break? You must be in the wrong queue.'

'I'm coming with you fellows,' the office manager assured them. 'Didn't the Lord Chairman tell you? You two are doing all the arty bits. I'm going to do the nuts and bolts of the business side. See you in Club Class.'

'We're not in Club Class,' Maggie admitted. 'We were told Klinsky's was cutting down on travelling expenses.'

'See you in Moscow, then. *Dasveedanya*.' And Shrimsley passed them to board the plane.

In due course the BA intercom told them to return to their seats, fasten their belts and extinguish their cigarettes as they were about to land at Sheremetyevo Airport. Summoning her charges, who had been gossiping and giggling in the aisles, the schoolmistress gave Ben another strange look of recognition.

'Mr Glazier. Miss Perowne. Welcome to Moscow. My name is Alyosha. The other name is too hard to say, so please call me Alyosha. I am here to arrange your programme and to look after you as well. I will be, as you say, your guide, philosopher and, I hope, friend. May I take your luggage from you, Miss Perowne?' Ben looked at the young man in dismay, disapproving of his large, soulful eyes, his dark, tousled hair and general appearance of a young Romantic poet out of the age of Pushkin, inappropriately dressed in jeans and an anorak, with a job as an Intourist guide. Why couldn't Merry Bland have arranged a bossy, middle-aged woman against whom he and Maggie could have formed an alliance? He tried to comfort himself with the thought that at least Alyosha had never been to Eton.

Alyosha's programme clicked into operation as soon as they had checked into the grand, art deco hotel, where the receptionist was delighted to see Ben's Visa card. It started on the great open waste of Red Square, among the crowds of Japanese, African and American tourists, by the van selling Coca-Cola and Snickers outside St Basil's Cathedral. It was afternoon, and the red stars weren't yet lit up on the steeples behind the Kremlin wall. Lenin, after so many years of shuffling queues paying him their respects, had been moved out of his tomb and put into storage. They walked across to the great glass department store, built on the lines of the old Crystal Palace or the hothouses at Kew. Gumm once sold little but fur hats, overcoats, huge bras and outsized nylon knickers. Now, Ben and Maggie found it housed branches of Benetton, Christian Dior and the Galleries Lafayette. There were queues outside all these smart shops and Maggie asked their guide who could afford to buy there. 'I think some hard-currency prostitutes,' Alyosha told them, 'small-time thieves and the Mafia.' At which Ben said that sounded rather like the clientele of Klinsky's auction house. He also said he needed, after so much excitement, a drink.

They went to a small, Scandinavian-clean bar, past the computer department of Gumm, and sat under a Smirnoff sign by a window which commanded an excellent view of Lenin's empty tomb. Alyosha, fixing his serious and soft-eyed gaze on Maggie, talked of the state of Russia since the Berlin Wall came crashing down and Communism was defeated. 'I am worried, quite honestly. I have to tell you this. In the old days we knew where we were.'

'In the Lubyanka?' Ben suggested, 'if you stepped out of line.'

'Ben, let Alyosha tell us,' Maggie shushed him and he muttered, 'Pardon me for living!' into his glass.

'Life was very hard for us,' Alyosha was speaking to Maggie. 'Very hard. There was nothing to buy. Nothing in the shops. Few motor cars, no stereo-sets or facsimile machines. Mr Glazier is right. You had to take care what you said. So all we could do was to lead a rich inner life. You saw people on the Metro, in those days, reading good novels and great poetry. What are they reading now? I think it will be soft pornography and computer magazines.'

'You're afraid you may lose your souls?' Maggie said, causing Ben to sigh and raise his eyes to heaven.

'*You* understand, Miss Perowne.' Alyosha looked gratefully at her.

'Please, Maggie.'

'Maggie! I may call you Maggie?' Alyosha was delighted. 'That is for Margaret, isn't it? A most beautiful name. Were you named after Mrs Maggie Thatcher? Older than you, of course, but many in Russia found her a most beautiful lady.' At which point Ben choked on his beer chaser.

'Are you feeling quite well, Mr Glazier?' Alyosha was concerned.

'I think another vodka. For medical reasons.'

Alyosha ordered it and then said to Ben, 'Perhaps the journey was difficult for you? At your age.' Before Ben could reply he turned back to Maggie, 'No, I'm not quite happy about our future.'

Ben, at this moment, was overcome with irritation at being treated as though he were in the geriatric ward and Maggie was listening to Alyosha. Neither of them noticed the young man reading the *New York Herald Tribune* at the next table. He wore a good deal of gold, having two gold teeth, a gold watch and a thick gold bracelet. He also had thick black hair, brushed back and sprayed into position. His name was Lubov and he belonged to one of the classes able to shop at Gumm. If either Maggie or Ben had noticed him, they would have had no reason to pay him any close attention. Maggie said, 'I don't think you're in any danger of losing your soul, Alyosha.' At which Ben groaned, 'Oh, my God!'

'Your God?' Alyosha was interested. 'You are a religious man, Mr Glazier?'

'He's Ben.' Maggie wanted them all to be friends.

'Ben is religious.' Alyosha nodded approvingly. 'That is good. You see, Maggie and Ben, my friends, we have suffered so much. Cold. Ice. Tzars. Stalin. I myself live in a very small apartment with my sister Tatyana, her two husbands, one of which she has divorced, my mother and all their children. Also a troublesome dog. But as I said, we have an inner life. We have curds and whey. Should we be better off with twenty different sorts of yoghurt to choose from at breakfast, as you have in the West?'

'Or muesli,' Maggie told him.

'Excuse me. What is this mu–es–?'

'Stuff that looks like the sweepings of bird cages,' Ben explained. 'Roughage. Some people in England like it for breakfast.'

'Muesli? In Russian we do not know that word.'

'That,' Ben told him, 'is, at least, one thing to be said in your favour.'

The next day Alyosha's programme began with work. They visited, as recommended by Merry Bland, the Ministry of Culture. After the statutory three quarters of an hour wait in a dusty corridor, being looked at with contempt by passing secretaries, they were admitted to a large, not to say palatial, office, with ornate furniture handed down from the upper bureaucracy in the days of the Tzars. There they met a fair, smiling, muscular man in his fifties who greeted them, with great enthusiasm, wearing a purple track-suit and trainers.

'I am Grekov. Please sit down, Mr Glazier, Miss Perowne. And your guide. I have been jahgging, you see. American-style. In the old days we used to goose-step. Now we have learned to jahg.' He waved at three small gilt chairs on the further side of his desk. When they were settled he said, 'Now we have the entrepreneurial society. Already we have Pizza Hut and MacDonalds. It would be an honour if we could also welcome the great house of Klinsky.'

'And no doubt all your citizens will be standing in line for a Picasso drawing and regular fries.'

'Ssh, Ben!' Maggie tried, as usual, to keep him in control.

'You are an entertaining fellow, Mr Glazier.' Grekov clicked on a smile. 'We give you both a warm welcome. We will cooperate fully with everything except money. You understand that?'

'I think so.' Maggie understood.

'We have enthusiasm. We have the love of art. We have adopted the great principles of your economy. Every man for himself. And woman, of course. Forgive me, Miss Perowne.'

'Don't give it a thought.'

'Now, there are others apart from me who must have a say in this. Other departments to be consulted. I will let you have a list of those to be visited by you. I'm sure you will find them very young and go-ahead. Very entrepreneurial guys, every one of them. Very thrusting, as I told your colleague Mr Shrimsley.'

'He's been here already?' Ben was surprised.

'Oh, yes. He is the early bird, Mr Shrimsley. And I am the poor worm! Amusing, didn't you find that? I have suggested to him premises in Petrovka Street. Once a department of the KGB. You see, we change from the secret police to fine art. What a world of difference!'

'I suppose both of them can be concerned with crime,' Ben suggested and Grekov leant back in his big carved chair and looked at him with some suspicion.

'So entertaining! Now, Miss Perowne. Is there anything else you wish to touch upon?'

'Someone suggested we ask what you know about a picture. An icon by Rublev.' Maggie was hesitant.

'I am a mind-reader!' Grekov smiled again. 'I am sure your enquiry is about "The Virgin of Vitebsk". It was one of our greatest treasures.'

'The man in our Icon department . . .'

'Mr Meredith Bland.' Grekov knew at once.

'Yes. He wonders if you've ever been able to trace . . .'

'A terrible tragedy! A small icon, by all accounts, but very beautiful, "The Virgin of Vitebsk". We have knocked over all the statues of Stalin. And why? Because he was a thief. Long before the war, he stole many great Russian works of art. I know he sold "The Virgin of Vitebsk" to line his own pocket! Who bought it? That is a mystery. But I have heard rumours that it may turn up in Germany. I hope so. Who else do you go and see?'

'Mrs Olga Krupenska,' Alyosha told him.

'At the Voynitsky Gallery. Dear Olga. An unreconstructed, old-style Communist, I'm afraid. But a great art expert. You will learn something of great value from her. I hope it. Give her my good love. Tell her to start jahgging and invest in foreign currency.'

A phone had started ringing. A secretary came up to the desk and whispered something to Grekov in Russian. 'Oh, the telephone!' Grekov was waving them away.

'Goodbye, colleagues from Klinsky. That is the trouble with the entrepreneurial society. The telephone never stops ringing! I wish you all the best, for your business in Moscow.'

In the passage outside Grekov's office a round, red-faced man in a worn, shabby overcoat, wearing his unwashed hair long, was standing by a window lighting a cigarette. His name was Tolyagin and his job at the Ministry of Culture was of a mysterious nature, except that he worked directly to (as Shrimsley would have said) Ivan Grekov. When Maggie and Ben and Alyosha got to the Voynitsky Gallery, Tolyagin was also there, but that might have been simply because the gallery houses the world's greatest collection of icons. They didn't notice him particularly, although they couldn't fail to see the English schoolgirls who were giggling and whispering their way round the solemn saints and placid Madonnas. Ben also saw that their schoolmistress gave him another look of curious intimacy as they passed through the gallery.

'From the days of the early icons we have been very religious. Our great writers – Tolstoy, Dostoevsky – they were religious. And this will surprise you. Mrs Olga Krupenska, who is an old-fashioned Communist, is religious also,' Alyosha told them. She's what you call a 'character'. I think you will get along together.'

Ben said, 'Cry God for Lenin, Stalin and Brezhnev? How very curious.'

On their way to the director's office, Angela Ridgeway, the tallest, thinnest and prettiest of the schoolgirls, who had her ears full of the taped commentary the gallery provided, ran into Ben coming round a corner. Although the collision was entirely her fault, he apologized and she uttered no word at all.

*

'Klinsky's! Of course, the name is famous.' Olga Krupenska had the fine bones, lustrous eyes and much-lined
face of an old woman who had once been a beautiful
young girl. She was smoking heavily, sitting behind a
desk on which the books and papers were stacked as
untidily as they were in Ben's office in London. Alyosha
was helping her pour out tea and hand round small
cakes to her visitors from England. She asked if Mr
Glazier would take a little vodka, and when he declined
politely she looked hurt. 'Why not? My husband, General
Krupenski, always took vodka for breakfast. Good on
the stomach. I tell you. We are giving away our country
to western politicians and the Mafia. We give them all
the treasures we have left. But such a house as Klinsky's!
Yes. I think we can do some business. We could trust
each other.'

'Of course,' Maggie began, 'there are many great works
of art in Russia ...' And Olga, looking at her with
interest, asked, 'You are his mistress?'

'I'm afraid not,' Ben had to admit. 'Maggie's the head
of Old Master Paintings. In fact, she's my boss.'

'Strange! I took her for your mistress. My husband the
General had many mistresses.'

As she turned away to pour tea, Ben whispered to
Maggie, 'Always took one for breakfast?'

Olga turned round to Alyosha. 'What did Mr Glazier
say?'

'He suggested that General Krupenski always took a
mistress for breakfast,' Alyosha repeated solemnly.

'Good! Very good!' Olga laughed, surprisingly loudly.

'There's one masterpiece we can't see, apparently. "The
Virgin of Vitebsk".' Ben changed the subject.

'Our greatest work of art! Stolen by the Germans.'
Olga looked disgusted. 'Looted. What for? To hang in

the lavatory of Field Marshal Goering, I shouldn't be surprised. Where is it now? Who can tell? We may never find it again, I think. Only by great good luck.'

'How did you come to lose it?'

'I tell you. It was in a monastery attacked by the Germans. Our soldiers fought to save it. They were good Communists, of course. But they fought to save that famous icon. Many were killed fighting in that monastery. Some were shot in front of the icon itself. "The Virgin" looked on as they were shot.'

'Is that the story?'

'It's the truth. My husband was there, a young officer, in that fighting. Look, here he is. With our heroic leader!' She stood up then and pointed to a large photograph hanging on the wall, framed in heavy, dark wood, ornately carved. It showed a number of young officers in a group with a jovial Stalin, then the hero of the West also. 'I have seen my husband weep when he told how the icon was lost.' There was a short, respectful silence and then Olga Krupenska became business-like. 'But now, of course, I should be pleased to help the great Klinsky's. I think we shall meet again now we have broken the ice. Is that that what you say? And I can decide exactly how we might work together.'

'If we did open in Moscow,' Maggie asked, 'are there people with money, interested in buying pictures?'

'Oh, there are enough people with money. When there are poor, there are always rich also. Now we have some in Mercedes cars and many sleeping on rubbish dumps.'

'It sounds just like home,' Ben added.

Olga had moved closer to the old photograph and was looking at it again with pride. 'Things were better in the time of the old Communists. When General Krupenski was alive.'

At the end of the day, long after Maggie and Ben had

left her, Olga Krupenska locked the door of her office against further intruders. She then went to the big photograph once more and pressed a spot on the heavy carved frame which swung back from the wall. In the space behind it hung a painting with a gold background. 'The Virgin of Vitebsk' was kneeling and holding a flower, listening to the angel who brought her astonishing news. Olga kissed the icon's frame and then, reverently, folded her hands in prayer.

Maggie, to Ben's silent regret, had invited Alyosha to join them for dinner at the Slavyanski Bazaar and now, after caviare and boiled fish, ice-cream and vodka, they were back in the foyer of their hotel. Alyosha, looking round at its green and gold, its chandeliers and marble floor, said, 'What a palace you live in! How either of my sister's two husbands would envy you such accommodations.' He was about to leave them to return to his overcrowded flat when Lubov emerged from the shadows with a smile which fully exposed his gold teeth.

'You English?'

'No,' Ben said truthfully, 'Scots.'

'I can show you round this town.' Lubov was undeterred. 'You guys want to know how to have a good time in Moscow?'

'These are *my* clients!' Alyosha was pale with anger. 'I arrange their programme as their guide, officially credited. You are not needed here!'

'OK. Keep your cool!' Lubov was laughing as he moved away. 'See you around.'

'I know that sort,' Alyosha said. 'This is a good time for no good people. So, now he has gone, I will leave you.'

He left. Maggie smiled after him and Ben didn't mutter

anything so crude as 'alone at last!' He did say that the fridge in his room was overflowing with beer and champanski, and would she care for a nightcap?

'Oh, Ben, darling, I'm exhausted!' Maggie stifled a yawn.

Agreeing that too much Alyosha did wear a person out, Ben went off to the bar, sadly unaccompanied. When he got there he found the plump schoolmistress who had, from time to time, shown such a curious interest in him nursing a small glass of vodka. He had only just sat down, a few stools away from her in the empty bar, when she began a conversation he found frankly mystifying. She opened with 'Hallo' in a throaty voice, and went on in almost a whisper, 'How *are* you?'

'Well, rather tired.'

'Yes, you would be.' She moved herself and her drink to sit beside him. 'Got my girls settled in for the night in the students' hostel. I came here for a breath of civilization.'

'I think I've seen your schoolgirls,' Ben admitted.

'School young women, actually. Highly privileged daughters of television executives and brain surgeons, about to go mad on Russian interpreters. I teach modern languages at St Peter's, Bayswater. For my sins.'

'Do Russian interpreters have that effect on girls?' Ben was worried.

'Oh, yes! English girls especially,' the mistress told him. At which bad news, he asked for another large vodka and drank it quickly as she said, 'How are you these days? Still chasing girls, are you?'

'I beg your pardon?'

'I suppose they can run too fast for you now, eh? I was never a great runner. But, anyway, you're happy. That's good. I'm glad of that. Very glad. Is that your daughter I saw you with at the airport?'

'No. Well, no, I haven't got a daughter. As a matter of fact, I never had a wife.'

'Lucky you. I married a Russian. I thought he looked like a prince. Ten years later, as a result of vodka and sausage, he looked like a frog. It was a fairy-tale in reverse. The story of my life. Oh, we split up years ago.'

'I'm sorry.' Ben wasn't sure how to react.

'Don't worry. It's not your fault, darling.'

Ben looked at her apprehensively, finished his vodka and got off his stool. 'Well, actually, I *am* rather tired.'

'It was wonderful to bump into you. See you around.'

'Yes. Well, yes, perhaps.'

She looked after him, smiling, as he walked towards the lift. Ben was still puzzling over this conversation when the memory of it was blotted out by a new and deeper anxiety. Maggie's room was next to his and as he approached it down the long, dimly lit corridor, he heard the distinct sound of revelry by night. Now he stood in front of number 406, listening to high-pitched giggles and deep male laughter. This was followed by music and unsteady singing. He clenched his fist and knocked on the door, again and then again, but he got no answer. Then, feeling ashamed, he stooped to peep through the keyhole and saw an empty champanski bottle on a threadbare square foot of carpet. There was the sound of further laughter and he went to his room, number 405, in the worst possible temper.

The telephone by the bed started to ring. Ben ran at it, hoping it was Maggie inviting him to a party which had been nothing to her without him; but all he heard was the distant voice of Meredith Bland. His opening line was also mysterious, 'What about the virgin?'

'What do you mean? I don't think I know any virgins.'

' "The Virgin of Vitebsk", Ben! What did Olga Krupenska tell you about that?' Merry Bland was in no mood for banter.

'Oh, that the Germans stole it.'

There was silence and then Merry spoke more quietly, 'Will you be seeing her again?'

'She said so.'

'Give me a ring at Klinsky's when she comes across with anything definite. Promise me that. Good-night, Ben.'

Ben said, 'God rest you, Merry,' and put down the phone. He looked up, startled. Who had hurled a glass against the wall between him and the woman he so inconveniently loved?

Breakfast at the hotel was well stocked with bacon and eggs, ham, herrings, liver sausage, black and white bread – food available to those with dollars, American Express or Visa cards. Breakfast for two would cost in roubles more than the monthly salary of a professor at Moscow University. Ben, sitting at the marble-topped table under the high, mirrored ceiling, saw Maggie help herself to the full English, Russian-style plate and join him with it. He gave her no smile of welcome but asked, 'You're hungry?' in a meaningful way which was quite lost on her.

She nodded and started to eat.

'I thought you might be. We've got a week's work ahead, you know ... by the way, Merry Bland rang up last night. I might have put him on to you, if you hadn't been otherwise engaged.'

'I was asleep.'

'Oh, were you? Boring as that, was it?'

'We'll get going soon. When Alyosha turns up.' Maggie was spreading butter on black bread, apparently calm.

'Turns up? Don't you mean "comes down"?'

'I left a note at the desk. Inviting him to join us for breakfast.' She looked at a glowering Ben. 'I say, you don't mind, do you?'

'Mind? Why on earth should I mind? I'm delighted to spend every waking hour with Alyosha, getting a fascinating insight into his soul. I'm sure you're thinking of taking him back to England. Perhaps you'll get him a job at Klinsky's, so he can teach us all spiritual values.'

'Ben, dear. Are you feeling quite well?' Maggie looked concerned.

'Perfectly well, thank you,' he told her. 'Of course, *I* wasn't up half the night throwing champagne glasses at the wall.'

'No, I don't suppose you were.'

He thought that her face lit up as Alyosha approached and put down a tray loaded with bacon and eggs.

'You got the message?' Maggie asked him.

'I think he got it yesterday.' Ben gazed unhappily at the ceiling.

'*Dobray outra*, Ben.' Alyosha was unfailingly polite. 'You are looking well and healthy, I must say. Are you ready for our programme?'

'Haven't I read of people starving in Russia? I'm glad your soul can cope with bacon and eggs, and' – Ben glanced at Maggie – 'all the other little luxuries.'

'It's very true, Ben. Some of our old pensioners are hit by inflation. They are going hungry. They would be grateful for a well-cooked breakfast, as I am. Many thanks to your good company, Klinsky's.'

Ben might have said more but Maggie was giving her room number to a waiter, and he heard her say, 'Number 404.'

'That can't be right,' Ben interrupted this routine

exchange with rising excitement. 'I'm 405. You're next to me. You must be 406.'

'Next to you on the *other* side, Ben.'

'The *other* side.' Really the other side? Excuse me, both of you. I think . . .' He stood up as though the news were too good to be true. 'I've left my notebook upstairs.'

He was still anxious as he came back down the corridor. He passed 406 and his door, 405. The door to 404 was open and a maid was dusting the wardrobe. He was delighted to see Maggie's coat on a chair and a book on icons. Then, as he turned back towards his room, the door of 406 opened and Keith Shrimsley came out wearing his fur hat and carrying a briefcase.

'*Dobray outra*, Ben,' he said. 'Can't wait to chat. Got plenty of work to do.' He didn't wait to hear Ben break into the opening bars of ''S Wonderful! 'S Marvellous –' and even got as far, with considerable optimism, as 'you should care for me!'

Over the next week Moscow became a way of life; Ben thought he could hardly remember living anywhere else. The trees were still black and bare but the spring sunshine shone through them strongly enough to melt most of the snow, some of which still lay in grey heaps at the roadside or powdered the ground in patches of shade. He and Maggie waited in numerous corridors and called on numberless secretaries at the Department of Trade, at the Ministry of Economic Cooperation and the Council for the Encouragement of Foreign Business. They received glasses of black tea and the warning that someone else, someone very high up indeed, would finally have to say 'yes' and such things couldn't be hurried. Ben thought they were getting precisely nowhere. Shrimsley, however, seemed to be doing rather better. He stopped by their table one day at breakfast and announced he'd got very close to Grekov at the Ministry of Culture. He couldn't promise but Klinsky's might have the chance of selling a work of enormous importance. 'One of the finest examples of its genre. Typically Russian, of course.' And then he was off, apparently to jog with Ivan Grekov.

'I'm not sure I like that,' Ben told Maggie when they were alone. 'Merry Bland only seemed interested in "The Virgin of Vitebsk" and now Shrimsley's talking about her. She just might be the real reason for our visit.'

'What do you mean?'

'If she turns up, someone might expect us to take her back to England.' And before they could discuss things further, Alyosha joined them.

Alyosha was with them for every meal. He was there when they visited the onion-domed churches in the Novodevichy Convent, and later when they walked round the lake outside its thick, grey walls. Ben remembered that Olga Krupenska had wanted to see them again, and time was getting short.

'I am so sorry,' Alyosha told him. 'I think she has not been too well. I will make inquiries.'

'Merry Bland apparently thought she had something important to tell us. What do you think it was?'

'I have really no idea.' Their guide smiled engagingly. 'Now. As we are getting near the end of the tour, I want to discuss our programme for tomorrow night. What would you like? In the theatre there is an interesting play about agricultural workers. Exceedingly controversial.'

'Please, Alyosha!' Ben begged him. 'Have mercy on us.'

'Or I might suggest the jazz club in the Arbat. Would you like it?'

Maggie said it sounded interesting but Alyosha looked

at Ben with deep concern. 'Perhaps you would prefer to rest?'

'What? Twiddle my thumbs in the hotel while you go out dancing with Maggie? It may come as a surprise to you, Alyosha, but I have always been able to fox-trot with the best of them!'

'What is fox-trot, exactly?'

'A dance that was popular,' Maggie explained, 'in the Stalin era.'

The jazz club in the Arbat had a small, brightly lit dance floor, a bar doing a brisk trade in Pepsis and beer in plastic mugs, and a platform on which three youngish musicians were playing Deep Purple numbers. There was a family audience, with small children running between the chairs and getting in the way of the dancers. Maggie sent a request to the band by way of Alyosha, so that Ben, to his great joy, was able to hold her in his arms and croon the words of 'Nice Work If You Can Get It' in her ear.

When the music changed to 'Long Ago and Far Away', Ben and Maggie joined Alyosha at a table. They had noticed a little group of girls in a dark corner by the band. One of them emerged, hugged by a glittering mini-dress. She climbed on to the platform, unhooked the microphone, clutched it, fondled it and sang to it with surprising power, flicking her hair, strutting the stage, pointing a triumphant finger at the ceiling and generally giving a performance of uninhibited professionalism.

'Who's that girl singing?' Ben asked, but Alyosha had invited Maggie to dance to 'A little more up-to-date music' and he was left alone. Then he remembered where he'd seen the girl before.

When the number ended to a smattering of applause, she came off the stage and walked to the bar, where she was bought a beer by a waiting man, who kissed her and had his arm round her as she drank. They had their backs to Ben but Angela Ridgeway turned as he came up and spoke to her, 'Shouldn't you be asleep?'

'Why on earth?' She freed herself from her friend's embrace.

'Tucked up in the dormitory of the students' hostel,' Ben suggested. 'What in heaven is that schoolmistress of yours going to say?'

'Oh, Batty!' Angela flicked on a quick smile. 'She's quite broad-minded. Well, you should know that as much as anyone.'

'Should I?'

'She knows I've been here before. Last year, in fact. After O-levels. I've made quite a few friends and, well, they asked me to sing here. It's a lot more exciting than plodding round icons.'

'So, sir. I hope you enjoy the evening.' Her companion smiled, exposing his gold teeth in a friendly fashion.

'Very enterprising,' Ben was talking to Angela.

'I suppose I ought to ask Batty to come along. She gets quite lonely. Why don't you do something about her? She's always talking about you.'

'Is she really? How extraordinary. What does she say?'

'That you know all about pictures.'

'Well, that's entirely true.'

Alyosha and Maggie came back from the dance floor and joined the group. Alyosha looked with intense dislike at Angela's friend, who was still smiling at Ben. 'I think we bumped into each other in the Hotel Lermontov. You are an art dealer? An art dealer from England?' He got a card out of his wallet and handed it to Ben. 'I am Vassily Lubov. My business card. I import and export works of art.'

'I thought there was some law against that.'

'There are many laws. They make very little difference to life in Russia.' At this, Alyosha could no longer contain himself and he shouted at Lubov, 'Thief! Crook! Mafioso! You keep away from these people!' Then he grabbed Lubov by the lapels of his jacket and started to push him away. They were shouting at each other in Russian. Lubov swung a fist at Alyosha and missed. Then the barman was parting them and Angela, who had been watching the fight with pleasure, moved back to the stage and started to sing again.

'Alyosha!' Maggie was frightened and concerned as their guide, philosopher and friend emerged from the fray.

'His soul's broken out,' Ben told her with some satisfaction. Alyosha was breathless and apologetic. 'Ben. Maggie. My friends. Perhaps we should leave here now and interrupt our programme.' And so, rather earlier than expected, they went.

The drama, whatever it had meant, was over. Maggie had gone up to her room and Ben, once again, was sitting over a lonely nightcap in the hotel bar. There, perched on a stool, was the plump schoolmistress whose prize pupil was hitting the high notes in the jazz club. Ben ordered another vodka and said, 'Batty!' to her by way of greeting.

'Did you hear my girls call me that?' She seemed pleased.

'Your girls get around, don't they?'

'You never called me Batty, did you?'

'Of course not!' Then he asked, for information, 'What did I call you, exactly?'

'I'd better not remind you.'

'No? Why not?'

'Mightn't it be a little dangerous, at our age?'

As Ben was silenced by this mysterious remark, Maggie, on her way to bed, got a phone call from Alyosha, who was still downstairs in the lobby. He said he wanted to talk to her urgently, so she invited him up. When he came, they drank beer from her fridge and she made sure that Ben hadn't seen him on his way. She asked him what the quarrel in the jazz club had been all about. He stood up and and paced the room in anger.

'Such people are ruining our country! They think every-thing can be bought. Everything! We don't want Commun-ism back. Secret police! Never! But we don't want to be bought and sold. Like – what was that breakfast dish Ben was talking about?'

'Muesli.'

'Muesli. That is a word I must try to remember.'

'I shouldn't bother, Alyosha. But why the hell were you attacking that man in the jazz club?'

'Because he wanted to do some dirty business with you. To help you smuggle some part of our soul out of Russia! Listen, the magician's soul was hidden in an egg. You know the story? Well, I think the Russian soul is in our icons.'

'But why should he be after us?'

'He had probably found out something about you. He's that sort of crook. A Mafia man. Maybe he knew you're interested in "The Virgin of Vitebsk". He thought you were dealers who'd do anything for money.'

'But we aren't.'

'I know *you* are not, Maggie. I felt that when we first met in the bar on Red Square. Remember? I knew that. Here is someone who cares about all the things that are important to us.' He raised his glass. '*Prosit!*'

'*Prosit*, Alyosha,' Maggie said.

*

'Smart-arse!' The schoolmistress in the bar spoke after a long silence.

'What did you say?' Ben was startled.

'"Sally Smart-arse". That's what you used to call me.'

Ben stared at her, incredulous at first, and then, looking at her, he saw a vision out of his past. 'Sally Smart-arse! Looked a little like a Botticelli nymph. Out of "Primavera".'

'Nice of you to say so.'

'Thin and dreamy and smoked occasional cigars. Called "Smart-arse" because she attracted money.' The memories came flooding back.

'Until the Russian came along.'

'That's who you are! Of course, I didn't remember Batty.'

'I thought, for a moment, you'd forgotten me entirely.' She looked at him accusingly.

'I can't imagine how you got that idea.'

'You know what, Ben? You haven't changed a bit.'

'You haven't changed either.'

'You were always an appalling liar. I wonder . . .'

'What?'

'I wonder if we should go on from where we left off.'

'I wonder . . .' Ben was doubtful.

'Probably not,' she decided.

'Probaby not.' Ben was relieved.

'I suppose there's bound to be someone else in your life?'

'Well, not exactly.'

But she was sure of it. 'There's someone else in your life,' she said.

'Thank you. Thank you for listening to me.' Alyosha stood up and finished his beer. 'I think now I must go back to my apartment.'

'Isn't it a bit overcrowded?' Maggie looked up at him, surprised at his sudden decision.

'Very much so. But they are expecting me back. Some time, perhaps, I can stay with you longer.'

'Some time?'

'When we have had a better evening.'

'I enjoyed myself. Honestly I did.'

'Apart from the presence of the Mafia. Good-night, Maggie.'

'Good-night, Alyosha.' She kissed him then, a conventional goodbye kiss. He enveloped her and kissed her hard. For a moment she returned his enthusiasm. Then he released her. 'Oh, Maggie. *Ya tebya liyubliu.*'

'I haven't had time to learn Russian.'

'*Ya tebya liyubliu.* I love you.' Then he went very quickly, before she could say anything.

That night someone got into the Voynitsky Gallery, carrying a torch and a bunch of keys. The light passed the enigmatic saints and the still madonnas with their stiff babies. The Director's office door opened to one of the keys. There the round-faced man with long hair, Tolyagin, Ivan Grekov's shadowy servant, started on a search, opening drawers and pulling pictures from the wall. The photograph of smiling Stalin and his young officers was hard to move, but his hand found a spot on the frame and it swung open like a cupboard door. And behind it, there was nothing to be found, nothing but an empty space which had once sheltered the long-lost 'Virgin of Vitebsk'.

Late that night Maggie was woken by the telephone beside her bed. 'Alyosha speaking. Can you meet me tomorrow? The Novodevichy Cemetery, near to Chekhov's grave. Please come alone.'

'All right. I'll tell Ben I'm going shopping. He hates shopping.'

'I have something to tell you of great importance. Something that will change our lives. Shall we say three o'clock. *Ya tebya liyubliu.*'

'*Ya tebya liyubliu.*' Maggie repeated the scrap of Russian she had so recently learned.

Outside the walls of the Novodevichy Convent, next to the Smolensk Cathedral, among naked birch trees, under the black earth and a powdering of snow, between weedy paths and struggling hedges, the great and the good, and the not so good, lay under elaborate tombstones. A stone general was to be seen forever answering some eternal telephone, and Khrushchev was trying to struggle out of a great block of marble. The actors and writers were huddled together. The bust of Gogol, with long hair, looked handsome and romantic. Chekhov was hidden beneath a little roofed hut, a primitive tomb he had seen on his travels into the heart of Russia. Beside him lay his wife and Stanislavsky his actor. And there it was that Maggie found Alyosha, sitting on a broken bench, smiling up at her, taking her hand and drawing her down beside him. 'You're alone?'

'Yes.'

'And tomorrow you go home?'

'I'll be coming back,' she promised him, 'if we open the gallery.'

He was looking at her, his excitement spilling over as he told her, 'I've got it!'

'What?'

'You are the only person I could trust with it. It'll be for both of us. For us to share. Some time, we said. Now I can tell you. That time has come.'

'Alyosha. What are you talking about?' She was horribly afraid.

'Oh, nothing very much. Just "The Virgin of Vitebsk". To be honest with you, I stole it.'

'You *what*?'

'Oh, it has had such a history of stealing. The Germans didn't steal it. You know who did? Old General Krupenski, Olga's husband! He told everyone the Germans had taken it from the monastery. What nonsense! He took it and kept it for himself. But you know what? This brave officer lacked the courage to sell the icon! But Olga didn't. She was going to sell it to you. And you know what she would have done with the money? Use it for her stupid politics. To help the old women in woolly hats who want Communism back, and their friends who put Jesus, as well as the hammer and sickle, on their red banners. What a waste! We shall sell it together, Maggie. Just you and I. I could come to England. We could live in some big apartment without any of my relatives. Perhaps. In the end, we could go further. To America! What do you say to that?'

'Alyosha. Have you gone completely mad?'

'I think, suddenly, I have gone completely sane. Look, tonight, I will bring the picture to you. It's not large. We shall think of ways of getting it to England. We shall give it a history, quite legal. Such documents are easy to get hold of. Perhaps your Mr Meredith Bland will help us.'

'My God! You're the one who was afraid of being corrupted by the West! You were the one who talked about the Russian soul!'

'You liked that, didn't you?' He smiled charmingly.

'It seems I was fooled by it.'

'You wanted me to have a soul, so you could feel good about me. So you could feel better about all our family squashed in three rooms in a block where our drunk neighbours use the lift for a toilet and we shall never afford a Mercedes car. Where my sister could not give a year's wages for a silk shirt like you are wearing.'

'So you set out to fool me.'

'I set out to make you love me. I know what English girls like about us. And it's true also, it will be true for both of us, when we have sold the icon we can afford to live a rich inner life. Together!'

'On stolen property?'

'There is no one in the West does that?'

'Some people, perhaps. That's not the point.'

'They can't preach to me. They beat us in the arms race, they destroyed Communism, they pulled down the Berlin Wall. They think it's their great triumph. But, after that, what do they expect us to live on? Honesty? Please don't make me laugh! Do you think there are honest livings to be got in Russia nowadays?' He stood up. 'I must go now. Tonight I bring the picture.'

'No, Alyosha. No!'

'I come tonight.' She saw him moving away, down the path between so many graves, and called after him helplessly, 'No. Listen. It's impossible. It's ridiculous. I'm sure you're joking. It's quite impossible!'

'Don't follow me now! It might not be safe for you.' He started to run and she was still calling, 'Alyosha! Come back. Alyosha. I don't even know your name.'

'Konchalovsky. Alyosha Konchalovsky. That's a funny name to you, isn't it?'

'No! No, it's not funny. Come back!'

'Tonight!'

She could see him no longer. The paths twisted and he was out of sight. He ran out of the cemetery gates and, as he did so, an old Mercedes car came to life and moved after him. It was driven by Lubov.

*

Maggie had decided that she couldn't believe a word Alyosha had told her. He had tricked her about his 'soul' because he wanted her to love him. Couldn't he have told her an absurd story about the icon for the same reason? The idea that he was going to turn up at the hotel with 'The Virgin of Vitebsk' was part of a ludicrous seduction technique. Of course, he wanted her to take him back to England, where they would wait for a picture which had, in fact, disappeared long ago. She decided not to be in that evening and asked Ben to take her to the circus.

'Without Alyosha?'

'Definitely without Alyosha!' When she said this he started to hum 'Nice Work If You Can Get It' and went to change into his most flamboyant tie.

So they fought their way through the crowds, past the circus horses stepping delicately on the pavement, and sat staring up and up to the immense height at which girls with strong thighs and square-shouldered men twisted and somersaulted and performed what seemed incredible feats of bravery in the air. And Maggie tried to forget all about that afternoon.

At which time Alyosha left his apartment block near Mayakovsky Station and started to walk to Maggie's hotel. And the battered Mercedes, with Lubov smiling at the wheel, started quietly and moved after Alyosha as he made his way to Tverskaya Street, once called after Maxim Gorky, a writer considered too left-wing for the brave new capitalist world. Quite soon, Lubov became aware of the fact that there was someone else intensely interested in Alyosha's journey.

At the end of Tverskaya, Alyosha turned into narrow streets by the Moscow Arts Theatre, a short cut to Theatre Square and Maggie's hotel. And it was in one of these, a silent empty place, that he heard footsteps behind him, looked round and started to run because of what he saw. The long-haired man shouted at him to stop and then raised the gun he took from the pocket of his battered overcoat.

Alyosha fell running and his briefcase tumbled open, exposing a glimmer of a gold picture. And then the Mercedes' lights lit up and, before Tolyagin could reach his prize, 'The Virgin of Vitebsk' was swept up and driven away by Lubov, the English schoolgirl's lover, to an unknown destination.

A few people heard the shot, but such sounds are common in the Moscow of today and they took no notice of it at all.

The next morning, the day of their return to England, a strange woman introduced herself to Ben and Maggie at breakfast. 'I am Ursula Mamentova and I am your Intourist guide for today. Our programme is: I take you to the airport and see you safely on to the flight for England. BA 873 it is, surely?'

'Where's Alyosha?' Maggie asked.

'Who?'

'Our guide was Alyosha.'

'Mr Konchalovsky,' Ursula told them, 'is not available. He has another client. Now. Shall we start our programme?'

Angela Ridgeway remembered the procedure for baggage inspection when you depart from Moscow Airport. The big suitcases go through an X-ray machine some fifty yards before the check-in, but not the hand-luggage. You then have to carry, drag or somehow hump your big case to the check-in and put it on the conveyor-belt. It won't be examined again and your hand-baggage doesn't get Xrayed until you're on your way to the final point of departure.

The important parcel, square, flat, and wrapped in brown paper, which Lubov had given Angela was in her shoulder-bag while her big suitcase was examined and found innocent. Half-way to the check-in, she put it down, apparently exhausted by its weight, and a well-briefed selection of her friends crowded around her. It was then that the parcel came out of her shoulder-bag and went into the big zipped pocket on the front of her suitcase, which was sent on its way to London.

Maggie and Ben saw none of this. They had passed through and he was saying goodbye to Russia with a small Guinness in the Irish bar, which was doing a roaring trade in the duty-free area. 'So Alyosha deserted us,' he said.

'Yes.'

'Were you in love with him?' he felt it safe to ask.

'I suppose so.' Maggie stared down at her coffee. 'A little.'

'I'm sorry.'

'Thank you, Ben.'

They were both silent. Suddenly, and unexpectedly, he said, 'Smart-arse!'

'What did you call me?'

'I suppose I was in love too, once. With a girl called Smart-arse. Now she's old Batty. Oh, well, it happens to all of us.'

Maggie had stopped listening. She was thinking of someone else. Then she said, 'Alyosha told me he'd stolen "The Virgin of Vitebsk".'

'He *what*?'

'I suppose you'd better know the whole story.'

*

It was on an easel in Lord Holloway's office: the small golden picture of the kneeling girl and the angel lit up the room. Ben and Maggie were looking at it for the first time, as were the Lord Chairman and Shrimsley, the office manager. Meredith Bland had received it into Klinsky's and he looked at it with the pride of ownership. 'The provenance is absolutely fascinating,' he told them. Stalin sold it in the Thirties. He looted so many Russian treasures.'

'However, it was a perfectly legitimate sale by a head of state,' Shrimsley assured everybody.

'Oh, entirely legal,' Merry agreed. 'It was bought by a Dutch gallery owner.'

'German,' Shrimsley suggested.

'No, Dutch,' Merry Bland insisted. 'He sold it to an Orthodox family who'd left Russia at the time of the Revolution and taken up residence in South America.'

'Leipzig!' Shrimsley was sure.

'Rio. The grandson of the original purchaser sold it to a dealer in New York,' was Bland's version.

'It was recovered by the Russian Army during the war and recently came into the hands of the Ministry of Culture.' Shrimsley apparently knew the full story.

'My dear Shrimsley. It was brought into Klinsky's by a representative of the New York dealer.' Bland was certain of the story.

'Ivan Grekov sent me certificates, authenticated!' Shrimsley opened the file on his lap.

'The New York provenance is fully documented,' Merry assured them.

'There would seem to be some conflict of evidence.' Ben looked amused.

'What did you find out about it, Ben?' the Lord Chairman asked. 'I assume you were doing *something* in Russia.'

'Apart from dancing and drinking vodka? Oh, yes. Maggie and I came to the conclusion that – it's a beautiful work of art.'

'I don't see what that's got to do with it.' Shrimsley was impatient.

'No,' Ben told him, 'I don't suppose you do.' And then he told the story as far as he knew it. 'Records in the Academy of Arts show it was still in Vitebsk when Hitler invaded Russia. It was fought over, soldiers died for it, but I don't think the Germans got it. A young Russian officer looted it. His name was Krupenski, the husband of Merry's friend Olga Krupenska. After his death she hung on to it. Waiting for the moment to sell.'

'But she never did?' Holloway asked.

'No. Someone we met told me he'd stolen it from her.' Maggie spoke for the first time.

'Who told you *that*?' Holloway was losing patience.

'Alyosha. Alyosha Konchalovsky. Our interpreter. He said he was going to bring it to our hotel.'

'And did he?'

'No.'

'Why did *we* have to go to Russia, Merry?' Ben asked in the silence that followed. 'Why didn't you get a visa?'

'Some bureaucratic nonsense.'

'About smuggling icons in the past?'

'That's a perfectly outrageous suggestion!'

'Please! Please, both of you.' Holloway tried to reach a solution. 'Let's be realistic about this. We're not detectives, Ben. Is it up to us to inquire too deeply?'

'It depends on whether you think we're honest dealers or receivers of stolen property,' Ben told him.

'So. What should we do?' The Chairman was undecided.

'Do? I'll tell you what we should do.' And Ben asked,

'Haven't we done enough to Russia? We've beaten her, defeated her, seen her split up. We've given her all the benefits of our civilization, crooked currency deals, pornography, crime on the streets. But, for God's sake, don't rob her of all her art. Maggie can tell you I got a bit bored hearing about the Russian soul. But leave them a bit of it. Do with this lady? Only one thing to do. Send her back to where she came from. The monastery of Vitebsk. I'm going out to buy a large drink. At least I'll know the pub came by it in a lawful manner.' And that was the point at which he banged out of the room. The meeting was adjourned, so that they could go away and come to the clear and independent conclusion that they could sell 'The Virgin of Vitebsk' in close collaboration with Meredith Bland's dealer.

Wonders in the Deep

These see the works of the Lord,
and his wonders in the deep.

Psalms 107:24

It was a fine spring morning in Wedensbury Park, Somerset, the dawn chorus was over but the early sunshine still sparkled on the dew, the daffodils were in bud and the azaleas looked promising, when Lady Pamela Wedensbury threw the entire contents of her husband's wine cellar into the lake.

She didn't do it in person. She marched – an elderly, grey-haired lady with the profile of a bird of prey, sensible shoes, a tweed coat and skirt and two rows of pearls – at the head of the procession. Behind her came the butler, Dennis. He was followed by two gardeners whose wheelbarrows were loaded with cases of Pichon-Longueville, Château Palmer, vintage port, Hermitage, Château Yquem and similar treasures. The rear was brought up by the miserable and long-suffering Lord Bertie Wedensbury who had long struggled against his wife's Puritan principles and had, at last, given up the battle. He had lived through her various campaigns for many years, from the early days of Decency on the Wireless to Sentence Smokers, Keep Sex out of the Sitting-Room (concerned with television) and The Bloom of Youth (forbidding the sale of contraceptives to those under twenty-one). Her latest enthusiasm was Sober Sanctity,

Lady Wedensbury having come to the conclusion that the consumption of alcohol was a clear defiance of the will of God. Bertie's spirit was so far broken that he forbore to bring up the subject of Communion wine and attended, however reluctantly, the ritual drowning of his famous bottles.

There was a little jetty on the lake for the mooring of boats. Lady Wedensbury stationed herself at the end of it and quoted Scripture in her support, speaking in the ringing tones of a minor prophet: '"Wine is a mocker. Strong drink is raging; and whosoever is deceived thereby is not wise." Proverbs.' She turned to the butler and issued a brusque command, 'In!'

The butler made a signal to the gardeners, who lifted a case and threw it into the lake. Bertie Wedensbury winced as though in acute pain as his wife came out with another question, '"How long wilt thou be drunken? Put thy wine away from thee." The Book of Samuel. In!' Another case splashed and sank into the bosom of the lake.

Klinsky's auction house was about to mount a sale of Old Master drawings. Ben Glazier was in the viewing gallery, straightening some frames, checking the catalogue against Annabelle Straddling-Smith's sometimes slapdash notes. He came on a sudden space, an empty square of red damask wallpaper, and called out to the porter who was bringing more pictures to hang, 'What the hell's happened to the Carracci "Satyr Frolicking"?'

'Was that the bloke with the goat legs doing naughties?' the porter inquired politely.

'I suppose you might describe it like that?'

'The Chairman had it put away. He reckoned it might cause embarrassment.'

'Did he really?' The porter was startled by a rare sight at Klinsky's: Ben Glazier in a towering rage.

In the Lord Chairman's spacious office, decorated with some of the best pictures passing through Klinsky's, Bernard Holloway and Camilla Mounsey, now head of Modern British Paintings, were engaged in a delicate encounter; it was particularly delicate for Bernard because Camilla had come to him with a serious complaint. 'Your wife gets everything,' she said. 'Weekends. Holidays away. Bloody Christmas!'

'She's given me the best years of her life,' Holloway excused himself.

'She's given them to someone. I mean, *she* certainly hasn't got them any more.'

At which awkward point the door was banged open and Ben Glazier was among them. 'Satyr frolicking with a young female faun!' he said dramatically.

'Really, Glazier! I have no idea what you're talking about.' Holloway moved away from Camilla and Ben explained, 'The Carracci drawing. It's not in the viewing gallery.'

'I know,' Holloway admitted. 'I've had it removed.'

'May a simple-minded art expert ask why?'

'My wife found it offensive,' Holloway said with dignity. To which Camilla added a bitter rider, 'Oh, well. Of course. That settles it!'

'Please, Camilla.' Holloway told the story. 'We happened to walk through the viewing gallery and my wife was upset by that revoltingly explicit drawing. She found it deeply offensive. She stared at it for a long time.'

'So,' Ben asked, 'what did her Ladyship say?'

'She didn't need to say anything,' the Lord Chairman explained. 'I knew her thoughts exactly. We can't display intimacy just because it's in a work of art. The public won't stand for it.'

'The Puritans!' Ben looked up to heaven in despair. 'The Puritans have come back to plague us!'

'No one could call me a Puritan, could they?' Holloway looked to Camilla but she failed to come to his support.

'Remember what the Puritans did?' Ben spoke with deep feeling. 'They knocked the willies off all the statues in the British Museum. You know what they've got there now? Drawers and cupboards full of broken-off willies.' Holloway looked pained. 'I thought that would make you wince.'

'Please, Glazier.' The Chairman sat at his desk and did his best to look busy. 'I have got rather more important things to do.'

'I wish to register a serious protest,' Ben said with dignity and was constrained to ask, 'May I borrow your loo?'

'No!' The Chairman was in some respects a hard man, but Ben had already gone through a door at the back of the Chairman's room. As he stood at the porcelain he saw, hanging above the tank, the drawing in question. Ludovico Carracci, born in sixteenth-century Bologna, was a master of chiaroscuro and a warm and passionate painter of religious works who, Ben knew, sometimes turned his attention to a happy pagan subject. The satyr frolicking with a faun was drawn with the accuracy and attention to detail which would have brought down the wrath of Lady Wedensbury's campaign and had caused Lord Holloway to transfer it to the Chairman's facilities.

Maggie hadn't exactly made peace with Nick Roper. She just hadn't felt up to continuing the war, especially as he seemed maddeningly unmoved by her hostility. She didn't feel she ought to forgive him, and yet the effort of not forgiving sometimes seemed too much. With the guilt a paid-up member of Alcoholics Anonymous might feel as he slinks towards the pub, she allowed herself to wander into the Wine department; there Nick seemed to pay less attention to her than to a single bottle which he had taken from an open wooden case and was now holding up to the light, smiling at it and saying, 'Beautiful stuff.'

'What's so good about it?'

'How can you ask such a question, Maggie? It's Petrus '61.'

'Well, I can't see it's beautiful,' she told him. 'If I showed you a Matisse, or a Rembrandt drawing, well, you know what you're getting. Immediate pleasure. All *you're* offering is a black bottle with a dirty old label. Can't we have a swig or something?'

'Good heavens, no!' Nick flinched.

'Not even if I bid for it?'

'Certainly not if you bid for it. We wouldn't let you open the case. You wouldn't even be able to go and visit it in the vaults.'

'How do I know it was Petrus 19–, whatever it is?'

'Because of the label. And because, well, you'll just have to trust me.'

Maggie looked at him. 'Famous last words,' she said.

'Maggie!' Nick looked injured and tried to look innocent. 'I know I cut a few corners over the Bronzino business, but you've had nothing to complain of since then, right?'

'Oh, yes, I have! I've got a great deal to complain of. I don't know why I'm still speaking to you.'

'Come off it. You called in to the Wine department. Entirely of your own free will.'

'It's contemptible. I mean, I gave up smoking, for God's sake. How can I be so entirely weak-willed as to want to light you up again? You ought to have a government health warning on you.'

'Should I really?' Nick felt deeply flattered. 'That's the nicest thing you've ever said about me.'

'Don't let it go to your head.'

'I mean, you don't have to give me up entirely. You could just cut me down to a couple after dinner.'

'You're ridiculous!' But she was laughing in spite of herself.

'Or even one before lunch?' At which he put his arm round her shoulder and they were kissing as Ben burst into the room, full of bad news. 'For heaven's sake! It's going on everywhere. Except on the walls of the gallery.' He looked at Maggie with deep disapproval as she separated herself from Nick. 'I thought you were here. Miss Annabelle Snotty-Smith said you were "in a meeting". I thought you'd be meeting someone in the Wine department.'

'I was showing Maggie our wonderful haul of Château Petrus '61. You interested, Ben? It's a snip at around eight hundred and fifty quid a bottle. No? You're sticking to Scotch ale. How sad.'

Ben ignored him, and spoke to Maggie as though she were alone, 'I came to tell you. We've been taken over by the Puritans!'

'Ben, what *are* you talking about?'

'Oh, nothing much. Only the Lord Chairman's censored the Carracci "Satyr Frolicking". Or rather, his wife has. Bloody woman in a hat who thought I came with the catering. Last time she had lunch she met me on the stairs and complained about the vichyssoise.'

'What's he done with the Carracci?' Maggie was puzzled.

'Oh, the satyr's still having it off with the young nymph. Now he's doing it in the Chairman's bog. The Puritans have taken over. From, now on, it seems, in Klinsky's art house pleasure is out!'

'Not for all of us?' Nick looked at Maggie.

'You be careful, Nick Roper.' Ben was still angry. 'Our good Lord Chairman might censor you. Even if you do keep your goats legs neatly tucked away in your Savile Row trousers.'

Anyone wandering through Wedensbury Park that night might have seen an unusual activity at the side of the lake. Three frogmen, with lights on their belts, climbed out of a parked van and waded into the dark water. Then they disappeared under it, leaving only a small ripple on the still surface.

Ben Glazier and Maggie Perowne were making a final check on the Old Masters drawings in the long gallery at Klinsky's, when he raised the question that was uppermost in his mind. 'It's not really all on, is it? You and the noissome Nick. Don't tell me you're an item all over again?'

'I suppose it's on the cards.' Maggie admitted.

'What's on the cards? A warning of forthcoming disaster.'

'You do exaggerate sometimes, Ben.'

'Exaggerate? After that exhibition you made of yourselves in the wine department! Absolutely disgusting!'

'You're an extraordinary chap.'

'You noticed that?'

'You rail at the Chairman for hiding the "Satyr Frolicking". You think the walls here should be covered with full-frontal drawings of satyrs and female fauns, and then you see me and Nick in a modest clinch and you behave like Queen Victoria confronted by a male stripper performing in the Albert Hall.'

'It's not because you were kissing, it's because you were kissing a cad. That satyr may have had a high degree of testosterone, but he wasn't necessarily a cad.'

'Neither's Nick,' she told him. 'Necessarily.'

'Oh, for God's sake, Maggie. Pull the other one.'

'Perhaps he's changed. You believe people can change, don't you?'

'Not really. They just grow older – and more irresponsible.'

'Speak for yourself.' She hung the drawing she'd selected in the empty space.

'St Anthony in His Cell,' Ben looked at the title and said, gloomily, 'Struggling against Temptation.'

'Where're you going?' Maggie asked as he left her. 'Back to my cell.' He went on his way to his small, lonely and quite disorderly office, where he might comfort himself with, perhaps, Ella singing 'Let's Call the Whole Thing Off'. He was going through a gallery showing a collection of French posters and, among the can-can girls, singers, dancers, jockeys and cyclists, a small, slightly grubby man with powerful glasses importuned him. 'Mr Glazier. You don't know me, sir. But I know you, of course and your article on "Old Gods and New: The pagan content in the religious art of the Italian Renaissance".'

'That goes back a few years.' Ben was puzzled, but flattered to be recognized.

'Been my constant bedtime reading. I go back a few years too. I'm not a renowned expert like yourself, Mr Glazier. A humble dealer, sir. In a very small way of business. But we have something in common, I believe. A love of beauty. The name's Johnson. Christened Oscar William Leonard and therefore known as Owly in the profession. A play on my initials, you see, but I take it in good heart, most of the time.'

'Very amusing. What can I do for you, Mr Johnson?'

There was a short silence and then Owly came out with one word, mysteriously emphasized, '*Condiments*.'

'I'm sorry?'

'You don't know what I'm talking about?'

'I'm afraid I have no idea.'

'Pepper, salt and mustard! You think I'm mad, don't you, Mr Glazier? You think I'm eccentric. But didn't a certain great sculptor make a salt cellar for the King of France?'

'Cellini?' Ben didn't know why he bothered to answer the question.

'None other than that famous rogue, womanizer and sword-fighter Benvenuto Cellini? You know your Italian Renaissance inside out. No one better.'

'You mean the salt cellar in Vienna?' Ben couldn't imagine what this well-known masterpiece had to do with the obsequious Owly.

'There's one there, of course,' Owly agreed. 'But why don't you call at my business address? At your own convenience, Mr Glazier. Entirely at your convenience, and satisfy your curiosity.' Owly produced a battered business card held delicately between a black-nailed finger and thumb.

Another salt cellar? Ben didn't believe it possible but, to escape the dealer, he took it.

Maggie had gone to dinner at Nick's flat and, without any further discussion, without terms agreed or treaty, stayed the night. She was woken up by the telephone ringing at his bedside. Nick picked it up, muttered, 'Nick Roper.' and then became monosyllabic. 'More of the same? Fine ... Good ... Well, round to the vaults, of

course. We should meet ... The club ...? That's fine.
Oh, well *done*!' As he put down the phone, Maggie
asked, 'You up to something?'

'What?'

'You?' He rolled towards her, and took her in his
arms. 'I very much hope.'

Peter Pomfret's picture restorers had, since the unexpected
death of Sarah Napper, been sold and boarded up, to
re-open shortly as a video store. Next door to it,
in the street full of fairly unsuccessful shops off the
Portobello Road, was O.W.L. Johnson's antiques and,
on the other side of Owly, an equally dingy premises
entitled Print-U-Like. The proprietor of this concern:
HAND BILLS AND POSTERS PRINTED, PAMPHLETS,
BUSINESS CARDS AND LEAFLETS OUR SPECIALITY was
Lenny Lockyer, a tall and cadaverous man, whose pro-
nounced nose and sunken cheeks twitched nervously at
moments of bewilderment or distress. He was enjoying
a mug of tea with his next-door neighbour and mentor
Owly Johnson when Ben came roaring along the street
on his motor bike, parked and pushed open Owly's
shop door.

For a moment he stood, surveying the chaos in Owly's
shop, and then the proprietor emerged from the back
room where he had been entertaining Lenny. 'Welcome,
Mr Glazier. You're very welcome, sir. Come in here,
won't you? Where we can talk private.' And he led Ben
into the inner office, where a bulky ginger cat nestled on
the top of the safe and Lenny was smiling and twitching
energetically. 'I'm sorry, this is Lenny from next door,'
Owly apologized for his visitor. 'I have an interest in his
little printing business. You might not think it to look at
him, but Lenny knows his printing. This is a famous art

expert from Klinsky's great auction house, Lenny. Knows all there is to know about works of art.'

'Klinsky's? Isn't that where that job –' Lenny began but Owly stopped him briskly. 'Oh, no, I don't think so, Lenny. I think you're confused with all the work we get in. Mr Glazier's here for something a good deal more interesting than having a few business cards run off. Lenny's thick as two short planks on the subject of art, but he knows his printing. Say good day to Mr Glazier, Lenny, and clear off out of here.'

'Good day, Mr Glazier.' The obedient Lenny was on his way.

'Oh, yes. Pleased to meet you.'

As Lenny went, Ben wondered why the hell he'd come. Was he simply bored in the office, where nothing much was happening, and the sight of Maggie made him think, with some pain, of her renewed friendship with the ghastly Roper? Was he really interested in what Owly had to show him, or was he trying to escape for a moment from the devout and rarified atmosphere of a 'high art' house. His thoughts were interrupted by Owly congratulating him on his politeness to Lenny, the printer.

'That was good of you, Mr Glazier. That 'pleased to meet you'. Not meant, of course. There's not much pleasure for an expert of your standing meeting a person as thick as Lenny. But he's a good boy in many ways. Yes, I depend on Lenny. He can print up anything. And he minds the shop for me when I'm out on a sweep. Now, then, I'll introduce you to the object in question.'

As he opened the safe, the cat awoke and leapt to the ground. Owly brought out something wrapped in newspaper. Unwrapped, this proved to be a lead box with the lock broken. 'Only once in a lifetime,' Owly was saying, 'once or twice, perhaps, does something nice cross my path. I remember when I picked up that picture down in the Caledonian. Sir Joshua Reynolds, but no one else could see it. As for this particular treasure trove, quite honestly, there can be no doubt about it.'

He had lifted out the glittering silver object which might have once been used for the mundane business of passing the salt. On its lid, a silver Neptune lolled, naked, supported by sea horses, pointing his trident and his solemn, purposeful gaze at a naked nymph who, thoughtfully fingering one nipple, staring back at him with equal concentration. Below her, on a triumphal archway, another nymph sprawled with her breasts erect. There were also silver waves, a turtle, and further nymphs prone around the rim. 'Amazing preservation of a beautiful work of art, wouldn't you say, Mr Glazier?' Owly put it on the table.

'Silver?' Ben looked at it doubtfully. 'The King of France's salt cellar was gold.'

'This one was made by Cellini for another customer. A dummy run, that's what it was.'

'Is that your story?'

'I've read a bit about Benvenuto,' Owly told him. 'Nothing to match your expertise, of course, sir. But from what I get from his writing, he made a wax model of this particular condiment and flogged versions around.'

'That's what you'd've done in his position?'

'Come on, Mr Glazier, confess you're interested.'

'Which lorry did it drop off?'

'You're not suggesting that a work of art of this distinction is going to be carried about on lorries?' Owly looked hurt.

'Then who did you get it from?'

'Silence on that subject, as you well know, Mr Glazier, is as sacred to me as the secrets of the confessional.'

'Sorry, your Reverence. But you'll have to tell us sooner or later.'

'It's old, isn't it? Anyone can see that.'

'So far as the period goes, I could take it for an opinion from our silver lady. We'd keep it safe for you.'

'A silver lady? You've got one of those, have you?' Owly picked up the salt cellar. 'Like this little bird on here?'

'Not much. Her name's Dorothy Entwhistle and her husband's a judge, so you'd better watch your step. She'll want to know where you got this desirable object.'

'It's part, sir, of the collection of a gentleman,' Owly said with dignity.

'Is it really? And how did the gentleman collect it? By climbing up a drainpipe of some stately home in the South of England?'

Maggie was spending another night with Nick in Pimlico. They thought of dinner at his local bistro, Les Deux Amants, an invariably overcrowded Sloane version of a French café, decorated with brass cooking utensils, dried flowers and blown-up photographs of sunny Provence. The waitresses, who wore blue shirts and jeans with striped aprons, looked very like some of the girls who worked at Klinsky's and were inclined to treat their clientele with similar, icy contempt. Nick was trying to thaw out their leader with a nicely judged mixture of anger and charm, 'We booked a table for nine o'clock. It's just not bloody good enough.'

'There *are* other people waiting, sir!' The head waitress was not yet charmed.

'But we're not other people, are we? We're *us*.'

'Oh, Nick. For God's sake!' Maggie couldn't stand scenes in restaurants.

'Don't worry, darling. She's going to help us.' It was then he decided to fall back on flagrant charm. 'You know I only come here because you're so gorgeous. *Love* the new hairdo.' This produced a slight thaw and, 'The couple in the corner got their bill ages ago. You can have their table.'

'All right, Mags. Forward march!'

Nick set off, squeezing his way between tables, to the corner, with Maggie following, protesting. Then she saw the back of an older man with a pink, bald head and a younger brunette at whom Nick shouted, 'I say. Are you planning to spend the night here?'

The man looked round, revealing himself as Bernard Holloway, the Lord Chairman, about to panic. Camilla, who was with him, smiled a welcome. She had drunk most of the wine and spoke loudly enough to make her lover look about him in a hunted fashion. 'Hallo, you two! Lovely to see you. We were just off, but why don't you let us buy you a drink? We'd love that, wouldn't we, Bernard?'

Bernard, who obviously wouldn't, said, 'I expect they'd rather be on their own.'

'Oh, no, they wouldn't!' Camilla disagreed. 'They see each other all day, anyway. Just as we do, don't we, darling? Pull up a couple of chairs. Lovely jacket that, Maggie. They put really good things in Selfridge's sale now, don't they? This isn't your local, is it?'

'No, it's mine.' Nick had gathered two chairs from other tables and Holloway was looking increasingly wretched.

'If Bernard had known that, he'd never have brought me here!' Camilla laughed. 'He only wants to take me out to places where I'll never be spotted by another human being, don't you, darling?'

'I read a write-up about this little spot in one of the Sundays.' Lord Holloway was, at least, trying. 'I thought it sounded fun.'

'No, you didn't, Bernard,' Camilla contradicted him. 'You thought it sounded like the sort of place none of your wife's friends would ever come to.' At which, Camilla grabbed a passing waitress, intent on not having her eye caught, by the wrist. 'This girl speaks French. Rather appropriate, isn't it? What's it to be? Pastis? *Très Provençal. Quatre pastis, s'il vous plaît, cherie.* Big ones.'

'I hope you'll excuse us.' Holloway looked at his watch. 'I don't really think we've got time.'

'Oh, yes, we have, Bernard. The night is young. Enjoy yourself for once in a while. Bernard's still jumpy in case we run into Muriel,' Camilla told Maggie in a penetrating whisper. 'That's the story of my life, isn't it, darling?' She put her hand on Holloway's, who moved his away rapidly and tried to sound businesslike, 'Well, Roper.'

'*Nick*, darling. His name's Nick,' Camilla told him. 'You know what this little bistro's called? Les Deux Amants. Well, now we're *les quatre amants*, aren't we, Bernard darling?'

'Well, Nick, how are things in the Wine department?'

'Very good, thank you, Lord . . .'

'Thank you, *Bernard*,' Camilla insisted. 'Forget the handle to his name.'

'Just laid hands on some Petrus '61,' Nick told the Chairman. 'Estimated ten thou a case.'

'Petrus? I don't think we did that at Come into the Garden Foods when I was Managing Director.'

'Oh, Bernard, darling. Do shut up about Come into the Garden Foods,' Camilla purred, 'it's not really a *romantic* subject.'

'Nevertheless, I have to tell you young people, it's where I made my money.' At which the Chairman stood up with as much dignity and determination as he could muster. 'Are you coming, Camilla? I mean, can I drop you off somewhere?'

'No, Bernard. Much as you'd like to, I'm afraid you can't drop me off. Ever!' And, as she explained to Maggie and Nick, 'I'm sticking to Bernard and there's not a thing he can do about it.'

'I can't give either of you a lift?' Holloway looked pleadingly at Maggie.

'Actually we haven't had dinner yet.'

'No. No, of course not. Well. It's a pleasure to see you both. Oh, by the way, there's no need to mention the fact we bumped into each other.'

'Poor old Lord Chairman!' Nick said when they were alone.

'What a ghastly fate! Torn between Lady Holloway and Camilla. Makes my problems with you seem almost bearable.'

'What problems are they?' Nick was studying the menu.

'Too many to remember.'

'You mean, you've forgotten?'

'Perhaps. For this evening,' she told him.

Dorothy, wife of the ferocious and well-feared Mr Justice Entwhistle, was a grey-haired, motherly, untidy woman with a high, authoritative and upper-class voice, much loved by her family and respected by the staff at Klinsky's where she was head of Silver. She was examining the salt cellar produced from Owly's shop as Ben looked on with interest.

'Benvenuto Cellini arrived in France in 1540 with the

salt cellar unfinished. It was completed in gold in '42, was it?' Ben felt he was being taught by a particularly nice headmistress, but he was glad to be able to say, 'In 1543, actually.'

'Thank you, Ben. He'd certainly made the design for the Cardinal of Ferrara and I suppose he might have cast another version in silver. He said he'd make one for "whoever was destined to possess it".'

'I bet he never thought it would fall into the sticky hands of Owly Johnson.' Ben smiled.

'And the provenance is?'

'Murky. Owly says that to talk about it would be to give away the secrets of the confessional.'

'He's going to have to tell us some time. As I'm sure you know, the gold salt cellar is the supreme example of Renaissance work. Worth God knows how much. He's going to have to answer some questions.'

'I'll ring him tomorrow.'

'Please do.' She lifted the salt cellar and looked under it. 'If it was made in England it'd have the lion's face and maker's mark, date letter and all that sort of thing. Nothing like that in Italy. We just have to go by how it looks.'

'Well, how *does* it look?' Ben ventured to ask her.

'What do you think?'

'I think it looks stunning.'

'Yes, God damn it, Ben. I think it looks *right*!'

Owly was sitting at the table in his inner office that night, eating fish and chips and reading an old copy of the *Connoisseur*. There was a sudden crash and the sound of glass broken. He stood up and opened the door into the shop. The cat jumped from the top of the safe, and stood, its back arched and its fur rising. Three substantial men wearing balaclavas were advancing through the bric-à-brac towards Owly Johnson.

The next morning Ben kept his promise to Dorothy Entwhistle and telephoned Owly. The phone rang for a long time in the back of the shop. The safe door had swung open, drawers and cupboards had been ransacked and many objects broken. An unconscious Owly was lying on the floor, blood dried and caked on his mouth and forehead. The cat was curled up and asleep beside him.

When he got no answer to his call, Ben, remembering all that Dorothy Entwhistle had said about the salt cellar, got on his bike. He found Lenny Lockyer in his doorway, where he had been watching the comings and goings of the police and the ambulance. Ben followed the restless and twitching man into his print shop. Lenny started to boil an electric kettle. 'Poor old chap. He didn't deserve that, Mr Glazier. I don't mind what he'd done, he didn't deserve that treatment. You're welcome to step in here, sir. Not that there's much more I can tell you. Late last night, it was. Of course the police don't have a clue who did it. They got Owly in intensive care. Terrible times we live in, don't we, Mr Glazier? Scares me to think about it. Luckily I don't have valuable objects like what Owly got. I've only got my printing but, as I say, you never know these days, do you?'

Ben didn't answer this question. He was standing at the counter looking at various bits of print work. What interested him most was a small box of wine labels, obviously freshly printed, on which Château Petrus 1961 was clearly written.

'I'm having a cup of instant to calm my nerves, like. Care to join me in a cup of instant, Mr Glazier?'

'Yes, thank you. Thank you very much.' And then he

asked; as he pocketed a few of the labels, 'I suppose you haven't got any very special claret at eight hundred and fifty quid a bottle?'

Maggie was having a lonely lunch, tomato and Mozzarella salad, a glass of red, and a quick look at the *Guardian*, in the Italian café round the corner from Klinsky's, when Camilla, carrying her coffee as though it were an unexploded hand grenade, joined her. When she had taken a tentative gulp, she said, 'Sorry about last night.'

'Don't worry.' Maggie was unused to the role of Camilla's comforter.

'You probably didn't notice, I'd had rather a lot to drink.'

'You amaze me.'

'And I was a bit desperate. I mean, I'm sick of keeping it a secret, about me and Bernard. It's time people *knew*.'

'If it's any comfort to you, I think most people at Klinsky's have known for a considerable time.'

'No! Is that honestly true?' Camilla seemed amazed.

'Well, almost everyone,' Maggie was careful not to exaggerate. 'I mean, there might be someone in Antiquities who hasn't heard. No, I think I heard them discussing it over the necklace of Queen Hatshepsut.'

'I'm jolly glad!'

'*What?*'

'I'm glad everyone knows. Then Muriel might get to hear of it and he'd be forced to *do* something. Till it all comes out in the open, Bernard just creeps around being scared she'll find out.'

'He did look rather nervous,' Maggie noticed.

'Yes. Sweet, isn't it?' Camilla smiled lovingly. 'He's dead scared of Muriel and he's dead scared of me. Poor darling. He's like a rabbit caught between the gun and the ferret. All big eyes and shaking with fear. I suppose that's what makes me want to stroke him, to try and calm the poor trembling little creature.'

'We *are* still talking about Bernard Holloway?' Maggie was puzzled.

'Of course, we are. I don't suppose if he wasn't such a pathetic, frightened little animal I should love him half so much. Oh, God, Maggie. Isn't life *hell*?'

In spite of this gloomy pronouncement, Camilla had become quite calm by the time she walked into Lord Holloway's office. He, on the other hand, was in a state of near panic, and had been since that unfortunate dinner at Les Deux Amants. He was doubtful if they should ever be seen together, certainly not alone in his office, and he announced in a voice of doom that Muriel was on her way back from her holiday. Camilla did her best to soothe his nerves. 'Poor sweetheart,' she said. 'How very scary for you.'

'She'll want to come to one of our lunches. And if Maggie Perowne, or Nick Roper, has told anyone about, well, about that unfortunate encounter . . . Then I'm very much afraid . . .'

'Of course, darling. You usually are very much afraid. But you're not to worry.'

'Aren't I?' The Lord Chairman was doubtful.

'I had breakfast with Maggie. I made quite sure she and Nick won't say anything.'

'Oh, you did? You're so wonderful!' Holloway's relief was so great that he embraced the head of Modern British Paintings with some enthusiasm. But then panic fear returned when there was a knock at the door which he had carefully locked so that he might not be disturbed during this important conference.

'Lord Chairman?' The noise off was Shrimsley's.

'Yes, what is it? Hold on a minute.' And the Chairman whispered to Camilla, whom he was still holding tightly, 'It's Shrimsley! He mustn't see you in the room.'

'I've adjusted the personnel timesheet figures to the artwork output ratios, Lord Chairman. I thought you'd like to see them before the meeting,' Shrimsley called out.

'I'll go, then,' Camilla offered.

'Not out of the door. He'll see you.'

'Then *where*?'

'In . . .' And then Holloway had one of those brilliant inspirations which had made him such a successful businessman, 'In the toilet.'

'Do I *have* to?' Camilla wasn't best pleased.

'I'm very much afraid so.'

'Do give up being afraid, darling. It may be the death of you!' So Camilla went to keep company with the 'Satyr Frolicking' and, when she was safely stored away, Bernard unlocked the door and said, 'Come in, Shrimsley! I can't think what you're doing lurking about in the passage.'

Ben Glazier had called on Nick in the Wine department and asked if he could take a look at a bottle of the legendary Petrus '61. When he was given it, he studied the label with particular care.

'I told you the price, Ben. Do you want some for your cellar? So you can invite Maggie and me for a really *special* little dinner?' Nick was being quite gently mocking.

'The label looks fairly convincing.' Ben chose to ignore the idle chatter and get down to what he now suspected was the dirty business in hand. 'Nicely stained, of course. But suppose it was printed last week, dirtied down a little, and stuck on a bottle of plonk?'

'It wasn't.'

'Wasn't it? You don't happen to know a little firm called Print-U-Like, do you? Or a couple of characters called Lenny Lockyer and Owly Johnson?'

'Of course, I don't. I have no idea what you're talking about.' Standing with his hands in his pockets, resplendent in scarlet braces and a striped shirt with a white collar, Nick, Ben thought, looked the very picture of public school unreliability. He carried on with his inquiries, 'By the way, Owly's met with a nasty little accident. Have you heard about that?'

'What the hell are you suggesting?'

'Just a fairly simple fraud. That's all.'

'Fraud? No way! We know exactly where this wine came from.'

'Oh, yes? Where exactly?'

'The cellar of a gentleman.' Nick wouldn't incriminate himself, Ben thought.

'Has this gentleman got a name?'

'He has. But he doesn't want me to divulge it.'

'All the same, divulge!'

'I couldn't. You know that, Ben. It would be like giving away the secrets of the confessional.'

'Oh, yes? Owly was terribly keen on the secrets of the confesssional too. It was so convenient' – he looked hard at Nick – 'for crooks.'

At the reception desk Lucy was intoning, most dramatically, the words from the book she was holding flat against her chest and only consulting in case of dire need: 'I believe it. I believe it ... Poor Uncle Vanya, you're crying. You've had no joy in your life, but wait, Uncle Vanya, wait ...'

Maggie, who had gone to buy a long-desired jacket after her talk to Camilla on the hellish nature of existence, was stopped in her tracks by Lucy's news. 'Maggie! I've got Sonia in *Uncle Vanya* at the Lame Duck in Hounslow. You will be at our first night, won't you?' She was saved from a commitment by Ben coming down the stairs and telling her he'd made an extraordinary discovery.

'The salt cellar? Dorothy Entwhistle told me. Could it possibly be right?' Maggie was interested.

'No. No, not the salt cellar. This is something far more important than the salt cellar. It's about your little friend.'

'Which little friend?'

'Nifty Nick Roper. The elegant no-good and fake artist.'

'Shut up, Ben!' Maggie was serious. 'Do you want everyone in Klinsky's to hear you?' Maggie started up the stairs and he followed her saying, 'You don't want to know what he's done?'

'No, I don't think I do.'

'Come into my office. I'll tell you.'

'I said, I don't think so.'

'You want me to shout it into Straddling-Smith's ear-hole? Or on the stairs?' So she went into his small untidy office and Ben shut the door. 'It's true,' he said. 'I know about Nick.'

'I know about him too,' Maggie told him. 'Do you think I've got illusions about Nick? I've got no illusions. He takes life as it comes. He thinks it's all a bit of a joke. He's slightly mad and quite dangerous to know. He may have sailed rather close to the wind during the Bronzino business, but he is not a faker!' It was then that Ben told her about Owly, Lenny at Print-U-Like and the Petrus labels. To his intense disappointment she seemed unmoved.

'For God's sake, Ben. All right. Some crook's been printing Petrus labels. How many wine dealers are there in the world?'

'Some crook who's got a connection with Klinsky's?' His partner came here with the salt cellar.'

'That doesn't prove a thing.'

'And when I asked your little friend . . .'

'He's quite big, actually.'

'When I asked your big friend where his supply of Petrus '61 came from, he didn't dare tell me.'

'You mean he didn't *want* to tell you.'

'Comes to the same thing.'

'No, it doesn't! You're trying to rubbish him.'

'Don't blame me! I didn't make him . . . Blame his parents. Blame God. I'm only pointing out his glaringly obvious defects.' And then, when he had run out of breath, Maggie looked at him and said, 'You know why you're trying to rubbish Nick, don't you? It's because you're jealous.'

'I'm what?'

'Well, perhaps, a *little* jealous.' She didn't, after all, mean to hurt him.

But Ben was outraged. 'You mean, I'd like to be a Hooray Henry? An old-public-school yobbo. An over-privileged prat with less idea of morality than a pimp doing the three-card trick on Brighton racecourse? Jealous of Nick? Why should I be jealous of him?'

'Because we're having an affair.' And Maggie did her best to explain, 'I wish you could understand, Ben. I do love you, in some sort of way. I don't know, it's probably a much better sort of love than what I feel about Nick. I don't know how to say this. You haven't got a cigarette, have you? No? Well, that's all right then. It's just that there's something about Nick I can't actually give up. He may have behaved badly once. But now I can tell you he's going straight.'

'Are you really sure of that?' Ben spoke with measureless contempt and Maggie seemed, as she said, 'Yes,' only a little uncertain.

One of the things that most depressed Ben Glazier was that Maggie had taken up jogging, not because she liked it much, but because Nick thought it was good for them both. After a damp and exhausting run round Hyde Park, they swam and had a shower at a Health Club, and then arrived at work with slightly-out-of- breath and glowing health. It was on one of these runs that Maggie asked Nick where the Château Petrus came from.

'I made it absolutely clear to Ben I'm not telling.'

'I'm not Ben.'

'No. You're his mouthpiece, aren't you? His little ventriloquist's dummy. "See if you can get it out of him." Were those his instructions?'

'All right, Ben has got some far-fetched idea in his head. He's suspicious.'

'He would be. The old chap fancies you.'

'That's got nothing to do with it,' she panted. 'I told him you weren't up to anything iffy. All you have to do is tell him where it came from.'

'I don't think my client would like that at all. Just tell poor old Ben Glazier to mind his own bloody business. Speed up, Mags, or would you rather jog with the elderly?'

However, in the gentlemen's shower-room after the jog, dressed only in a bath towel and smiling broadly, Nick Roper could be heard talking to the telephone attached to a pine-covered wall. 'Ben? Oh, this is Nick Roper speaking. Now, don't ring off in a huff or anything. I just think we should have, well a bit of a heart-to-hearter. Why? Because you're upsetting Maggie. I thought I'd take you to lunch and we could sort of . . . get it out in the open. My club. Yes. Brummel's. St James Street. Shall we say, one o'clock?'

*

While the Sheridan Club caters for lawyers, judges, publishers and the occasional actor, Brummel's serves nursery food and adult wines to the aristocracy, many of them Nick Roper's cousins or mere distant relatives, Conservative politicians of the old-fashioned sort, retired generals and admirals, a smattering of journalists who write for the *Daily Telegraph*, and one or two quite dangerous financiers. The premises are a good deal more elegant than the dusty old Sheridan. Brummel's boasts white walls, Regency furniture, chandeliers and some impressive portraits of long-dead military men and well-bred racehorses. Members and their guests sit side by side at a long table down the centre of the dining-room, and there Ben, only slightly embarrassed, found himself sharing a meal with his least favourite male person. When he asked Nick why he had invited him, he got a charming old Etonian smile and another question, 'Why did you accept?'

'Out of curiosity, perhaps. I'm on a mission to find out much more about rare and fine wines. I'm after some of your secrets.'

'Give it a rest, Ben, why don't you?'

'Why should I? Give me one good reason.'

'All this business about labels. You've got Maggie running after me asking questions. I asked you out to lunch, Ben, to tell you to stop interfering, because there's no real point in it is there? You don't really want Maggie all to yourself. You wouldn't know what to do with her.'

'I suppose I could protect her.' Ben did his best to sound dignified.

'From what?'

'Bad company.'

'She *is* grown up, you know.' Nick smiled tolerantly. 'She is over twenty-one and she holds down a pretty important job at Klinsky's. She's perfectly entitled to fancy whoever she likes, and it's one of the facts of life you'll have to get used to that she fancies me. So why don't you lay off and enjoy my bad company over a bottle of the club claret?' Nick turned to a small, weather-beaten club servant in a white jacket, a man who walked with a curious rolling gait, as though he were serving lunch on board a ship. 'Liver and bacon, I think, Gilbert, and the bread and butter pudding to follow.' At which point the man on Ben's other side, uttered in a high bleat, 'Has anyone in particular died at Klinsky's recently?'

'Unfortunately not,' Ben muttered, and his neighbour, who had grey hair, a long upper lip and was decorated with a Brummel's club bow-tie, introduced himself, 'I'm Parsifal Mallows. I do the obituaries in the *Informer*. We specialize in reminding the world of the dear departed's eccentricities and disgraceful scandals. Anyone with that sort of record in the art world been looking rather peaky lately? Tip me the wink, if you can think of anyone.'

'The one I'm thinking of is looking rather well at the moment.' Ben glanced at Nick as he ordered the lamb cutlets, and his host, filling his glass with the club claret, said cheerfully, 'So what's it to be, Ben? Peace and goodwill all round?'

Determined to make no concessions, Ben turned his attention to the Georgian loving cup which had been presented to the Club by a winner of the Derby, who had subsequently shot himself. 'That's a beautiful object,' he said. 'But not quite as beautiful as the object we've got from that Owly Johnson I was telling you about.' At which, a voice came floating across the table, 'Awful responsibility, silver. Got to have a chap in the pantry going over it again and again with a toothbrush.' The elderly member who spoke looked irredeemably boyish, with untidy grey hair and small, darting eyes. Nick said, 'Hallo, Bertie. My guest, Ben Glazier. This is Bertie Wedensbury,' introducing the long-suffering peer whose wine had been consigned to the deep.

'Glazier. Not Shropshire, at all?' Bertie peered at Ben suspiciously.

'The Glasgow Glaziers,' Ben told him.

'Your family keep a lot of ornaments, do they?'

'Ornaments? As a matter of fact, my family rather went in for china ducks flying across the wall.'

'China ducks, eh? Damned original. We had a lot of silver once. Lost it unfortunately during the war.'

'You were bombed out?'

'Bombed? Good God, no! They didn't have bombs in the war when we lost our family silver. Pikes and halberds and, well, a few muskets, I suppose.'

'I think Bertie's talking about the Civil War. You know, Cavaliers against Roundheads,' Mallows explained.

'That's it! Charles I versus Oliver Cromwell. Roundheads? I don't know about Roundheads. Bloody Puritans, that's what I call them! Killjoys. Party-poopers. You don't like Puritans, do you, Glazier?'

'As a matter of fact, I can't stand them,' Ben told him.

'Good. Good man! I say, Roper, your friend here tells me he doesn't care for Puritans. Let me tell you, it's the whole history of my family, the curse of the Wedensburys: Cavalier husbands married to killjoy, Puritan wives. And that doesn't lead to a happy home life.'

'You were telling us about your silver?' Ben tried to keep a grasp on the subject.

'Oh, yes. Before the bloody Puritans got at it! My ancestor, Henry Wedensbury, was a pretty close friend of Charles I, who was a great collector, as you know. They got on like a house on fire but, of course, Henry's wife didn't like it. She was of the Praise God and Shut Up on Sunday school of thought. Women like that can't stand anything beautiful.'

Lunch was over without any sign of peace having broken out between Ben Glazier and his rival, Nick. They were together by the porter's box in the black-and-white tiled entrance hall, and Nick was leaving his guest and returning upstairs to a meeting of the wine committee. Ben thanked him for an interesting lunch in a place, it seemed, where time stood still.

'Does that mean you'll stop filling Maggie's head with unnecessary suspicions?' Nick asked.

'Of course. I'll stick to the necessary ones.' As Ben's host left, Bertie Wedensbury, on his way out, approached Ben as though he were an old friend and said confidentially, 'Can't stay here and drink. Not all the afternoon. Someone's bound to notice and report back to the leader of the opposition. Look here, why not come and spend a happy hour in my other club?'

'Your other?'

'Monica's Bar, Frith Street.' Bertie came close to Ben and whispered, 'Very discreet. Harder to get in there than it is to Brummel's. Good atmosphere. Not Puritan. And not a word to Pamela.'

'I don't suppose you'd drink Petrus '61 at Monica's?' Ben asked.

'Petrus at Monica's? Not bloody likely.'

'I'm afraid I've got to get back and work,' Ben apologized.

'Puritan!' Bertie was searching for his wallet. 'Never mind. Another time, perhaps. Monica's Bar. I'm there most afternoons when I'm up in town. Just mention my name.'

He gave Ben a card from his wallet.

*

Maggie was alone in Old Masters when Ben got back and she received his news with amazement. She said, 'Nick actually bought you lunch? I mean he *paid*? He must be extremely fond of you.'

'Nonsense! It was a first sign of weakness. He knows I'm on to him and he's trying to buy me off.'

'I told you' – Maggie was sure of it – 'Nick's going straight.'

'Prove it!' Ben challenged her.

She looked at him in doubt for a moment and then said, 'All right. We'll prove it.'

'You and Nick Roper,' Ben smiled. 'That wouldn't be very satisfactory.

'No, you and I. We've proved things together in the past. We'll find out about these damned labels and clean up the salt cellar business. Then we'll discover that Nick has absolutely nothing to do with either of them.'

'You want to bet?' Ben didn't believe it.

Maggie took what she was afraid might be a risk because she wanted to end the warfare between the two men who were most important to her. She believed Ben was wrong – all right, she told herself, she hoped he was wrong – and, when he found that out, she could settle down again, more or less easily with the friend she couldn't help loving and the man whose friendship she most enjoyed. So she perched herself on the back of Ben's Harley-Davidson as he made his return journey to Print-U-Like, and was with him when he confronted Lenny with one of the Petrus labels. 'Your work?' Ben asked, without preliminary introductions.

'I'm not too sure . . .' Lenny looked at it as though he'd never seen it before.

'I am,' Ben told him. 'I got it from a box on your counter. The 1961 wine. Printed now. Bit of an odd thing to do, wasn't it? Didn't it strike you as a little strange?'

'That's the job the client wanted. So that's the job I carried out.'

'So it *is* your work?' Maggie wanted to get this clear.

'Well, I did the printing. Yes,' Lenny admitted.

'Who was your client?' Ben asked. 'And, for God's sake, don't give us the spiel about "secrets of the confessional".'

'Was it anyone from Klinsky's?' Maggie asked and was half afraid of the answer she might get.

'Don't look so surprised,' Ben warned the printer. 'When we first met, Owly told you I was from Klinsky's and you started to say you'd done some work for us. Owly shut you up pretty damn quick, as I remember.'

Lenny, twitching energetically, looked at Maggie for help, and she was brave enough to ask, 'Does the name Nick Roper mean anything to you?'

'Roper?' Lenny frowned.

'Yes.'

'No. No, it doesn't ring a bell at all.'

'There! You see?' Maggie looked at Ben, triumphant.

'Perhaps he didn't tell you his name?' Ben tried again. 'But he was from Klinsky's?'

'No, I didn't mean as we was printing for Klinsky's,' Lenny spoke carefully. 'I mean, the client reckoned he needed labels like that because of something he was going to auction. Anyway, that's what Owly told me.'

'Someone appears to have been contemplating a fraud, and getting Klinsky's to sell wine with forged labels,' Maggie summed up. 'You said it wasn't Nick Roper, didn't you?'

'He hasn't said *that*,' Ben told her.

'You said it was someone outside Klinsky's.'

'That is true, Miss. That is too very true.'

'If we find out who this trickster is, we can go to the

159

police and tell them. At the moment, the only name we can give them, Mr Lockyer' – Maggie smiled in a way Lenny didn't find encouraging – 'is yours.'

'Mine?'

'Get the big fish and a little tiddler like you could swim away and hide under the rocks.' Ben also wanted a name.

'I never dealt with the man. Not personally.'

'The man?' Ben asked.

'Owly dealt with him. It was always Owly.'

'Owly's in intensive care. He can't talk.'

'Owly always called him the Captain.'

'That's not a great deal of help.' All the same, Maggie was relieved. The Captain didn't sound much like Nick.

'But I know where Owly went to meet the Captain.' Lenny was anxious, now, to sound helpful. 'He used to ring him and tell him to get his skates on and come down.'

'Down where?' Maggie asked.

'Some sort of afternoon drinking club, I think. Down Soho. Owly said the Captain's there most afternoons. Holding court. Frith Street, was it?'

It was an outside chance, but Ben tried it. He opened his wallet, took out a card and asked, 'Does Monica's Bar mean anything to you?'

Half-way up Frith Street in Soho, between an adult video store and a betting shop, a discreet doorway had a similar card pinned above the bell. Ben rang and told the answerphone they were friends of the Captain's, and asked if he was in by any chance. 'Captain said he'd be in after lunch. Want to come up and wait for him? First floor,' said the disembodied voice. The street door clicked open and they climbed up a dark staircase to where an ageing Peter Pan, a timeless, boyish figure wearing jeans, a black T-shirt with 'Monica's' written on it and an insecure toupée, was holding a door open. 'You're not members?' he asked them.

'Well, no, not exactly,' Maggie had to admit.

'Don't worry. We'll just charge you exorbitant prices for the drinks. My name's Martin, by the way.'

Monica's club had none of the facilities of Brummel's, or even of the Sheridan. It was a small airless room, and the pink lampshades and the string of fairy lights over the bottles failed to give it a festive appearance. It hadn't changed much since it was fashionable in the Fifties, and photographs of the youthful Francis Bacon, Lucien Freud and George Melly, all signed 'To Monica', hung, as they had for years, on the blotched wallpaper. At three o'clock in the afternoon, there was only one other customer, a dangerously thin woman in her sixties perhaps, sitting on a bar stool with her legs crossed, a cigarette dangling from her pillar-box red lips and a beret on the side of her head, looking, for all the world, as though she were hanging out in the Deux Magots waiting to get a distant glimpse of Juliette Greco. Martin had hardly got himself behind the bar when she called out, in a threatening baritone, 'Bloody tide's gone down in my G and T!' When she had been attended to, Ben got a beer and Maggie thought she'd have a white wine. 'Whaite whaine!' the woman in the beret put on her poshest voice. 'How terribly, terribly. Who *are* these people, Martin?'

'Friends of the Captain, Betsy. So you'd better watch it, hadn't you?'

'Oh, are they? Splice the mainbrace. How do you know the Captain? In the war? You a frog?'

'Actually, I'm Scottish,' Ben told her.

'How killingly funny. I meant, were you a frogman ever? A diver?'

'No.'

'Well, don't go on about it. Nothing's more boring than what some ancient fart did in the war. Packet of Silk Cut then, Martin.'

'There's another friend of ours who's a member of this place.'

'This exclusive members club, do you mind?'

'Lord Wedensbury.'

'You're Bertie's friends? He hasn't got many.' This got a throaty laugh from the woman on the bar stool. 'Pamela sees to that.'

'You expecting him in this afternoon?' Ben asked Martin.

'He rang for the Captain, seems his wife's poorly.'

'Of course she's poorly,' the woman said. 'They're both poorly. That bloody stately home of theirs is mortgaged up to the chimney-pots. Wedensbury Park! Why did he ring for the Captain?'

'Some deal they got on, I suppose.' Martin slapped her packet of cigarettes on the counter.

'What deal?'

'How should I know? I mind my own business,' Martin shrugged.

'No, you don't! You haven't got any business of your own. You mind other people's business. That's about all you're capable of.' The other customer lit a cigarette and introduced herself. 'Sorry, we haven't been introduced. I'm Betsy Pitt-Plummer.'

'Pitt-Plummer? Doesn't your family own a Rubens?' Maggie seemed to remember.

'"The Wise Virgin". Not a portrait of either of us, I'm afraid! Oh, yes, I'm terribly top drawer!' Betsy laughed and then looked seriously at Ben. 'When you were young, I was extremely beautiful. Can you believe it?'

'I think I can.'

'Oh, listen to you! Mister Smoothy-Talker. Are you rogering that young girl?'

The answerphone behind the bar spoke, Martin replied to it respectfully and pushed the button to open the door. Ben answered Betsy Pitt-Plummer's question with a regretful no.

'I bet you wish you were!' Betsy coughed in her cigarette, and the door swung open to admit a short, close-cropped, grey-haired man with the shoulders of a PE instructor, dressed in a blazer bearing some sort of crest, grey flannel trousers and a turtle-neck sweater. Following him was a younger, taller and broader man with hair over his ears and a gaucho moustache who gave off a deafening smell of after-shave. 'Captain' – Martin was already pouring out a large Bells whisky – 'there's friends of yours here.'

'Friends of mine?' The man who'd been called the Captain sat next to Ben. 'Do I know you?'

'Perhaps not yet,' Ben told him. 'We're also friends of Lord Wedensbury.'

'Bertie? You know dear old Bertie, do you? Did he send you?'

'He said this was an excellent place for getting drunk in the afternoon.'

'Why only the afternoons?' Betsy asked loudly.

'His Lordship's not coming,' Martin told the Captain, ignoring her. 'Her Ladyship's ill. That was the message.'

'Oh, well. Bertie's not going to break his heart about that, is he? Not seeing as how she treated him. Know her too, I expect?' He turned to Ben, smiling.

'No, I never met her.' And then Ben said, 'But I did meet Owly Johnson.'

'You seem to have friends up and down the social ladder, you do.' Betsy raised her eyebrows and Maggie told her, 'We get to know all sorts of people in our business.'

'What's your business?' the Captain happened to ask.

'The pursuit of beautiful objects' – Ben described it carefully – 'a pretty tough trade.'

'Does that mean Owly Johnson and Bertie?' The Captain was looking worried. 'They never got together, so far as you know?'

'Not as far as we know.' Maggie looked at him and said, 'Owly's in hospital, isn't he? That's what we heard.'

'We were wondering why?' It was the question Ben had been waiting to ask. 'We also wondered why you ordered a lot of wine labels to be printed for Petrus '61?'

Maggie added, 'And whether the name Nick Roper means anything to you?'

'Wine labels.' The Captain was no longer smiling. 'Is that what you came here about?'

'One of the things.'

'You came here to ask questions. Not to see me or your old friend, Bertie. This is a good place, this is. A nice safe place. Except for people who come here asking questions. Martin!' he called to the barman, without taking his eye of Ben.

'Yes, Captain?'

'Are these people members?'

'No, Captain. I don't know why they came in, really.'

'Seems they came to ask questions.' The Captain issued a brief order. 'See to it, Robin. They've been taking liberties.'

From that moment, Maggie noticed, things began to happen with great rapidity. The smell of after-shave became stronger as the tall man with the gauche moustache advanced on Ben, and he only hesitated for a moment when half of Ben's beer arrived in his face. Then Ben had her by the wrist and was dragging her down the stairs. The dark hallway was filled by an extended Chinese family loaded with shopping. As Ben pulled her past them, they started to struggle up the stairs, holding up the Captain's man. They were out of the door before Robin had extricated himself from the crowd, and Ben pulled her through the curtain of hanging plastic strips into the adult video store, and, to her immense relief, they saw their hunter run past it.

Then they were out and retreated down Bateman Street and into Mead Street, where the Harley-Davidson stood waiting. As they roared away they just missed Robin who was pounding back up Wardour Street, running incautiously in the middle of the road.

When he had washed his face, straightened his tie and recovered his breath, Ben took his mug of tea into Dorothy Entwhistle's office and got a short lecture on King Charles I. 'Rotten king and first-class patron of the arts. Bought as much as he could afford: Italian paintings and other Italian works of art, including silver. You look tired, Ben. You've been working too hard?'

'Above the call of duty,' he told her. 'I mean, I didn't spend all those years studying Piero della Francesca and the science of perspective to be chased through Soho by a frogman's bouncer.'

'What on earth were you up to?'

'Investigating the provenance of the salt cellar. But go on. Did the King make presents of works of art?'

'Sometimes to people he stayed with,' she nodded. 'Or loyal Cavaliers.'

'Or at least to husbands who were Cavaliers. And when the Puritans took over, they got rid of the precious silver?'

'Church candlesticks and chalices, of course. Anything that struck them as ornate, erotic or extravagant.'

'You want to make sure that the Puritans don't get at the Cellini lookalike, whoever it really belongs to.' Ben finished his tea and stood up.

'It's locked up in the vaults,' Dorothy told him. 'You can feel perfectly safe about it.'

'Safer than I can feel about myself. I've got to ask a few more questions.'

'Not in Soho?' She looked at him, worried.

'Not there, thank God,' he assured her. 'In a frightfully posh gentleman's club.'

But when Ben presented himself in the marble hall of Brummel's, the porter told him he doubted if Lord Wedensbury was in the Club, although he consented to send some underling off to make sure. Ben took a seat under a portrait of a whippet-thin Derby winner and, after some delay, that busy obituarist, Parsifal Mallows joined him with news: 'If you're looking for Bertie, he's not coming up today. Pamela's been taken worse and I bet he hopes it's nothing trivial. As a matter of fact, and this might interest you, I've just been up in the library roughing out Pam's obituary. Of course, you know the *terrible* thing she did to him?'

When Ben confessed he had no idea of Lady Wedensbury's crime, Parsifal Mallows proudly produced a sheet of Brummel's notepaper and, for the first time, he read of Bertie's tragedy:

Pamela, Lady Wedensbury, came from the North-ampton branch of her husband, Bertie Wedensbury's family. The Northampton Wedensburys fought for Cromwell in the Civil War, but the Wedensbury Park branch was devoted to the Cavaliers. Lady Pamela carried on the Puritan tradition of her relatives. She disapproved strongly of drinking, smoking and short skirts at Wimbledon, which, she said, had 'become more of a strip-show than a decent sporting occa-sion'. Recently, she had the entire contents of the famous Wedensbury Park cellar thrown into the lake, where some great vintages of classic wines still lie 'full fathom five'. She is survived by her husband, Lord Herbert 'Bertie' Wedensbury, who has never been known to object to drink and who had to witness the fate of an historic cellar.

'That's due to go in on Thursday.'

'Has she died already?' Ben wondered.

'No, but it's as well to be prepared.'

In fact, Parsifal Mallows hadn't wasted his time in the library at Brummel's. Pamela Wedensbury died, having extracted from her husband a solemn promise not to touch strong drink after she had left him. Her funeral in Wedensbury church was attended by only a few relatives and a scattering of villagers. But Ben Glazier and Maggie Perowne might be seen in a pew at the back of the church and, later, at some distance from the grave.

After his wife had been committed to the earth, Bertie, alone in his library, removed the brandy from its hiding place behind the books and poured himself a stiff one with soda. He was enjoying it when there was a knocking at the French windows which led out on to the terrace, and there stood Maggie and Ben, clearly anxious to talk. Displeased at the interruption, he let them in.

'Lord Wedensbury' – Maggie sounded particularly serious – 'we're from Klinsky's, the auction house.'

'We'd like a word with you on the subject of a serious wine fraud,' Ben added, 'before we go to the police.'

'The police!' Bertie was worried and then cheered up as he said, 'Oh, I recognize you. You're that fellow Glazier I met at Brummel's who doesn't like Puritans. I recommended my favourite watering-hole.'

'You did that,' Ben agreed. 'And that's why we've got to ask you some serious questions.'

'Oh, have you, really? What a pity! I thought that after Pam died, I needn't do anything serious again. But if you insist. Anyway, do sit down.'

Bertie returned to his fireside. Ben and Maggie perched together on the sofa.

'We've been asked to sell some wine as Petrus '61,' Maggie started.

'At an astronomical price,' Ben said.

'We've discovered that the labels on the bottles were printed quite recently, Lord Wedensbury. We have reason to believe, good reason to believe . . .'

'Yes! Excellent reason' – Ben chimed in – 'that you put a large quantity of fine wines, including the Petrus, into our house for auction.'

'Well, of course, I did!' Bertie seemed quite untroubled. 'I'd like to drink it all. Of course, I would. But, well, we live in hard times. The roof. And the home farm. Disaster. Terrible losses on the pigs.' And then he asked Maggie, 'You don't know a decent pigman, do you?'

'I'm afraid not,' she had to confess.

'Bloody hypochondriacs, pigs are,' Bertie complained. 'Finicky about their food. Malingerers, I call them. We had a pigman, but he left us to go into the church.'

'Lord Wedensbury' – Maggie returned to the matter in hand – 'we believe you ordered a number of Petrus '61 labels to be forged by a printer called Lenny Lockyer in London.'

'Hang on a minute!' Bertie looked deeply hurt. 'Not forged. I wouldn't say forged. I'd say, well, done artistically to look like the real thing.'

'Why on earth did you do that?' Maggie asked.

'Because the old labels got washed away, of course,' Bertie told them. 'They got washed off when Pam chucked the cases into the lake. She'll be happy now she's in heaven, along with all those bores drinking Diet Coke. You can't imagine what it's like to see your entire cellar, brandy as old as Napoleon, port that was offered to Edward VII, all chucked into the bloody lake! Drowned. I'd have rather seen Pam drown some of her ghastly relatives.'

'The Puritan branch of the family?' Ben asked.

'Cromwell's men and women. The women were the worst,' Bertie said gloomily.

'So I suppose you hired the Captain to dive for the booty?'

'You know the Captain?' Bertie frowned.

'Rather too well,' Ben remembered.

'Chap I knew was in the Navy, Banjo Buckleworth. Banjo put me on to this frog feller. He'd been Banjo's petty officer but he always called himself the Captain. Gave himself promotion. Bit of a chancer, in my opinion, but he got hold of some divers and they pulled the stuff out for me. While Pam the Puritan was asleep, you know. She never heard a sound from the lake. Terrible shame I had to sell most of the stuff.'

'So what you sent to Klinsky's was genuine Petrus '61?' Maggie was smiling with relief.

'Of course, it was.'

'Our man in the Wine department, Nick Roper,' Ben asked, 'did he know anything at all about the forged labels?'

'Why should he?'

'That's exactly what we wanted to hear!' Maggie was still smiling. 'Isn't it, Ben?'

'What *you* wanted to hear, anyway.' And Ben had something else to ask, 'We've got sound reason to think that claret wasn't the only precious thing the captain of the frogmen fished out of the water?'

'Really?' Bertie was puzzled. 'Wine was the only thing he told me about.'

'Oh, we're sure of that. But we think he might also have found a piece of silver. A salt cellar.'

'Valuable?' said Bertie.

'Oh, extremely,' said Ben.

'Well, go on. You do interest me.'

'Has your family a habit of throwing valuable items in to the lake?' Ben was curious to know.

'Well, yes, now you mention it.' Bertie gazed back into history. 'Terrible lot, the Northampton branch of the family. My ancestor in good King Charles's days married one of them, Lady Susannah. He had a famous bit of silver done by some Italian fellow. Very well known. Chap who murdered a few people and had lots of sex. Artists do, I suppose.'

'Murder people?' Maggie frowned.

'Have all this sex.' Bertie shook his head sadly. 'Models and all that type of thing. Gives them the opportunity, of course. I've never gone in for all that. Well, this bit of silver. Mustard pot or some such thing.'

'Salt cellar?' Ben suggested.

'You know a lot about it!'

'I know a little,' said Ben.

'That old bloody God-bothering, Cromwell-loving Lady Susannah Wedensbury took exception to the starkers lady carved on top of it and chucked it in the lake. Beautiful girl, that silver one, from the drawing we've got of it.'

'You've got a drawing?' Maggie could hardly believe it.

'Somewhere. Tucked away in the old archives. Of course, the thing's gone forever now.'

'Unless the Captain dragged it up from the bottom of the lake?' Ben suggested. 'Safe in its steel box?'

'Good heavens! I thought he was a bit of a chancer.' Bertie said.

'Enough of a chancer to give it to a dealer called Owly Johnson to get rid of'– Ben told the story – 'and to have Owly beaten up when he hadn't got it in his safe. As a matter of fact, he'd sent it to us. You'll have to tell us what you'd like to do with it.'

'Do with her? A silver lady, starkers?' Bertie looked at them proudly. 'Present to my old ancestor who died at Naseby from King Charles the Martyr. I say, do you think you could get a spot of cash for it?'

The table in the Lord Chairman's office was laid for a lunch party. The door was once again locked as he embraced the tender and yielding head of Modern British Paintings. And then the doorhandle rattled and the stern voice of Lady Holloway was heard without, calling, 'Bernard!'

'Muriel, is that you?' The Chairman panicked easily. 'It's too early for lunch.'

'Maybe it is. I got bored in Harrods.' The answer came with alarming clarity. 'What on earth are you doing in there?'

'Nothing. Absolutely nothing!' And then, whispering fearfully, he once again begged Camilla to take refuge in his personal gents.'

'Not *again*!' she protested.

'What else can we do?'

When Camilla had vanished, he unlocked the door to a wife who asked him what on earth he was up to. 'Just trying to work, Muriel, without interruption,' he answered with dignity. And she looked at him with some fondness and said, 'Bernard, what a funny little man you are!'

Later the lunch party was held in honour of a respected customer, a Mr Wang Chai Ping, who had bought the Petrus. 'It will be on my dinner table in Hong Kong,' he said, 'when some big Communist cheese from Beijing comes to dinner.'

'And you might be inclined to bid for the Cellini salt cellar?' Dorothy Entwhistle suggested. The glittering silver object was on the table and Ben told them its provenance.

'A Puritan threw it in her husband's lake because she didn't approve of the naked goddess. Divers stole it. An antique dealer received it, knowing it was stolen, and passed it on to us to sell for his own profit. So he was beaten up. Crime, theft, violence and all because a lady in the seventeenth century had absurdly strict standards of morality.'

'So it belongs to who?' The Hong Kong client was not entirely clear.

'Oh, old Bertie Wedensbury,' Ben told him. 'A fairly undeserving old cove.'

'The wine came from his cellars too. It's got a perfectly genuine pedigree.' Nick looked at Ben and said quietly, 'To your extreme disappointment, Ben.'

Lord Holloway started to talk to Dorothy and the

gentleman from Hong Kong was being charming to Muriel. 'You mean, I'm disappointed that your wine department is actually honest?' Ben asked Nick for clarification.

'Of course you are,' Nick told him. 'So is Maggie, as a matter of fact. You like me to have a slightly dicey reputation, don't you, Maggie?'

'Slightly dicey, I suppose,' Maggie admitted. 'But not the whole game of backgammon.'

'I do hope you're right, Nick Roper,' Ben told him. 'I do hope we've proved you too virtuous to be interesting.'

'Bernard' – Lady Holloway said, much to her husband's surprise – 'I passed through that gallery of lovely old drawings. One was missing! The "Satyr Frolicking".'

'Yes, indeed, Muriel' – Holloway was on his best behaviour – 'I saw the way you looked at it and –'

'And what?' Lady Holloway asked.

'Well, we took it out of the public view. I thoroughly agree with you.'

'Do you? I'm so glad!' And Lady Holloway went on, surprisingly, 'It was such a lovely, joyful thing. Nymphs and satyrs, thoroughly happy in the morning of the world. Even when we get middle-aged and a bit creaky and thoroughly, well, married! We can still enjoy such things, can't we? Even if it's only in pictures. Where did you put it, Bernard? I hope it's somewhere where everyone can enjoy it.'

'Well, not everyone,' Ben whispered to Maggie. 'Not the general public. Only the lucky few who happen to be caught short in the Chairman's office.' But, by then, Lord Holloway had promised to put the 'Satyr Frolicking' back on the open market. And Camilla, turning over the pages of the *Connoisseur*, as she sat on her hard seat, really felt inclined to stop frolicking for good and all.

After Titian

If you get simple beauty and naught else,
You get about the best thing God invents:

Robert Browning, 'Fra Lippo Lippi'

New York. In ravines and crevices, between the glittering glass of tall buildings, and the casual mess of quick-food outlets, laundries, delis and cafés, where the customers and the piles of rubbish spilled out on to the pavement, the traffic was becalmed, sending up hoots of fury, wails of sirens and the throb of frustrated engines towards the distant sky. And in the back of one of a thousand yellow cabs, Maggie Perowne and Ben Glazier sat and gave up hope of reaching the New York branch of Klinsky's in time for the day's Old Masters sale.

'Klinsky's?' the bearded Russian driver frowned and made a huge effort to remember. 'That's the big deli on Fifth and . . .?'

'No,' Ben told him, 'not exactly.'

'Restaurant, is it?'

'It's a place for selling pictures,' Maggie explained.

'Picture house?'

'Auction house, as a matter of fact,' Ben told him. 'Gallery.'

'It's a way up past the Plaza Hotel.' Maggie tried to help.

'What makes you think he knows where the Plaza is?' Ben tried to keep his voice down, but the taxi driver asked, 'Where's that located?'

'Klinsky's?'

'No. What you said. Plaza Hotel.'

At which, Maggie told Ben it would be quicker to walk and he said, 'Have you completely lost your nerve? Are you suggesting I take *exercise*?'

All the same, when they only inched towards Klinsky's, Maggie made Ben get out and they did better, although he complained of being in constant danger of death from killer cyclists who reared up out of the traffic to terrorize the pedestrians.

The Old Masters sale was beginning in a room which was lighter and glitzier than its London equivalent: the pictures were displayed on a turning rostrum and the auctioneer's podium had KLINSKY'S, NEW YORK emblazoned on it in lights. If the handsome, sun-tanned and grey-haired auctioneer looked almost too English, that was his intention. With his Savile Row suit, his Turnbull & Asser shirt and tie, the Dunhill pipe in his pocket, and his accent which seemed quite English to Americans and quite American to the English, Charles B. Whiteside, known as Chuck since his Harvard days, was proud of his extreme anglophilia. He looked at the Sale Room, filling up with more shoulder pads and Dallas-style outfits than would be seen in London, patted the silk handkerchief in his top pocket and gave himself a cough sweet of the sort he always bought in London, rustically called a Fisherman's Friend.

Some late arrivals were still struggling into the Sale Room, giving their names to the girl at the reception desk and collecting the numbered paddles which they would raise to bid. Among them was a man who wore a shapeless grey suit and scuffed shoes. He carried his belongings – some books, a catalogue and a spectacle case – in a plastic shopping bag. He might, in fact, have been about the same age as Chuck, but he looked older, far less sure of himself, and he gave his name in a soft Southern accent. He was awarded a paddle by the girl who was too busy to pay much attention to him. All she said, without looking at him, was, 'Duck? How are you spelling that, sir?'

Once the sale started, Chuck Whiteside forsook his casual, Bostonian manner and his almost English accent. He sold rapidly, with great attack, and on each side of the room young henchmen in suits pointed to the bidders of the moment and shouted, 'You!' The battle for Old Masters was in full swing when Maggie and Ben arrived at the reception desk. Chuck's assistant Gloria Shallum was waiting for them. She was a dark, willing girl in a plain black suit with glasses and scraped-back hair. Her intelligence and good spirits were always at war with her political correctness and the extreme seriousness with which she took her job at Klinsky's, New York. Maggie greeted her, kissed her and said, 'Terribly sorry we're late, Gloria. Traffic.'

'I know. You don't have that in Britain, do you? Not traffic.' Gloria started to lead them into the Sale Room.

'You know Ben Glazier?' Maggie said.

'Of course I know Ben.' Gloria smiled at him. 'You came over with the Tintorettos, didn't you? 1989? Chuck's sure going to be glad you got here. We're in dire need of you, Ben. Absolutely dire need.'

As Ben and Maggie took their seats, a portrait of a young man in a helmet and breastplate came round on the revolving rostrum and Chuck fired off the news that it was 'Lot 12. The Parmigianino portrait. Starting at twenty-five thousand dollars for it'. Ben, tilting his glasses to see the picture more clearly, said, 'Rather a plucky attribution.'

'Ssh!' Maggie whispered. 'Chuck Whiteside's a splendid chap. He knows his business.'

'But are we sure he knows Parmigianino's business?' And then Ben noticed an untidy, grey-haired man in front of him, who was struggling to his feet and, waving his paddle vigorously, called in a half-strangled Southern accent, 'I want to tell y'all . . .' A young man pointed to the bidder and said, 'You!' As though the word had exercised some fatal magic, the man who had given his name as Duck clutched his chest and subsided slowly, turning his face in Ben's direction as he collapsed. For a moment Ben had a curious feeling of recognition, but then it went. The people around him stirred. Gloria Shallum came quickly down the aisle with a porter, and the bidding moved elsewhere in the room. Ben got up and went to help, but Gloria calmed him, 'It's kind of hot in here, I'm afraid. Sure, he'll be all right.' She and the porter half-helped, half-dragged the unsuccessful bidder out of sight.

There was the wail of an ambulance in the street and a youngish man with a pony-tail, wearing a red baseball cap and a T-shirt with Van Gogh's self-portrait on it, was cycling rapidly towards Klinsky's. His name was Peter Pollack. When he got to the auction house, he chained up his bike and, coming into the entrance hall, he saw the ambulance men carrying a stretcher on which lay, under a blanket and with a face the colour of putty, the elderly bidder whom he clearly knew, because he called out, 'Don! For God's sake!'

'I guess he's not in a state to converse,' a tall, lanky ambulance man told him, sadly chewing.

'Where're you taking him?' Peter asked.

'Lennox Hill. Mind yourself. He's in a hurry.'

The stretcher was carried out of the doors into the street. Peter Pollack stood in silence for a moment and then followed.

*

The sale stopped at lunchtime. Chuck Whiteside had filled his pipe from a tobacco jar and was looking down from his office windows on to Sixth Avenue. Maggie told him it had been an exciting day.

'So exciting,' Ben added, 'that some old buffer nearly passed out.'

'So Gloria told me! I didn't really notice.' Chuck returned to his lazy mid-Atlantic accent.

'Odd thing,' Ben told him, 'I'm sure I've seen him before.'

'I expect you've met a good many old buffers in your time, Ben. All the same, you're looking well.' Chuck gave his visitor a friendly punch on the arm. 'Keep yourself in good shape, do you? Jog, of course?'

'Certainly not!' Ben was clear on the subject. 'I'd put jogging high on the list of fatal diseases.'

'Still the same old Ben, isn't he, Maggie?' Chuck smiled at her, exposing almost perfect teeth. 'Never changes.'

'I'm afraid not.'

'Not since the great days of our youth. Remember, Ben?' Chuck put his smouldering pipe carefully in a deep glass ashtray and took a photograph in a frame off a shelf to show Maggie. A group of men in their twenties were in front of an Italian villa and among them stood a young Chuck and a young Ben. 'Bright young things, we were,' Chuck remembered. 'Learning our trade, visiting Italy to pay homage to Bernard Berenson. It was a great summer. Then we went our separate ways and got older.' He put the photograph back, a little sadly.

'Older, not much wiser, perhaps.' Ben was still looking at the photograh.

'Great days. But let me tell you two. *This* is a terrific moment of time in the history of art!' Chuck went to his desk and sat smoking with his feet up. 'You know what

New York is? It has to have some religion. Once it was just God, I guess, and all the old money did charitable works. Then it was opera and they paid out millions to wear their diamonds at the Met. Then it was civil rights and they discovered they cared deeply about blacks on buses and sent donations. And now, thank heaven for it, it's art. Forget God. Forget the Ring Cycle. To hell with the urban ghettos. They worship at the shrine of the Blessed Giovanni Bellini and Saint Picasso and All Angels. If you're not on the Board of the Museum of Modern Art or the Lemberg, you're a social pariah. And how do you get on the Board of the Lemberg, I hear you asking?'

'As a matter of fact you don't,' Ben assured him.

'I heard Mrs John T. Flecknow III ask it,' Chuck went on. 'From the depths of Cleveland, which isn't exactly the address from which to start a brilliant career in the art world. The answer is that John T. Flecknow has done bloody well. Isn't that what you English say? *Bloody* well?'

'I really wouldn't know,' Ben said. 'I'm not English.'

'He's going to put in the top bid for our Titian,' Chuck told them proudly. 'Then he'll present it to the Lemberg, Mrs John T. will get her seat on the Board and they'll be received into the Eternal Kingdom of Art and be sitting on the right hand of the Curator of the Getty Museum.'

'I've got some clients in London to bid for,' Maggie said. 'John T. Whatsit's not going to get an easy ride.'

'All the better. The price will mount as–tro–nomically. But it depends on just one thing.' Chuck blew out smoke and looked up to heaven as though in prayer.

'On what?' Ben asked.

'On you! John T. Flecknow has got it into his head that you're the greatest living expert on Old Master paintings. He's only going to buy the Titian if you tell him it's authentic.'

'A man of great good sense and discrimination,' Ben thought.

'Of course, you'll have to see the painting.'

'It might be a help.'

'They're doing a bit of work on the frame,' Chuck told him. 'But Ben, you're going to . . .' He sat up straight. 'I mean, you're certainly not going to have any doubts about it?'

Ben said nothing, but Maggie asked, 'How can you be sure of that?' Before Chuck could answer, Gloria Shallum came in.

'Oh, Gloria sweetheart,' Chuck greeted her, 'I seem to have misplaced that new tobacco pouch. Red and green, remember? From Dunhill's. I was kind of proud of it.'

'I'll ask around,' Gloria promised. 'And, by the way, the ambulance took the old guy to Lennox Hill Emergency. That was all we could do.'

Chuck said 'Oh, sure. Thanks, Gloria.'

And Ben asked her, 'Have you any idea who he was?'

'We checked his paddle number at the desk. He gave the name Don Duck. Sounded a bit curious to me.'

'Sounds like someone's last joke.' Ben went to the photograph and looked at the picture again. He looked particularly at a young man with glasses and untidy hair, smiling uncertainly at the end of the row. 'Was there any Don in our group of hopeful young art experts?'

Chuck shook his head. 'God, it's so long ago. You and I were close, Ben. I can't recall too much about the others.'

'You don't remember a Don?'

'Not really,' Chuck had to admit.

'I've got a feeling.' Ben started trying names, 'Estmore.

No. Estragon? That nervous little American? Wasn't he Donald something?'

When Ben got down to the entrance hall, the man with a pony-tail, a red baseball cap and Van Gogh's earless portrait on his T-shirt, was saying to the receptionist in a slow voice, full of hatred, 'In a meeting, is he? Mr Whiteside is in a meeting? Well, you let him know. Don's dead. He died before they got him to the hospital.'

'I'm sorry,' Ben had heard.

'You work here?' Peter Pollack turned, his eyes full of tears. 'You work at Klinsky's?'

'At Klinsky's, yes. But not here. I'm from London.'

'OK, you tell them. Let them all know the good news. Don Estover's dead and Klinsky's got what it wanted.' He turned then and walked quickly to the door. Ben followed, but when he got to the top of the steps Peter Pollack's red cap was disappearing among the traffic. Ben was left alone, remembering Donald Estover.

Chuck had taken Maggie to lunch at the Plaza Oyster Bar. They sat up on stools and drank Napa Valley Mumm, and ate Blue Point oysters, and she asked him if he always lunched in such style.

'Only when we get beautiful visitors from England.'

'I'm sorry Ben's missing the oysters.'

'I've loved Ben,' Chuck said, 'since we made our pilgrimage to Berenson, the great BB whose word on pictures was law, who lived like a king in his Italian villa, ruled his little court. You know the art world hasn't been quite the same since BB died.'

'Ben says Berenson sometimes adjusted his attributions to market forces?'

Chuck didn't answer that. He smiled and said, 'Great to have you here. Maggie, I wish we saw more of you.

And God, I miss London. The smoky little pubs. The old roast beef and two veg. The pints of beer and great theatre.'

'It's not exactly like that anymore.'

'It's not?'

'Not really. The pubs are empty and everyone's at home thawing out frozen lasagne and drinking New Zealand Sauvignon and watching soft porn videos.'

'It's not true!' Chuck was appalled.

'Not altogether true,' Maggie agreed. Then there was a silence, he speared an oyster and said quietly, 'Ben's not going to be any trouble, is he?'

'Well, he might be quite jealous when he finds out we were eating Blue Point oysters together.'

'Jealous?' Chuck was puzzled. 'You two haven't got something going, have you?'

'Well, we're great friends,' she told him.

'Friends . . . Is that all?'

'It's quite a bit.'

'Of course. Friends.' Chuck laughed. 'That's all it is. Ben's a much, much older man.'

'He's not much older than you, in fact.' Maggie looked him over.

'But that's entirely different.' Chuck could hardly take her seriously. 'I mean, I work out. I watch what I eat. I've been doing this relaxation technique. You kind of empty your mind, you know, and think young. Rediscover yourself. I go out with twenty-five-year-old dates.'

'Do you really?' Maggie asked. 'I'd've thought you'd have more fun staying in with them.'

Chuck ignored this for a more important matter. 'What I meant, Ben's not going to have any trouble attributing the Titian, is he?'

'Not if it's right.'

'We just can't afford any of his precious doubts over this one. Not "school of", not "circle of", not "after Titian". Not any of that damned double-talk. "*By* Titian"! Straight down the line. That's all he needs to say. He won't have any trouble about that, will he?'

'I'm afraid, you'll have to wait until he sees the picture.'

'Until then?' Chuck frowned and then clinked his champagne glass on Maggie's and smiled at her with great charm. 'Yes, of course. We'll just relax and leave it all to dear old Ben.'

That afternoon, dear old Ben was holding transparencies to the light and giving his view on Titian's later period to Maggie and Chuck. 'He was an old man when he painted like that. A very old man. Vasari called on him when he was over eighty and found him still working hard, with brushes in his hand. We keep going, you know, we old war horses.'

'Don't show off, Ben. You're really not that old.'

'What's old age? The period of liberation. The time when you don't have to pretend to be grown up, or serious, or responsible in any way.'

'Speak for yourself!' Maggie told him.

'Old Titian was liberated. He gave up the classical ideal. He painted like an Impressionist, splashes and dots of colour against a thunderous sky. Great figures looming up out of the night. Paint was hurried on with a smudged finger. Old age for Titian was a time for magic, and he still found women beautiful.'

'What you're saying is, it's a late Titian?' Chuck was reassured. 'Well, that's OK! So long as it's a Titian, we don't care how late.'

'"Naiad Bathing in a Stream".' Maggie took a

transparency. 'He was still painting nymphs when he was an old man.'

'He couldn't resist them. It's hard to tell until you see the paint.'

As if in answer to Ben's request, Gloria opened the door to let in two porters with a big canvas in a heavy gold frame. 'See the service you get at Klinsky's?' Chuck was delighted. 'Let me introduce you to your Titian.'

Ben stooped, tipped his glasses, looked into the deep-green glade in which a half-naked nymph was bathing under a stormy sky. 'You know what the Romans thought about nymphs? If you were unfortunate enough to see one undressed, it led to madness. I can understand that.'

'It's perfectly right, isn't it?' Chuck wanted to be sure.

'I don't know yet. I'd have to spend some time alone with her.'

'What are you looking for?'

'All sorts of things. Perhaps a smudged finger.'

Chuck told Maggie they should leave Ben to his thoughts on Titian and suggested they go for a little exercise: 'You go mad in this city if you don't keep in shape.' So he let Gloria know that they could be found in the New York Athletic Club, if anyone wanted them. He said they intended to play around a little, because he thought that was funny.

Left alone, Ben ignored the Titian. He got hold of a New York telephone directory and found a number of Estovers, including one in Jackson Heights he thought might be possible. He sat down at Chuck's desk, got a line and dialled a number.

'What is it?' The woman who answered didn't sound entirely friendly.

'Oh, hallo. Look, I'm sorry to disturb you. But does a Mr Donald . . . Don Estover live there?'

'Donald? I don't know no Don. Donald's out at work. Who are you, for heaven's sake?'

'An old friend of his, actually. I just wondered if Mr Donald Estover . . . had, well . . . He hasn't died, has he . . . in any way?'

'Who are you?' The woman's voice rose in fury. 'Funeral business, is it? Hustling work? We don't want you! You hear me? We don't need you. We're in beautiful health. Every one of us. Donald checks up regular. Heart, lungs, everything. You hustle business for dead people someplace else!' The telephone buzzed angrily and Ben put it down. He went back to the directory, found a D. Estover in Greene Street and dialled.

The phone rang in the living area of a shabby and old-fashioned apartment. Half of the room was tidy, with some carefully arranged art books, a well-organized desk and a neatly arranged collection of tapes and records. The other half was a tip, with a chaotic paint table, heaps of scrumpled newspaper and an easel on which stood an abstract painting, consisting only of strips of colour. In his half of the room, Peter Pollack sat, still wearing his baseball cap, grief-stricken and inert. He let the phone ring, but finally picked it up and heard Ben say, 'Oh, could I speak to Mr Donald Estover, please?'

'Don won't be back. Never! Never! Never be back.' And then Peter Pollack put down the phone.

In the Athletic Club Maggie and Chuck were playing squash, whooping, shouting, bumping into walls and into each other. Then Maggie glanced up to the gallery over the court and saw Ben looking down on them. They finished their game quietly, in a most restrained fashion, and then Chuck invited Ben for a decaf.

'What's the point of coffee, if there's no coffee in it?'

Ben asked and got no answer but allowed himself to be led to the health bar, which contained a number of obese people in lurid anoraks, as well as slimmer and more athletic members.

'It seems an odd way to spend the afternoon, breathing in the delightful smell of ageing gym shoes.' Ben looked at the passing scene with deep disapproval.

'He means trainers,' Maggie translated for Chuck.

'I know. I've made a close study of the English language. OK, Ben. So is it a great Titian? A one hundred per cent, straight up, genuine masterpiece? Of the final period? Like you said, when he was a great old man but still with a fine taste in nymphs?'

'Oh, you're talking about the picture!' Ben raised his eyebrows.

'Of course, I am.'

'I haven't really had time to think about it. I've been busy.'

'Busy?' Chuck was puzzled.

'I remember a rather shy young American. He asked an awkward question. Something like, "Mr Berenson, when you make an attribution, who are you trying to please? The dead artist or the living dealer?"'

'I don't remember.' Chuck smiled and shook his head. 'I know you and I were there, of course. And Ed Bachman, he was there. But none of the others come back to mind.'

'Wasn't there an evening' – Ben pushed away his decaf – 'when we all went to a local trattoria and got shamelessly drunk on Italian brandy? Don didn't say much. He was probably the one who staggered out and vomited in the olive grove.'

'Don?' Chuck frowned.

'Don Estover. He was with our group. I saw him yesterday.'

'Can't say I recall.' Chuck smiled at Maggie, as though he was thinking of other things.

'He was taken ill in the Sale Room while you were auctioning. It seems he died on his way to the Lennox Hill Hospital.'

'That's terrible!' Maggie put a hand on Ben's arm.

'Sure. I'm sorry.' Chuck sounded suitably concerned. 'I just can't remember the guy. Of course, you may be right. But has it got anything to do with the attribution of a Titian?'

'I honestly don't know the answer to that,' Ben told him. 'I'm trying to find out. If you're not too exhausted, Maggie, we might go and hear a little jazz later. I thought perhaps a trip to SoHo and the Village? You wouldn't enjoy that, would you, Chuck? It's so terribly un-English.'

That evening Maggie and Ben visited the Village and were walking south from Bleecker Street Station to Greene Street in SoHo. There they saw a young man in a business suit, who was leading, with a chain attached to a dog-collar, another young man on all fours wearing a singlet and Y-fronts. Maggie was unused to such a spectacle. 'Strange things people do,' she said, 'in search of pleasure.'

'Oh, I know.' Ben was unforgiving. 'They knock small rubber balls against a wall in the company of men in smelly gym shoes.'

'They weren't noticeably smelly.'

'Elderly men. Trying to sweat away the years with unnecessary exercise.'

'Chuck looks good on it.'

'Good? You think he looks good?' Ben over-reacted. 'Shining with purity. Saint Chuck of the art world.'

'All of which means you don't like him.'

'Not all that much,' Ben had to admit.

'He's been very kind to us in New York.'

'He's been very kind to you.'

'Is that the trouble?' she asked, and, when she got no answer said, 'He desperately wants the Titian to be right.'

'What do *you* think?' Ben asked her.

'It looked fine to me.'

'So he's got your vote at least. I told him I want to find out more.'

'You said you wanted to find out about this man who died.'

'Don Estover? I met his friend. His boyfriend, I suppose. I think that's what he was. Anyway, he said that Klinsky's had got what it wanted because Don was quiet for good now.'

'What did that mean?'

'I don't know. Have you got any ideas?' Ben asked her. 'Here we are.' They went up the front steps of a dilapidated townhouse. A couple, entwined, were coming out of the front door and left it open for them to walk into the dingy, unswept hallway. There was a row of letterboxes. Ben found the one on which was written Estover/Pollack, Apartment 3B. He led Maggie up the dark stairs. They rang and waited.

There was a sound of music from inside, the Brahms Violin Concerto. Ben rang the bell again. The music stopped, but no one opened the door. 'He's in there, but he's not coming out.' Ben tore a page out of a notebook, wrote on it and pushed it under the door. Then he said they'd go and find some jazz, the older the better.

There was only a pianist in Vintage Village, grey-haired, black, with a voice which poured out as slowly as treacle, and with dancing fingers. Ben forgot to be irritated by the afternoon's squash game and talked about Italy and Berenson, and some long-gone art deals, as they listened to variations on 'A Slowboat to China'. At last his patience was rewarded and he looked up and saw a red baseball cap in the doorway. He raised his hand and rose to greet their guest. 'You've come to join us. That's good. You must be Mr Pollack.'

'Sure, I'm Peter. You said you were Don's friend.' Peter pulled Ben's note out of the back pocket of his jeans.

'Years ago, many, many years. We were in Italy together.'

'I've got an idea Don mentioned your name. He said you were OK.'

'That was good of him.' Ben ordered white wine and a Michelob and a Tab for Peter Pollack.

'This your girlfriend?' Peter Pollack looked at Maggie.

'No. She's my boss, as a matter of fact. Maggie Perowne. Head of Old Master Paintings.'

Pollack was unconvinced. He said, 'Your girlfriend looks a good deal younger than you.'

'In certain lights, I'd have to admit it.'

Maggie explained, 'We work together, that's all. We were so sorry about your friend.'

Pollack looked from one to the other and then the words poured out of him, as though he had found no one to understand his grief. 'I was a lot younger than Don. Maybe over thirty years younger. People used to laugh about it, but he was the child in a way. It was like having a child about the place. Money! He didn't know the first thing about money. He'd write an article for some obscure magazine: "Erotic Influences on Mannerist Paintings of the Sixteenth Century". Stuff like that. And as soon as he got paid, which was peanuts, he'd rush out and buy me presents: paints, canvases, music. All stuff like that. Couldn't look after himself, of course. I don't think Don had ever learned how to boil water. He just lived for art. No wonder Klinsky's hated him. I have to tell you guys, Klinsky's is strictly for cash. Klinsky's hates art. My art they would certainly hate.'

'You're a painter?' Ben asked.

'I make images, sure. Images for our time. Of course no one wants to buy them. If you're worth anything, you don't sell. Look, I've got him on my shirt here. Vincent van Gogh. One of the greatest. And he only sold a single picture.'

'I think that's one of the tragedies in the history of art,' Maggie felt herself driven to say.

'Oh, sure. I bet your heart bleeds for him.'

'. . . Because most great painters made quite a good living: Raphael, Titian, Leonardo, Rembrandt. But just because Van Gogh never sold, everyone thinks you're a genius just if no one wants to buy your stuff.'

'Maggie!' She could be impossible at times, Ben thought. 'Mr Pollack's here because I think he's got something to tell us.'

'Peter. I guess you can call me Peter.'

'It's just that I don't think Klinsky's is all that bad.' Maggie, Ben thought, suffered from occasional loyalty.

'Then you don't know what Klinsky's in New York City is *doing*. Or what they did.'

'Which was?' Ben's voice was gentle.

'I should never have let him go. After he left the apartment, I decided to go after him. To stop him doing anything stupid. I went to your glitzy art shop on the bike. When I got there, Klinsky's had done it!'

'Done what exactly?' Ben asked.

'Murdered him!' Peter Pollack almost shouted. Then he got up suddenly and left before they could say anything or ask another question.

The nymphs and shepherds dancing in the dark glade were still on the easel in Chuck's office. Ben was examining the picture with his magnifying glass. On the desk behind him, books and transparencies were piled in no sort of order. Chuck was out to lunch at his club. Ben was engrossed in the picture and Maggie was thinking about something entirely different when she said, 'It's the most ridiculous suggestion I've ever heard!'

'Titian and his pupils, Titian and the Titiani,' Ben said, and asked her. 'You know them all, of course.'

'What's Klinsky's meant to have done?' Maggie couldn't be bothered with the Titiani. 'Launched poison darts at him through a blowpipe from the rest-room? Smeared the handle of his paddle with some rare Mexican tincture that produces immediate death? Your friend with the pigtail, the producer of unsaleable works, who probably has absolutely nothing else in common with Van Gogh, must have read far too much Agatha Christie.'

'Oh, I thought what he had to say about murder was the least interesting part of the conversation.'

'What on earth do you mean?'

'Come and look at the painting of the hair over the neck, Maggie. Tell me what you think, quite honestly.'

Maggie joined him in front of the picture. Then the door opened and, elegant and cheerful as ever, Chuck came back from lunch. 'Hi, boys and girls.' He saw Maggie, stooping, intent on her view of hair through a glass, and said 'My God! You're looking beautiful.'

Ben said, 'Thank you very much!'

Chuck, filling his pipe with tobacco from the jar on his desk, was delighted to tell them, 'I've got a great invitation.'

'Please. Don't ask me to play squash,' said Ben.

'John T. Flecknow's hosting a party for us in Sutton Place. We can drink champagne and look out over the East River, and for God's sake, Ben, let's hope you'll have made up your mind about the Titian by dinner time.'

'Don't rush me!'

'OK. That's OK. Save the good news for the Flecknow dinner.' Chuck blew out expensive and perfumed smoke. 'Oh, his wife's just longing to meet you.'

'I find that extremely alarming.'

'Why?'

'Some eager trout anxious to get her foot into the art world.' And Ben prayed, 'Please God, I don't have to sit next to her.'

The Flecknow's house in Sutton Place was filled like a small museum, with paintings and antique furniture. Big windows opened on to a balcony with views of the Queensborough Bridge and the East River. John T. Flecknow was a large, grizzled man with one of those deep rumbling American voices which can make every word audible across the most crowded restaurant. He sat at the head of the table at which a dozen of his close personal friends, together with Ben and Maggie, were dining. Behind him was a huge painting of a Scottish glen, and the chair backs and place mats were in what might have been the Flecknow tartan. He had gripped Ben by the arm on his arrival and explained that they were countrymen, although he had no trace of a Scottish accent.

Ben found himself sitting next to Barbara Flecknow,

who, in spite of his fears, turned out to be a beautifully produced blonde of about Maggie's age. She was treating Ben with the most flattering attention, sitting very close to him and frequently laying a friendly hand on his arm. Owing to this and the proximity of her revealed shoulders and mostly revealed breasts, Ben had become noticeably more cheerful.

'I'm the fourth wife of John T. Flecknow III,' she told him. 'We go in for numbers in our family. As the years went by, John became more interested in youth. Do you find that yourself, Mr Glazier?'

'Perhaps so. In a way.' He was looking across the table to Maggie who was laughing, he hoped only politely, at some joke of Chuck's.

'I sure hope you like younger women! Then we can become really good friends. I'm going to have to keep coming to you for advice. When I'm on the Board of the Lemberg Museum.'

'Sadly, I'll be back in London.'

'Oh, I'll hop over. I just adore London. So quaint. There's a little hotel in St James's which is kind of quiet and, you know, tremendously discreet. Maybe you'll let me take you out to dinner and, well, next day I'd fly right back to New York and impress them with my marvellous knowledge of art.'

'You getting on the Board of the Lemberg doesn't really depend on the Titian, does it?' Ben never felt he fully understood American museums.

'Oh, yes! That's what's going to get me in, when Johnny buys it. You see Susie Elphberg over there? *Her* husband bought them a genuine Corot, I guess it was, and she didn't get on the Board. So she'll be sick as a cat, which won't cause me any real pain, I can tell you. Chuck told me that with a Titian, I'm a shoe-in. Go on,

Ben. Tell me honestly. What do you think of it?' Her hand, with sparkling fingers was on his, her eyes were appealing.

'I think it's very skilfully painted,' he told her.

She said, 'Go on. I love your accent.'

'I'm sure it was painted in the right period. Say, 1570 to 1576.'

'I just love it,' she said. 'It's genuine, isn't it?'

'Well . . .' he hesitated.

'I mean your Scottish accent. That's genuine?'

'It's certainly mine,' he was happy to tell her.

At which, John T. Flecknow III tapped his glass with his knife, a well-known New York sound which produces instant and respectful silence to go with the dessert. He rose majestically to speak. 'Tonight I feel kind of at home, because our guest of honour is a man from my own country! Our families come from those same misty Highlands. We once wore the sporran and hunted the deer. Since my grandfather's time we McFlecknows have given our loyal services to the retail food industry of America.'

There was a solo clap from a man called Louis Elphberg, James T. Flecknow's business partner. 'Thank you, Louis. Otherwise, my time is devoted to the great cause, 'The People versus Narcotics'.' More general applause greeted this worthy organization, and when it had died away, the speaker continued, 'However, as I'm sure is the case with our guest, my heart's in the Highlands!'

'Glasgow, in fact,' Ben said quite audibly, but the Flecknow oratory rumbled on. 'Now, I have done business with all sorts and conditions of men. With the people of Cleveland. And the people of England. And some citizens of Israel and Ireland and even of Canada. But I have to tell you folks. There is no one you can trust as you can trust a Scot. As Robbie Burns put it, "Princes and lords are but the names of kings".'

'"The *breath* of kings".' Ben's correction was unnoticed and Flecknow completed the quotation, '"An honest man's the noblest work of God." Now, when I wanted an art expert of complete honesty to pass judgement on a certain picture, I rang another great name in retail food outlets, my old friend and aristocrat, the noble Lord Holloway, Chairman of Klinsky's, London. And I asked him for a brilliant art expert who happened to be an honest Scot. "I have the very man for you", the noble lord told me. And, of course, he mentioned our guest of honour, who not only, the Lord Holloway told me, identified a most valuable . . . Bonze–?'

'Bronzino,' Chuck came discreetly to the rescue.

'Thanks, Chuck . . . but has some of Scotia's old grandeur about him. The point of these remarks is, if our guest of honour, as an art expert and a Scot, gives his opinion that a certain picture is not up to standard, then, as my grandfather used to say, "The jig's off". But if he gives it his seal of approval, then I don't care what price I pay. My lovely wife, Barbara, will carry the Titian into her first meeting of the Lemberg Board and hand it over with a skirl of the bagpipes. So, folks, will ye tak a cup of kindness to our guest of honour, Ben Glazier!'

Glasses were raised, the toast was drunk, and when the dinner was over, and the guests found places and coffee on the living-room sofas, Chuck invited Maggie out on to the plant-filled, glass roofed balcony to look at the lights on the bridge, the lights on the water and said, 'Wonderful, glittering, glamorous – and I don't mean the view.'

'You're looking particularly gorgeous yourself,' Maggie had to say.

'It's Savile Row tailoring. You can't beat it.' And then

he stopped smiling. 'What do you think Ben's up to exactly?'

'Taking his time.'

'No, not that. Why was he talking about the old guy that passed out in the Sale Room? Someone I swear I can't remember.'

'He's been listening to some absurd story about Klinsky's,' Maggie told him.

'What story?'

'It's so ridiculous it's not even worth repeating.' She decided not to tell him. 'Maybe we ought to go back to the party?' She turned to go, but he held her wrist.

'Stay a minute.'

'Why?'

He kissed her suddenly and seriously. She responded only for seconds and then moved away from him. 'When the party's over,' he promised, 'I'll show you the view from my apartment.'

'Not possible.'

'It might be fun.'

'It might.'

'What's the matter? You got a serious boyfriend in England?'

'I suppose I've got a boyfriend. Nobody could possibly call Nick serious.'

'You don't fancy me?' Chuck said it as though he didn't believe it were possible.

'It's not that either. You're very acceptable, Chuck. You wear nice clothes and you've got a great tan and your hair's survived. I bet you've picked up all sorts of tricks and I'm sure you'd make a girl feel very spoiled and popular. But . . .'

'What's "but" about it?'

'But you're the same age as Ben,' she said, as though that settled it.

'He's a year older. At least! Anyway, what's age got to do with it?'

'Well, Nick . . .'

'Your not serious boyfriend?'

'Yes, Nick. He's young. Younger than me, in fact. He's young and rather disgustingly attractive.'

'Oh, he is?'

'But Ben minds enough about him. If it was you – well, almost his age – I don't think Ben could take it.'

'That's distinctly unfair.' Chuck felt that, in some way he didn't quite understand, he'd been cheated.

'Terribly,' Maggie agreed. 'We'd better go back or they'll think we've jumped in the river together.' She slid back the glass door into the living-room, and he followed her reluctantly. John T. Flecknow was advancing on him in a purposeful manner. 'You said our guest of honour might give us his decision tonight.'

'Oh, sure.' Chuck called out to Ben who was on a sofa beside Barbara Flecknow. 'You must have made your mind up by now? On the Titian.'

'You mean you want to know the truth? Do you, Chuck?' Ben had seen them come in from the terrace together and wasn't best pleased about it.

'Of course, we do. Give it to us, fellow Scot!' John T. Flecknow was prepared to look delighted as Ben stood and crossed the room to deliver judgement.

'The truth is,' he began carefully, 'it's a very well-painted picture. But it lacks the freedom of old age and the courage of an old man. The painting of the hair falling on the neck is hesitant, over-careful and without Titian's perfect confidence. It's the work of a talented pupil, perhaps Paris Bordone, who trained in Titian's studio and learned about erotic painting in the court of the French king. Is it a Titian? No, I'd say it is a perfectly respectable contemporary repetition.'

'For God's sake, Ben.' Chuck looked betrayed, disappointed and deeply angry. 'Don't make jokes about it.'

Peter Pollack was painting strips of colour and playing, once again, the Brahms Violin Concerto. His doorbell rang and this time he opened it and let in Ben who looked round the room and said, 'Your favourite music?'

'It was Don's.' Peter switched it off. 'You come from Klinsky's?'

'No. No, I came straight from the hotel. I haven't been to the office this morning. I'm afraid I'm not their favourite art expert any more. I passed judgement on an alleged Titian. I don't think it was exactly what they wanted to hear.' He looked round the room, at the abstract painting and the neat, scholarly desk, 'What did Don do to annoy Klinsky's exactly?'

'He was angry at the way they attributed pictures. He told me they made false claims. Anyway, claims he didn't believe in. He was going to speak out.'

'That was asking for trouble.'

'He was going to do it at the sale. He was going to tell everyone that wasn't a Parmigianino. Old Don who was so quiet, so gentle. He was really angry. He was going to make a great scene in public.'

'That was brave of him.'

'And stupid.'

'Yes. Yes, I'm afraid so. Would you mind very much if I used your bathroom?'

'Oh, sure.'

The bathroom was in chaos and had lost all traces of Don's sense of order. Socks were soaking in the basin, shirts hung up and dripping over the chipped and greying bath. The cupboard Ben opened contained twisted tubes of toothpaste, dental floss, various herbal remedies and a bottle of pills on which he was able to read the word, Digoxin. He went back into the living-room as the tape started again in the middle of the slow movement and asked, 'How on earth do you think anyone at Klinsky's killed Don?', as though he'd just remembered Peter's accusation.

'I don't know. I don't know what they did when he got there. I don't know that. I only know . . .' Peter Pollack seemed on the verge of tears.

'What do you know?' Ben asked in a voice as sharply unexpected as a slap in the face.

The young man shook himself and answered the question, 'Someone from Klinsky's came to see Don. A week before the sale. Came to warn him off, I guess. But Don didn't heed the warning. I wish to God he had.'

'Who came to see him? Did you meet this visitor?'

'No. Don wouldn't tell me who he was. He wouldn't say much about it, as a matter of fact. Except . . .'

'Except what?'

Peter went to the paint table and opened the drawer in it. 'His caller left this behind. For roll-ups, I guess.'

And he handed Ben an expensive-looking tobacco pouch made of red and green striped leather.

'Roll-ups? Oh, I don't think so. That wouldn't be his style at all.' He opened the pouch, sniffed and looked at the maker's name. 'This is really rather upper-class, anglo-phile pipe tobacco.'

Maggie was in Chuck's office looking at the painting and thinking that Ben was probably right, but that Titian had had a marvellous influence on his followers. Chuck was restless, pacing the room. Anger and irritation, she thought, had aged him overnight. There was no trace of the cool, would-be lover of the evening before, only an anguished man in a good suit who asked, 'He's not in the office! He's not in the hotel! For God's sake, where is he?'

'I don't know. He'd gone out before I left.'

'Has he gone mad?'

'I don't honestly think so.'

'What did he mean by telling the Flecknows that nonsense?'

'I suppose he thought he was right.'

'He *thought* he was right! He wasn't right. Let me tell you, he's utterly and entirely wrong. That Titian was approved by Berenson.'

'Is it on one of the Berenson lists?' Maggie was interested.

'No.' Chuck hesitated. 'Well, no. Not exactly. But years ago, many years ago, Berenson saw that picture. The greatest art expert in the world, the man we travelled to Italy to worship, whose word was accepted as gospel by all the dealers of his day, saw that picture and said it was undoubtedly Titian. Isn't that enough for you?'

'Is it enough for the Flecknows?' Maggie asked, as innocently as possible.

'It would have been, if JT hadn't got that crazy idea about Scottish experts. And if Ben hadn't let us down.' Chuck stopped pacing. 'Do you think Ben did it out of spite?'

'Whatever do you mean?'

'Because you and I got kind of friendly. You said he wouldn't have liked it if we had?'

'But we haven't.'

'Hell, no! I haven't even got that consolation.'

'I'm sorry, Chuck.' She smiled at him. 'Our visit to New York hasn't been a wild success for you.'

'You can say that again.'

'My clients in England are going to be disappointed too. They sent me over to bid for a Titian.'

'What are you going to tell them?'

'The truth.'

'And not Ben Glazier's crazy ideas!' Maggie found he was very near to her, gripping her arm and desperately serious. 'You keep quiet about what Ben said. You don't work for him. You work for Klinsky's! That's what it'll pay you to remember.'

'What's that mean exactly?' Before he had a chance to tell her, the door opened and Ben was with them.

'Ben! Where did you get to?'

'I woke up early. Had breakfast at a deli. Made a call. Rather an interesting call, actually.'

'Have you sobered up?' Chuck asked him.

'Considerably.'

'You admit it. You were drunk out of your skull when you talked all that rubbish about Paris – Whatever his damn name was.'

'Paris Bordone,' Ben repeated it with relish. 'I've got a lot of time for him. A considerable second-class talent and lover of women.'

'Chuck says Berenson saw the picture and said it was right,' Maggie felt she ought to put the case.

'So that proves it!' Chuck was cheerful again.

'Proves what?' Ben asked. 'That Berenson liked a good Paris Bordone?'

'Ben. Look. My old friend.' Chuck put out a hand and kneaded Ben's shoulder. 'Will you call and tell the Flecknows the truth?'

'The whole truth? I don't think you'd want me to do that, would you, Chuck?'

'I don't know what the hell you mean.'

'You told us you didn't remember Donald Estover. You said the name meant absolutely nothing to you. It did mean something, didn't it?'

'Meant what?'

'An old expert who objected to your over-optimistic attributions. Objected so much that he was going to stand up and denounce them in public. And you called on him to persuade him not to do it.'

'That's ridiculous! Who said I called on Don –?'

'This says it.' Ben threw the red and green tobacco pouch on Chuck's desk. 'I don't think either Don or his boyfriend smoked Dunhill tobacco out of a Dunhill pouch. It doesn't go with the pony-tail and the red baseball hat and the Van Gogh T-shirt. Or an old man who had problems with his heart. I found it in Estover's apartment. It's the pouch you thought you'd lost, wasn't it, Chuck?'

The telephone on Chuck's desk rang then. Instead of answering Ben's question, Chuck spoke to it in sudden awe and respect. 'Yes . . . Yes, of course. They're here. I'll tell them to come at once. Thank *you*, sir.' He looked at Maggie and Ben. 'Emmanuel Klinsky's sent his car for you. You'd better go down to the entrance hall. We can't waste time chattering up here. Anyway, Ben, there are still a few smokers in New York. And some of them may even have tobacco pouches.'

When they had gone, Chuck filled his pipe from the pouch, whoever it belonged to. He sat still and blew out smoke, having a lot to think about.

There was a stretch limousine with darkened windows waiting outside Klinsky's and, sinking into the back of it, Ben felt they were being whisked to another country, to some remote area in the past, to meet a potentate they had all heard rumours of but no one, to his knowledge had actually met. The limo moved slowly through the traffic up Fifth Avenue and turned into 66th Street, where it stopped in front of an ornate house, built in a French Renaissance style for a nineteenth-century banker. Inside it was very quiet; the elderly manservant who received them spoke in a whisper and took them up in a silent lift. He opened a pair of doors as though ushering them into the presence of royalty and, at the end of a room furnished with Greek, Chinese and Egyptian vases and statues, a very old man with a scrap of a white beard and a shawl over his shoulders peered at them but didn't rise from his seat behind a bulbous desk. 'Mr Glazier, Miss Perowne. Kindly be seated.'

They sat on the sort of chairs which have silk ropes across them to deter the public in stately homes. Ben admired a medieval wood-carving of a Madonna and Child, and a small Fragonard of a seductive and ridiculously young shepherdess, behind the old man's head. Emmanuel Klinsky's fingers were busy, nervously threading paper clips into a long chain, but he spoke in a calm, amused voice and started to give them his guiding principles for success in the art world. 'My great, great-grandfather always said to tell a man his Rembrandt is doubtful is like telling him his wife is unfaithful. It is a crime to deprive people of their dreams.'

'I suppose that's one way of looking at it,' Ben allowed.

'You know he came from Vienna, that old Emmanuel Klinsky? On the way to London he bought all the paintings his pocket could afford. Pictures he thought would give pleasure to the dukes and lords. So much more pleasure if he also gave them the names they wanted to hear like Rembrandt, Raphael, Velasquez. That first

Emmanual Klinsky was never one to deny pleasure to the customer.'

'Even if it meant telling lies?'

'Lies, Mr Glazier? Such an ugly word! An unnecessary word when we are discussing the happy subject of art. You know, as I know, there is no such thing as truth in our particular business.'

'I can't agree with that!' Maggie protested.

'What is art? Colour stains on a bit of wood or canvas, pretending to be a Pope or a beautiful woman, or a storm at sea. Do you call that the truth?' Old Klinsky smiled at her tolerantly.

'I imagine all this is to persuade me to tell Mr John T. Flecknow he can bid for a genuine Titian?' Ben was anxious to get to the point.

'How perceptive you are! I am proud we still employ people of such intelligence at Klinsky's. And you too, Miss Perowne. Remarkably intelligent, I understand, for one so young and beautiful. What's your view of the picture Mr Flecknow wishes to buy from us?'

'Ben's the expert,' Maggie said loyally. 'He thinks it was done by a former pupil.'

'Perhaps by a pupil on a very good day, or by Titian when he was, let us say, not quite at his best? Of those possibilities which should we choose?'

'I think I can guess.' Ben had got the point.

'I would suggest, the one that gives the most pleasure. Many great experts have taken care to assure our customers that they spent their money wisely, when they bought a work of art.'

'Money and art.' Ben felt stifled in an airless room, surrounded by priceless articles, being the object of an attempted seduction by a very old man wrapped in a shawl. 'I sometimes wonder if they've got anything at all to do with each other? Berenson made that mistake. At the end he was attributing pictures for business reasons.'

'Very sensible of him,' Klinsky nodded with approval.

'We were brought up to worship Berenson,' Ben told him. 'We all went to pay court to him, we were young men with a hero. But two of us grew up to find his way of working suspect. The other one was called Donald Estover. Now he's dead. Killed by Klinsky's.'

'Ben! You know that's ridiculous,' Maggie protested.

'Oh, not by blowpipes or poisoned darts. Of course not. But he had a heart condition. Fibulation. Uneven heart beats. He was taking Digoxin for it. Any sudden excitement might have killed him. The excitement that did it was having to stand up at a sale and denounce the false claims being made for a picture.'

'He didn't *have* to do that, Mr Glazier.' Old Klinsky spoke softly.

'He felt he had to. He felt he had to tell the truth. Klinsky's had forced it on him.'

'He was taking unnecessary risks. I hope you're not tempted to do that.'

'It's a temptation I can't resist,' Ben was sorry to say. 'You see I feel I owe it to Don Estover, as well as to Titian.'

'And you, Miss Perowne?'

'I've got too used to working with Ben. He's probably right.'

'Then there's nothing more I can say.' Emmanuel Klinsky raised his hands in an almost comical gesture of despair.

'I'm afraid not.'

'You'll be going back to England soon?'

'There seems to be nothing much to keep us here.'

'Or perhaps not much to keep you in London. Who

knows? Perhaps in the end you will agree with me. The customer comes first. Good day to you. Oh, Miss Perowne. Just one moment. Don't let me detain *you*, Mr Glazier.'

Ben looked at Maggie. She gave a small shrug and a smile and he left her alone with the old man.

When Ben got down to the street there was no limo waiting. He stood in the entrance hall until Maggie joined him. He told her the car had gone, so it looked as though their days were numbered, and asked her what old man Klinsky had wanted.

'Me for dinner. Alone in his apartment. He wanted to get to know me. He said he didn't only give pleasure to customers.'

'Of course you're going?'

'I think not.' She gave a small shudder. 'It'd be like being groped by dead leaves.'

'Maggie. You stood by me.'

'Yes.'

'You said I was right. Do you believe that?'

'I suppose I believe in you, Ben. It's become a sort of habit. See you later. I'm meeting someone.'

'Not Saint Chuck?'

'Don't worry. See you round the Labour Exchange.'

While Ben and Maggie had been closeted with the father of their firm, Chuck called at Sutton Place and was received by Barbara Flecknow, a woman likely to be disappointed in her hopes of getting a seat on the Board of the Lemberg. Chuck did his best to comfort her, telling her that Berenson had attributed the picture to Titian, 'Berenson wasn't a Scot. He was a Lithuanian Jew, brought up in Boston. He was the greatest art expert the world has ever known. But JT would rather listen to Glazier.'

'He seems to think he's found an honest man.'

'Maybe he'll be disillusioned.'

There was a silence between them and then Barbara said, 'Is that possible?' He began to tell her how it might be, and, in consequence of what he said, she picked up the telephone and left a message at Ben's hotel.

Maggie's lunchtime date was with Gloria Shallum. They met in a glass-fronted café near Klinsky's, and Maggie felt they were part of the street, close to the traffic jam and the weaving cyclists. Gloria, picking at a Caesar salad, said, 'You're going back to England soon?'

'Very soon.'

'I know very well Chuck's been, well, after you. Hasn't he?' And when Maggie didn't answer she said, as confidently as she could, 'He'll get over you.'

'I hope so. I'll certainly get over him.'

'Level with me, Maggie. Did Chuck achieve significant otherness with you?'

'I'm not quite sure what you mean.'

'Did he screw you, is what I mean?'

'Of course not. Absolutely nothing happened.'

'Not for want of asking?'

Maggie didn't answer.

'The bastard. No, he is! He's all I've learned to hate since I went to college and became aware of my responsibility to the environment.'

'You find Chuck environmentally unfriendly?' Maggie smiled.

'He's ghastly! That tobacco pipe. He spreads death, throws it around like confetti at a wedding. And his attitude to women! I know you've had some experience of this, Maggie. He regards us as receptacles, an ever-open convenience, where he can deposit little bits of Chuck B. Whiteside.'

'I'm afraid I disappointed him.'

'Oh, he doesn't disappoint very easily, or for too long. Also, he eats the corpses of dead animals.'

Maggie looked down at her hamburger and pushed away her plate.

'He poisons his system with alcohol. He listens to Frank Sinatra tapes and he's infringed my human rights by telling me I have great tits and I should make more of them.'

'It's a pretty grisly indictment.'

'Then how come I love the bastard?'

'It does seem terribly unfair.'

'But I do. So naturally I want to help the creep. I figure help from me's the only hope for him.'

'That's very noble of you.'

'It means a lot to him, about this Titian.'

'*If* it's a Titian.'

'Oh, he's sure it is. You see, it was bought by someone he knew years ago. Some guy called Ed Bachman picked it up in Italy when they were both young and went to visit Berenson.'

'Berenson seems to get in everywhere.'

'Chuck says he gave the picture the OK and Bachman, who was some kind of rich nut, bought it. Well now, Bachman died in South America and left it to his old friend Chuck.'

'You mean Chuck's selling his own picture?' Maggie was astonished.

'Well, not officially, of course. Officially it was entered anonymously and all that. I'm telling you this because I want you to help Chuck.'

'He seems perfectly capable of helping himself.'

'I want you to persuade Ben to change his mind. I guess Chuck could make it worth his while.'

'I'm sure he could. And I'm sure Ben wouldn't.'

'But you will help me. After all, we're part of the great sisterhood standing shoulder to shoulder! I guess if you don't . . .'

'What do you think will happen?' Maggie asked and Gloria looked strangely alarmed: 'I'm just scared of what Chuck might take into his head to do.'

While Gloria was confiding in Maggie Perowne, the man who was causing her so much anxiety was paying an unusual visit to the Modern Art department at Klinsky's and having a private and somewhat guarded conversation with its head, Walt Wenzel. Chuck didn't like Walt, who was aggressively young, regarded New York as the centre of civilization, wore pink-framed glasses and unstructured suits and thought the place for Old Master paintings was on tea-towels and dinner mats. He looked amused when Chuck, after a good deal of elaborate stuff about living life to the full and all experience being an archway to the truth, got round to the request he had to make, believing, as he did, that Walt would know how to help.

'To be honest, Chuck' – Walt Wenzel looked astonished and then amused – 'I thought that disgusting pipe of yours was your only vice.'

'Well life is full of surprises.'

'If you like I'll have a word with my contact. But I've got to warn you, old boy. This is going to cost you.'

The Lemberg is a small but richly endowed gallery with pictures hung in an old New York mansion. It was fairly empty when Ben met Barbara Flecknow and they were able to sit on a couch in the middle of a room full of Dutch Old Masters and talk in private. He had got her message from the hotel and, though he thought she'd try to persuade him to change his mind about the alleged

Titian, he didn't resist the chance of meeting her again. To his surprise, she seemed to have taken his attribution quite calmly. She put her hand on his arm as affectionately as ever and, when he told her he was sorry for what he'd felt he'd had to do, said, 'Please. Don't apologize. It's always best to know the truth. Anyway, JT still thinks you're marvellous.'

'That's extremely generous of him.'

'Isn't this a great gallery?'

'Perhaps you'll still get on the Board?'

'Oh, yes. I'm perfectly sure I will. Come on. I'll show you around.'

So they saw some of the best that the Lemberg had to offer, and had lunch at an Italian restaurant round the corner, which Ben found an entirely pleasant experience. When they parted Barbara said, in a voice full of regret, 'You're going back so soon?'

'I don't think my services are required here any longer.'

'We'll meet over there then. We'll have lots more chances for our feet to get together under tables. Oh, by the way. You wouldn't do me an enormous favour, would you? Something I want to send to some friends of mine who live in my favourite London hotel.'

Later Chuck got out of his car in an underground car park in the Thirties. He looked down a row of cars and saw the man he had come to meet walking towards him carrying a brief-case. He put his hand in his inside pocket and felt for a long envelope. As Walt Wenzel had said, it was going to cost him.

Ben was packing in his hotel bedroom. Maggie had joined him for a cup of tea and an account of her lunch with Gloria, which caused him great amusement and some delight. 'Saint Chuck planning to auction his own picture? Oh, dear! He's rather fallen off his pedestal. It only goes to show. Jogging *doesn't* improve the morals.'

There was a knock at the door and Maggie went and took a small parcel from a bellboy.

'There's a packet for you.' She looked at it with vague curiosity. 'I suppose?'

'Oh, yes. She said she'd send that over. I've got to deliver it to someone in London.'

'Who's she? The cat's mother?'

'Well, no. As a matter of fact, she's Barbara Flecknow. We happened to meet at lunchtime,' he told her modestly.

'You mean you just bumped into each other on Fifty-second Street and she pulled you into the Four Seasons.'

'She wanted to see me and she was very decent about my view of the Paris Bordone. We're still good friends.'

'How sweet! And she asked you to take this to London. Who to?'

'Oh, a friend. In some hotel.'

'A friend without a name. She's set you a pretty tough assignment. There's not a word written on this package.'

'She must have forgotten. I'll give her a ring later.'

'Perhaps she won't be in.'

'Why ever not?'

'She might want you to be travelling with a totally anonymous package.'

'Why ever should she?' Ben had no idea what Maggie was talking about.

She looked at him severely and said, 'You really fancy her, don't you?'

'She's a remarkably attractive woman.'

'Quite young?'

'She looks young.'

'And apt to run her fingers over you in the course of a conversation, I noticed.'

'Some people are extremely tactile.' Was she jealous? Ben almost dared to hope so.

'And some people might want to ruin your reputation. Perhaps make it seem you weren't such an entirely trustworthy Scot! What did she say was in here?'

'She didn't say.'

'And you didn't ask?'

'Well, no.'

Maggie started to tear the brown paper open.

'Maggie, hold on. You can't do that! It's a private parcel.' And then he looked down and saw clear plastic packets of a whitish powder, one of which Maggie had torn open, saying, 'Surprise, surprise!' with some satisfaction.

'Probably one of her organic beauty preparations.' Ben was still prepared to think well of Barbara.

'You really are an innocent, Ben.' Maggie put a finger on the powder and tasted it. 'If you'd been at art school parties in my day you'd've learned to steer clear of this particular beauty preparation.'

She went into the bathroom and Ben followed her as she poured Barbara Flecknow's 'gift for her friends' down the loo.

Ben said, 'You don't honestly think?'

'I think you'll get yourself into serious trouble if you start fancying other women!' Maggie said, as she pulled the chain.

The next day they were back in London. Ben was saying goodbye in an unfriendly manner to the telephone in his office as Maggie came in. He put it down and she asked him who it was.

'The cat's mother, Mrs John T. Flecknow III. She said she was so terribly sorry she never got around to sending

me the parcel. They'd gone to visit friends in Palm
Springs and she'd forgotten all about it.'

'What did you say?'

'Pull the other one, it's got bells on it.'

'That must've made your meaning entirely clear. Do
you want to see the Lord Chairman?'

'Not in the least.'

'Well, he wants to see us.'

'Had a good trip?' Lord Holloway looked up from the
work on his desk as they came into his office. It seemed
to Maggie his look was moderately baleful.

'Hardly,' Ben told him. 'I was stopped at Kennedy
Airport and submitted to a search. About the most
intimate physical experience I've had for a considerable
time.'

'What did they find?'

'Happily they drew a complete blank. I think they
must have had an unreliable tip-off.'

'Well, you certainly endeared yourselves to our most
important clients, and an old friend of mine, as it so
happens. John T. Flecknow III and his lovely wife.'

'*And* his wife?' Maggie raised her eyebrows.

'Oh, yes. She told the Lemberg Museum a supposed
Titian was only the work of a pupil, based on your
opinion, it seems. They were so impressed by her expertise
that they put her on the Board. Johnny Flecknow is
extremely grateful. Congratulations, Ben.'

Ben absorbed the news in silence and Maggie asked,
'Chuck Whiteside wasn't disappointed at Ben's turning
down the Titian?'

'I'm afraid Whiteside has something slightly more
serious to think about.' The Lord Chairman assumed a
sorrowful expression, as though announcing a death in
the department of Egyptology.

'Losing weight? Hair implant? Going in for a face-lift?' Ben was curious.

'Hardly that. Gloria Shallum rang to tell me he's been arrested.'

'He's been *what*?'

'Some drug-dealer got caught and started naming names. He identified Whiteside as a customer. Of course, it's some ridiculous mistake.'

'Oh, of course.'

'It'll soon be sorted out.'

'I hear these things take time,' Ben said hopefully.

And then the Lord Chairman asked, in reverend tones, 'And it seems you met the great Emmanuel Klinsky?'

'Of course we did, didn't we, Maggie? He had us up for a chat. Wonderful old boy, for his age.'

'Did he seem to be fairly pleased, with the way things are going in London?' Holloway dared to ask.

'Oh, fairly pleased. There was one thing he was rather concerned about.'

'Oh, was there? What was that?'

'That I didn't have adequate space to park my motor bike. I assured him that the problem would be addressed. Nice to talk to you, Holloway, but we must get on. Maggie and I have so much work to catch up with.'

'Poor Chuck!' Maggie said, as they left the office.

'Oh, yes. My heart bleeds for him. Do you honestly think he wasn't behind Barbara Flecknow's little plot? The sinners have met their just desserts.'

'Only one of them. The other's got herself on the Board of the Lemberg. She's had a triumph.'

'There you are, then.' And Ben told her, 'That's more like the art world as we know it.'

Maggie put her arm in his and they walked up the stairs to work.

The Spectre at the Feast

Accidents occur in the best-regulated families.

Charles Dickens, *David Copperfield*

All these stories, Ben Glazier thought, about Chippendale tables hidden in the hen-house, the odd Canova used as a doorstep, the roll of tapestry plugging a draught in the scullery, the mysterious Correggio over which a dull portrait was painted, only waiting to be scrubbed off to leave the family truly famous, lead too many people to believe they're surrounded with hidden treasures. You may not think I look much, the inhabitants of old houses seem to say, but if only you knew what I've got stopping the draughts, or if that painting of a horse could be attributed to Stubbs, I would be rich and famous. You don't even need a house to think like that. I have a hidden talent, many people might say, if only I could remember where I've hidden it. Those with old family homes tend to breed the concealed masterpiece madness, and Ben never forgot the strange series of events, absurd and then alarming, which marked his brief association with the Bovingtons of Bovington Moat House.

The house was not grand: it had once been a fortified farm, built on and extended over the ages. In the middle of the last century the Bovingtons had owned a good deal of land and a factory in the local town. Now the land had gone; the factory, sold long ago, had become a shopping centre; the moat, once full of water and stocked with trout, had run dry. Hester Bovington fought gamely to keep the garden respectable and lived, for most of the year, alone with one old family retainer, her formidable family nanny. The place was well supplied with attics, lofts, sheds, cupboards and stables, where masterpieces might have hibernated, unnoticed, over the centuries.

Hector Bovington, MP, Hester's older son, was a youngish man who lived surrounded by a cloud of dissatisfaction, which moved with him wherever he went. He was dissatisfied with his job as a Parliamentary Private Secretary in some obscure department of a government with which most of the country was dissatisfied. He was dissatisfied with his wife, Mousekin, who, although over-anxious to please him, had grown larger than he hoped she would. He was dissatisfied with his son's progress at his prep school and terrified of having to pay his fees at Eton. He was not entirely dissatisified with his own appearance, his fair hair and regular features, although his pale blue eyes had the glossy look of boiled sweets.

He was dissatisfied with the length of the holiday he was spending at his mother's home and one afternoon he decided, after having read about forgotten treasures in an old copy of *Country Life*, to search the attics. Hours later, camouflaged with dirt so he looked like some long-abandoned object himself, he found among a pile of old canvasses behind a rusty iron bed what he had decided he was looking for.

Hester Bovington, wearing gum boots and an old mac, was burning the autumn prunings in the garden. In the library Hector was about to make a phone call when the real ruler of Bovington Moat House, a masterful woman, wearing a well-washed blue nurse's dress and a cardigan, put her head round the door and said in strict North

Country tones which could send the most wayward charge straight up to bed, 'Master Hector! Wherever have you been and got into that state?'

'Up in the attic, Nanny. I'm just making a call.'

'Well, keep it quick then. Think about your mother's phone bill. Now, wherever has your poor mother got to? Never out in the garden. Nanny Tucker went to the window and called out to ask if Mrs Bovington were determined to catch her death of cold, and Hector made his quick phone call to an old school friend at Klinsky's.

It was Maggie's birthday. She opened her cards in the Old Masters office and thanked Ben for the tapes *Ella Sings the Golden Years of Gershwin*, which, she assured him, she'd always wanted. Nick Roper came up from the wine department because he'd got a great surprise for her, which was going to be the best present ever. 'What would you say to a Rubens?'

'A what?'

'The chap who paints all these tits and bums of course. You know that.'

'Very funny, Nick.'

'I think I've found you one. In the Cotswolds, actually.'

'Where did you pick it up? A car boot sale?'

'No, darling, that's what I came to tell you. I keep getting phone calls from dear old Marilyn Bovington.'

'Some woman you're interested in?' Ben sounded hopeful.

'No, Bovington's not a woman. Not at all. He's MP for somewhere or other. Parliamentary Private Secretary to something else. He got the name Marilyn because he was rather a pretty boy in the Lower School. He's gone off a lot now, of course.'

'I don't have much to be grateful for,' Ben told him. 'I'm knocking on in years, I can't find a cleaning lady and my love life is somewhat frustrated. But how I thank my lucky stars I never went to your old school.'

'Don't worry, Ben,' Maggie comforted him. 'No one would ever have called you Marilyn.'

'Anyway, his real name's Hector,' Nick explained. 'And his ma owns the Moat House, which has been in the Bovington family since fourteen hundred and something. Now the point is . . .'

'Oh, there's a point, is there?' Ben was surprised.

'Yes. The point is, old Hector rings me to say he's unearthed this Rubens in his ma's attic.'

'Who says it's a Rubens?' Maggie asked.

'Well, he does.'

'Does a certain physical allure when an inky schoolboy make him an expert on Old Master paintings?' Ben wondered.

Maggie said, 'Well, he'd better bring it in and have a word with us.'

'Not a chance. He's keeping the whole thing dark from his family. For the moment. He doesn't know how his ma would take the idea of untold wealth in the attic.'

'So what does he suggest?'

'Well, that I just drop in as an old school chum and take a look at the hidden treasure. Portrait of a woman and kids apparently. Fully dressed.'

'That makes a whole lot of sense.' Ben was unconvinced. 'As an expert on highly priced booze, you're naturally qualified to judge a Rubens.'

'Oh, Maggie and I'll go together, of course. An away day in the leafy Cotswolds. I mean, this just could be a find.'

'So it would seem sensible if Ben came too?' Maggie suggested.

'Well, all right then.' Nick looked at Ben. 'I'm not jealous.'

Nick made further calls to the one-time Marilyn and Hector told him he'd shown the thing to a local antiques man, sworn to complete secrecy, who'd been extremely encouraging. Almost before he'd had time to consider the improbability of the journey, Ben found himself in an icy dining-room in the Moat House, among a family Tolstoy wouldn't have found like any other because it didn't seem to be a happy one at all.

There was clearly a deadly rivalry between Hector, the Conservative politician, and Mike, his younger brother, who wore a sweatshirt and leather jacket, taught English Literature at a North Country polytechnic, now turned into a university, and who had acquired, during a year at Philadelphia State, an American wife called Lucky – although, burrowing into a cocoon of a sweater and shivering ostentatiously, she looked as though she felt her luck was out. Ben sat next to Hester, who appeared surprisingly calm, perhaps because her mind was out in the garden. Maggie had drawn Hector who as he looked at her frequently, seemed to have difficulty in not licking his lips. Nick was next to Hector's wife, Mousekin, who was nervously loyal to her husband and had a body that was too large and voluptuous for her small-scale, diffidently pretty face.

'Art to me means an interpretation of society. To you, I suppose, it means money?' Mike, the academic, was haranguing Ben.

'I suppose to me it means pleasure.'

'Pleasure! You mean the whole world of art is just an enormous brothel?' Mike seemed full of contempt.

'Mike, try not to argue!' Lucky rebuked him and explained to Nick, 'My husband can't stop arguing. I tell him he could be teaching literature in Philadelphia State if only he wouldn't argue all the time. Or *any* place where they've invented central heating.'

'I thought chaps from auction houses were all frightfully intellectual and terrifying.' Hector felt he had to lean very close to Maggie to tell her this.

'I'm not exactly a chap,' she said.

'Well, that's wonderfully obvious, if you don't mind me saying so. I mean, *girls* like you . . .' At which, his wife Anthea, known as Mousekin, displeased Hector by breaking into this intimate conversation, 'I say, do you have to look round the room for bids? And bang with a hammer and all that? How enormously *impressive*!'

'My wife's so easily impressed.' Hector made excuses for her. 'Don't be silly, Mousekin. Miss Perowne – Maggie, may I? Maggie doesn't actually bang with a hammer.'

'Oh, yes, I do. All the time.'

'I'm awfully sorry.' Hector looked hurt. 'I didn't realize you actually did it.'

'Oh, yes. All the time.'

Ben found conversation at his end of the table flowing like cement and, looking round for inspiration, was delighted to see one of his favourite authors on the wall. 'Isn't that a contemporary photograph of Charles Dickens?' he asked Hester.

'Oh, you recognized his face? How clever of you!'

'He *is* quite well known. Who did that photograph belong to, I wonder?'

'Probably one of the maids,' Mike suggested. 'Someone who liked bad jokes and sloppy sentimentality.' Mike's special subject was D. H. Lawrence.

But now Hester began to talk in a gentle, distant voice. 'There used to be a story about Dickens coming to Bovington. My husband's great-great, whatever it was, knew Dickens at the Garrick Club and invited him down.'

'Thousands of people must have stayed here,' Mike protested. 'What on earth does Dickens matter?'

'And he took quite a shine to my husband's great-great-grandmother, Henrietta.' Hester ignored her son's interruption. 'They did some sort of theatricals together, out in the hall.'

At this point, Nanny Tucker came wandering into the room and started collecting up the plates.

'Ma, it's the *text* that matters' – Mike was giving a seminar – 'not gossip about the writers. Examine Dickens's *texts*! Then wash your sticky fingers and read *Sons and Lovers*.'

'I thought coffee in the library?' Hester suggested. 'Will that be all right, Nanny?'

'They haven't eaten up their puddings, some of your visitors.' And Nanny Tucker picked up Ben's plate and looked at it critically. 'Is that meant to be finished?'

'Thank you. It was delicious.' Ben surrendered his plate with guilt.

'If it was so delicious like you said, why didn't you eat it up?'

Happily for Ben, Hector created a diversion by inviting Maggie to come out and look at the rose garden, and Nanny Tucker became involved in finding her a pair of wellies to borrow as she couldn't possibly venture out in those 'useless little pumps'.

So Hector led Maggie out into the autumnal garden where the roses were almost over and the late blooms mildewed by the rain. He led her round the corner of the house into a stable yard and unlocked the old tack room to which he'd removed his treasure to show it, in strict confidence, to a local dealer.

'I'm not an expert in any way,' he said, 'but one picks up a sort of nose for what's right if you've got any taste at all. Anyway, I want you to be the first to see it. I don't want the others to influence you.'

'I'm quite capable of making up my own mind,' she told him. He'd shut the door and she smelled old leather and sour hay.

'Not a word about this to Ma,' he was saying, 'or to Nanny Tucker,' and then, like a triumphant conjurer, he whisked a piece of sacking off a canvas propped against the wall to reveal a dark picture, much in need of cleaning. 'It's the Rubens touch, am I right? Not *quite* as usual, because the girl with the kids kept her clothes on. Even her hat, would you believe it?' Maggie said nothing and he asked her, 'What do you think it is?'

'I know what it is.' She had no doubt about it. 'It's Hélène Fourment, with two of her children.'

'This Hélène, friend of Rubens, was she?'

'I suppose you could say so. He married her when she was sixteen.'

'Did he, by God! I suppose a lot of that goes on in the art world.'

'A lot of what?'

'Sex!' Hector was laughing. 'You know, the moment I saw you I knew we'd hit it off.'

'Did you really?'

'Of course, I could offer it to Sotheby's or Christie's.'

'I suppose you could.'

'But, well, I've always had a soft spot for old Klinsky's.'

'Very touching.'

'A Rubens would be a huge plus for you, wouldn't it? Picture of the year and so on.' He waited for her reaction and, when none came, he called the evidence in support of his great find, 'I mean, Rubens came to England, didn't he?'

'Knighted by Charles I,' she told him. 'Given a degree at Cambridge. Struck by the beauties of the English countryside.'

'So some of his stuff might have been picked up by the Bovington family?' Hector seemed to think the case was made out.

'It's possible.' At which he smiled and made her a proposition, 'Of course, if I promised you, you could sell this masterpiece at Klinsky's, you personally – and not any of your rivals. You and I could become really *close* friends, Maggie.' He put an arm tentatively round her waist. She moved away but looked at him with apparent interest. 'Have sex, you mean?' she asked innocently.

'Well, you do come straight out with it, don't you?' Hector was delighted.

'You're suggesting I'd have sex to get a Rubens for Klinsky's?' Maggie smiled at him sweetly.

'Wouldn't you?'

'I don't know.' She seemed to be thinking it over. 'Perhaps I might. I haven't really thought about it. Luckily the matter doesn't arise.'

'What do you mean?'

'I mean, whatever I'd do for a Rubens, I wouldn't do for that daub!'

'That what? Why do you call it a daub?'

'Because the real painting of the beautiful Hélène and her children is safely in the Louvre and what you were asking me to take my clothes off for is a rather indifferent copy. Bought by some gullible Bovington in the last century, I imagine.' She moved to the door. 'This visit has been a complete waste of time.'

'I'm so . . . I'm sorry.' He looked, unattractively, like a small boy caught out in some disagreeable net.

'So you should be, Marilyn,' Maggie said, and left him.

While Maggie was disappointing Hector, Ben had used his time to make a truly unexpected discovery. The party had coffee in the library, another long, icy room with leather-bound volumes which looked as though they hadn't been read for generations. Ben, bored with the after-lunch chatter about the strange absence of apples and of routes to London, wandered down the shelves and started to pull out some old family albums, bound books of watercolours, drawings, letters and poems left by visitors to mark a happy stay with the then prosperous family in the 1840s and 1850s. Some of the poems were illustrated with drawings. Here and there he found a pressed flower, a lock of hair or a marked dance card. And then there was something more substantial, about thirty pages written over with brownish ink, crossed out again and again, rewritten and clearly agonized over. They were held together by a strip of white ribbon and on the front page there was an inscription in the same small handwriting. Nick came up with a cup of coffee and looked over Ben's shoulder. They were both able to read a confident, unaltered dedication with much difficulty: TO HENRIETTA BOVINGTON. THIS LITTLE GHOST STORY FROM WHICH WE TOOK THE PLAY YOU ACTED IN SO CHARMINGLY. A TRIBUTE FROM HER FELLOW PLAYER AND A GREAT ADMIRER, CHARLES DICKENS. THE MOAT HOUSE, SUMMER '59. 'I say, Ben. Is that important?' Nick wondered.

'If it's right, it certainly might be. I mean, I'm not a manuscript man, but . . .'

'Not as important as a Rubens? I wonder where the hell Marilyn's taken Maggie?'

'Are you jealous?'

'Don't be ridiculous!' But Nick gulped his coffee. 'Yet she might like me to keep my eye on her . . . They always find a bit of anxiety flattering, don't they?' So Nick went. Hester had been drawn back to the garden, the two wives were talking and Mike had gone off somewhere. Ben sat in a chair by the window and started to read 'The Spectre at the Feast; A Ghost Story by C.D.'. And then he began to decipher an opening paragraph:

> It is not unknown for an aged relative to appear, unannounced, at a family board and require to be given pride of place at dinner. Such an occurrence would be by no means out of the way and would make but a tame beginning to a story which, in the telling, seeks to chill the bones of the most rational reader at the most cheerful fireside. But when I tell you that the life of the relative in question had undoubtedly been terminated by a ball shot from a French cannon some twenty years before the night I am about to describe, it may take on a different and more alarming complexion.

When Ben had read it, he looked through the window and saw his hostess cutting off dead heads with a pair of secateurs. He put the book he had found under his arm and went out to join her.

'Those dusty old albums,' she said when he'd shown it to her. 'Nanny Tucker wouldn't let the children touch them. She said they'd get their clothes grubby and we always thought they looked terribly dull.'

'Well, perhaps not so dull as that. You said Charles Dickens visited Bovington?'

'Well, that was the story we were told. It may have been pure fiction.'

'He certainly left some fiction here. A ghost story called "The Spectre at the Feast".'

'My father never read us that one.'

'So far as I know, it's never been published, Mrs Bovington, I've got it here.' He opened the pages of the album and showed her the loose leaves of the story. 'It would seem to be in his handwriting. I'm not an expert at all. Henry Quarles is our man on manuscripts. But an unpublished story by Dickens might be worth, well, a very great deal of money.'

The rain had stopped and the garden was lit by low sunlight. Hester Bovington looked distressed. 'Oh, dear. I'm so sorry to hear that.'

'Why?'

'Well, I haven't got a lot of money. We can't have the heating on much and Mike's wife complains. Usually we don't drink very much – an occasional sherry when we have visitors. But I've got this house and the garden, of course. We get on very well here and Nanny Tucker's a tower of strength. A lot of money? That might be very embarrassing. I really wouldn't want anything to change.'

'But would you let me show this to Henry Quarles?' Ben suggested. 'Then at least you'll know what *sort* of money we're talking about.'

'Well' – she was still doubtful – 'I suppose so. Is that what you'd advise me to do?'

'There's no harm in knowing.'

'I suppose not. Well, yes, then, Mr Glazier. But please don't say anything to the family about this. Especially not to Hector. I wouldn't want anyone to be upset.' She walked with him back to the house, and they passed

Nanny Tucker, well wrapped up, sitting on a kitchen chair by a yew hedge, doing a pile of mending.

Henry Quarles, in Manuscripts, was a pale young man who must have been born with the quizzical look, the lopsided smile and the myopia of the confirmed bibliophile. He wore a three-piece suit, boots and a gold watch-chain; he also had a surprisingly beautiful girlfriend and spent three evenings a week playing poker. He was holding the pages of 'The Spectre at the Feast', and telling Ben about a possible connection with Bovington Moat House: 'Ned Bovington was a member of the Garrick Club and had taken Dickens's side during the row with Thackeray. Charles was in a bit of a turmoil. Marriage broken up, in love with a younger woman.'

'Poor chap.' Ben was understanding.

'In 1859 he started *The Tale of Two Cities*, working flat out.' Quarles found a page in a book. 'But in a letter to Wilkie Collins he says this: "A friend from the Club is summoning me to a week in the country. A house among apple trees and flowering cherries, also ornamented by a flowering of daughters. There is a rumour that we may have theatricals!" That might be where he wrote this ghost story – at the house you went to.' Quarles picked up the manuscript again. 'The paper's right. The handwriting. The watermark. The history. Yes, Ben, you have dug us up a bit of buried treasure.'

'How much would you say?'

'A reserve of ... What? Seventy-five thousand? I'd hope we'd get more.'

Ben shook his head. 'I'm afraid the owner's going to find that rather worrying.'

*

Since her embarrassing visit to Bovington Maggie hadn't been hugely pleased with Nick who had taken her on a wild goose chase to see a man she described as a complete wanker. But Hector had called in at Klinsky's Wine department and, though he didn't dare approach Maggie again, asked Nick if he had any idea what Ben had taken from the Moat House because his mother was being distinctly cagey on the subject. Nick did a little research, having been promised a commission by Hector from any eventual sale, and got hold of Quarles.

When he heard the magic figure of seventy-five thousand, Hector said it was his mother's duty to arrange a family meeting so the Dickens manuscript could be fully discussed. As he was a hugely busy man it would have to be an evening. Ben was invited back to the Moat House to stay a night, give his advice, and bring the entirely welcome 'The Spectre at the Feast' with him.

The family gathered in the library after dinner, a company of which Hector, having had more than a little too much to drink, had appointed himself the chairman and managing director. Hester, sitting on the edge of the group, her attention often straying to the bulb catalogues on her lap, looked as though she would rather be anywhere else. Mike was scowling, Lucky was shivering, Mousekin was so supportive of her husband that it got terribly on his nerves, and Ben wandered up and down the shelves, found nothing else worth his notice, and thought he'd better leave the Bovingtons to make up their own minds, although he had a clear idea who was going to do it for them.

'The price seems excellent. Who knows what's going to happen in the future? As I read the market, now's the time to sell. Would Mr Glazier agree?' Hector opened the debate.

'It's not a bad time.' Ben told them. 'But whether we sell it for you is entirely Mrs Bovington's decision.'

'So what's it to be, Ma?' Hector hadn't got all night. 'I mean, it's not doing a damn thing for us stuck in the bookshelf, gathering dust.'

'I'm not sure. I can't be sure. What do you *really* think, Mr Glazier?' Hester asked.

'It's not what Mr Glazier thinks.' Hector stayed in charge. 'It's not only just what *you* think, Ma, quite honestly. This is family property. Like the house, it'll go to the family. Here's a chance for the family to improve its cashflow situation.'

'Improve yours, you mean?' Mike spoke with slow sarcasm in the classless voice he had acquired.

'I'm thinking of the *family*. People seem to forget family values nowadays and just run around joy-riding in other people's Volvos.' Hector slid easily into his political tone of voice.

'Personally I wouldn't give two p for a ghost story, scribbled by Dickens for so much a bloody commercial line.' Mike sighed, looked bored, and, to his surprise, Ben saw Mousekin grant him a quick little smile of solidarity.

'If you feel like that, Michael' – Hector was trying to sound entirely reasonable – 'there's absolutely no need for you to share in it.'

'Of course, there's a need for Mike to share in it!' Lucky was angry. 'He could take time off. He could do his book on Lawrence. That might get him tenure in California.'

'You and Michael don't have the same responsibilities as myself and Mousekin.' Hector stoked Lucky's rage. 'There are just two of you. Hardly a family in any meaningful sense of the word.'

'You mean, we don't have a brat to send to a highly expensive boarding school?'

'Malcolm isn't a brat, Lucky. Malcolm is the next generation – the future of England!'

'Tongue-tied, tedious and sexually frustrated!'

'Well, that's not a complaint *you* suffer from,' Hector told Lucky and Hester, confused and distressed, appealed to them both, 'Please. Oh, please. There's absolutely nothing for you to quarrel about.'

Lucky, however, could find plenty. She told Hector, 'I don't know what the hell you mean. Mike and I may have our ups and downs, but we've talked it through and we're committed to each other.'

'And you don't see why you shouldn't get your hands on some of the manuscript money?' Hector asked as Hester begged, 'I just want the *advice* of all of you.'

'We do have a brat' – Hector began a speech – 'as Lucky so delightfully puts it. He has been down for my old school since birth. Mousekin and I are determined to see him –'

'Buggered and beaten,' Lucky suggested.

'I don't think I heard that, Lucky.' Hector went on, 'If a capital sum is to come to the family, as a result of Mr Glazier's lucky find, then I suggest any division should take account of Malcolm's need to get a proper start in life.'

'What do you think, Anthea?' Hester, turned in her bewilderment, to Hector's wife.

'Oh, it seems such a pity to sell something that's, well, part of the family history.'

'Mousekin!' Hector looked at her as though she had suddenly appeared, for no reason at all, on the opposition benches.

'But, of course, Hector's right,' Mousekin retreated. 'We do need to think of Malcolm.'

'Well, I suppose . . .' Hester seemed on the point of surrender. 'What do you *really* suggest, Mr Glazier?'

'I don't think I can suggest anything, Mrs Bovington. It's really for you to decide what you want to do with *your* property.'

Hester was silent, drew in her breath, appeared to be about to speak, but, before she could, Nanny Tucker banged in to the room. 'Are you lot going to stay up all night wasting the electricity?'

'No, Nanny. No, of course we won't,' Hester promised.

'All right, then. Time to go up the wooden hill to Bedfordshire.' At which, she turned out all the lights and left them. Hester said, 'Good-night, Nanny,' in the dark and, as Hector turned the lights on again, he said, 'I do wish she'd stop treating us as though we were all about six years old.'

'Do you, Hector? Do you really?' Hester wasn't sure. 'Life seemed, well, a good deal easier then. I'm rather tired and I think Nanny's right. We can all come to a decision in the morning. Good-night, Mr Glazier. I do hope you'll be comfortable.'

The Moat House seemed to move and mutter in the night, and inexplicable sounds could be heard, which might be footsteps or nothing but the wind. Hector, having a very large, very late brandy alone in the library, looked up at sounds he thought he heard from a floor above. In the bedroom corridor a door opened and Mike, in his pyjamas, started on a journey to somewhere. Ben had finished deciphering the Dickens story, put it on his bedside table, switched the light out and went to sleep. Some time later, Ben's door swung open, letting in a wedge of light. There was a foot in the doorway and a hand came out of the darkness and felt for 'The Spectre at the Feast'.

*

There was sunshine in the room when Ben woke up. He was in a fairly cheerful mood. The family would make up their minds and he could get back to London to lunch, perhaps, with Maggie. And then he was staring at the bedside table where he'd put 'The Spectre' he'd finished reading, and he was out of bed, searching in his briefcase, his overnight bag, in drawers and cupboards, with a growing panic and finding nothing.

When he was dressed he went down to the dining-room. The family were sitting at breakfast like a commit-tee meeting, or a jury about to come to a verdict. Ben took his place. Hector scraped the last, searching spoonful out of his boiled egg, cleared his throat, and with all due solemnity, as though telling a packed House of Commons that war had been declared, he began, 'As the eldest son I think it is for me to announce the family's decision. The decision, I have to say, is unanimous. We are giving you formal instructions, as the representative of Klinsky's, to sell our rare and much-treasured Dickens manuscript. For the highest possible price, of course.'

'Oh, dear.' It was all Ben could think of to say.

'Why? What's "oh dear" about it?'

'I'm afraid I haven't got the manuscript. Have any of you?'

'Of course not!' Mike's voice was high and mocking. 'You told us you brought it down with you. To await our decision.'

'I feel sure I had it in my room. I was reading it before I went to sleep. I didn't dream that. And this morning it has slowly and silently vanished away.'

'It *can't* have.' Mousekin seemed on the verge of tears.

'If anything has happened to our manuscript, Glazier,' Hector told him with icy calm, 'we shall hold you person-ally responsible.'

The family were all looking at Ben with varying degrees of hostility. He got away from them as quickly as possible, sacrificing breakfast and promising to search and see if by any chance the precious manuscript had been left at Klinsky's. He would call them as soon as he had any news. It was Lucky who got him a taxi for the station and Hector who, with a set jaw, refused him even the coldest of farewells.

Back at Klinsky's, Ben made a cursory search of his office, but he knew when he had last seen 'The Spectre'. He was about to call on Maggie when Shrimsley entered the room in the manner of a brisk police inspector carrying out a dawn raid, and told him that the Lord Chairman wanted to see him at once. When Ben asked if he were under arrest, Shrimsley replied, 'Not yet,' and marched him off. Indeed the atmosphere in the Chairman's office was not unlike that in the interview room of a particularly unfriendly nick.

Holloway was outraged. 'A Member of Parliament! Parliamentary Private Secretary at what, Shrimsley?'

'European Union, Lord Chairman.'

'At European Union. A man of unimpeachable character who has made it pretty plain to me, on the telephone, Glazier, that he suspects you of having . . .'

'Half-inched?' Ben suggested helpfully.

'Of having stolen – I hope you realize the seriousness of the situation – stolen what he says is a valuable manuscript. Is it a valuable manuscript?'

'Extremely valuable.'

'And have you stolen it?'

'Not guilty! What's this? A judgement by my peers?'

'It was only by the use of the greatest tact that I managed to stop him calling in the police.' And Holloway, in a distinctly unfriendly manner, added, 'For the time being.'

'I went down there. I was reading it in bed. I put it on the bedside table and in the morning . . .'

'You're not suggesting that the family at Bovington stole their own property?' Shrimsley was at his most flatly ironic. 'I don't think you'll find your average jury would take very kindly to that idea.'

'Well, what idea *would* they take kindly to? One of the dogs ate it? A ghost? Why not?' Ben asked them, in all innocence. 'It's a ghost story.'

'I think I should tell the meeting that Mr Glazier asked Accounts for a certain amount of his salary in advance,' Shrimsley was delighted to be able to say.

'I had my eye,' Ben explained, 'on something rather glamorous.'

'You mean a woman?' Lord Holloway made what was, to him, a natural assumption.

'No, I mean a BMW K1100LT,' Ben told them. 'With an electronic windscreen.'

'Are we to understand that you stole a Dickens manuscript to buy a motor bike?' Like King Lear, the Lord Chairman seemed to fear the onset of madness.

'Of course not,' Ben reassured him. 'The idea is ridiculous!'

'In fact it's extremely serious,' Holloway corrected him. 'It's a case which, in our opinion, calls for a ruthless investigation.'

And then Ben, fed up to the teeth with all these absurd suspicions from the man who wouldn't know the Martini horseman from a cocktail, lost his temper, stood up, and decided to end his long and occasionally brilliant career at Klinsky's. 'Then let me tell you what you can do for a start. You can take my job and bloody catalogue it. You can put it in the next sale and knock it down to the lowest bidder and I hope you do a terrible deal. You can ask Hector Bovington, MP exactly where he intends to flog the precious manuscript he pinched off his dear old Ma. And when you've done all that, you can write me a letter of grovelling apology, care of the Uffizi Gallery, Florence, Italy. Sorry, Shrimsley, I've forgotten the post-code!' And with that he banged out of the room and, so far as he was concerned, out of their lives for ever.

People who leave their jobs, Ben knew, are meant to clear their desks. On the face of it that sounds a fairly simple proposition, sweep the notepad, the pen tray and the photo of the wife and kids into a briefcase and slope off. But when he sat down in front of his desk and started to grub about in it, he was faced with a job that would take at least a week and might call for packing cases and a pantechnicon. Just one deep drawer was found to contain a pullover, a spare pair of socks, three spectacle cases, a guide to Urbino, two tins of butterscotch, the remains of a bottle of Glenfiddich, shoe trees, a small watering-can, a tweed cap, a compass, about thirty tapes – most of which had been put in the wrong boxes – and a tinned Christmas pudding. He had taken a swig from the Glenfiddich bottle and was wondering how on earth Gregorian chants had got into *Golden Moments from 'French Cancan'.* when Maggie burst in on him, considerably aggrieved. 'You're not going to do it!' she ordered.

'Do what?'

'Leave?' The news had spread round Klinsky's like wildfire.

'Oh, yes, I am.'

'Where are you going?'

'I'll be perfectly content' – Ben did his best to sound

dreamy – 'cadging drinks in Harry's Bar. Showing rich Americans round the Botticellis. Sitting in the sunshine doing the *Daily Telegraph* crossword in the Piazza della Signoria. That's if I'm not arrested at the airport. If Lord Fishfingers down there doesn't get me sewing mailbags in Wandsworth.'

She looked at him then, in a way he found highly inconvenient. 'I'm going to miss you.'

'Oh, for God's sake, Maggie. Don't say things like that!'

'I'm going to miss you very much.'

'Shut up!' he said, and then talked about simpler, more practical matters. 'That manuscript didn't just melt into thin air, you know. "The Spectre at the Feast" didn't just glide into the other world. Our Hector stole it.'

'Why?'

'Why? Because he needed ready money to pay his young hopeful's school fees at some highly expensive penal colony. He wanted to steal it from Mrs Bovington, whose property it undoubtedly is. He didn't want to have to split his share of the boodle with his boring brother. He nipped into my bedroom when I was enjoying my beauty sleep and now he's off on a parliamentary mission to Tokyo, looking for an anonymous millionaire who has a secret store of Dickens manuscripts.'

Maggie thought about his scenario for a little and then said, 'I've had some dealings with Hector Bovington.'

'Of course you have! The Rubens that wasn't.'

'He made me a quite extraordinary proposition.'

'What do you mean exactly?'

'I suppose he thinks he rather fancies me.'

'It's not an uncommon complaint, unfortunately.'

'I might be able to find out if he's got it.'

'You have ways of making him talk.'

'Anyway, don't you leave!' Maggie's mind was made up. 'Not till I've had a go at it.'

'I'm not going to stick round here.' Ben was sure of that. 'I'm not going to give Lord Muesli the satisfaction.'

'Go home, say you're ill,' Maggie called out her instructions as she left. 'Skulk in your tent. Say you're dead. It shouldn't take me too long.'

Back in her office Maggie called European Union and got the Parliamentary Private Secretary with alarming rapidity. He came on the line, switched on and with his engine running, 'Hector Bovington, here.' Annabelle, the Old Master Number Two, was listening eagerly as Maggie chatted back, 'Oh, hello, Hector. This is Maggie. Maggie Perowne. From Klinsky's. Yes. Well, I know Klinsky's is a dirty word to you, but I've got an idea. I might be able to help. There's a party. Old Master drawings. We could have a drink and a quiet word perhaps. Around seven thirty?'

She put down the phone and made a small gesture of disgust. He had accepted with quite horrible enthusiasm.

The gallery was crowded with potential buyers and practising drinkers, but Hector Bovington, MP had Maggie in a corner and was making it clear that he was seriously angry. 'Not blaming you, of course, but I've told your Chairman straight. I told Holloway that unless Klinsky's and your friend Glazier cough up our manuscript in forty-eight hours I'm turning the whole shooting match over the the police.'

'Quite right!' Maggie agreed heartily.

'What?' Hector was surprised.

'That's the best thing for you to do. Oh, by the way, *that's* a Rubens. Just in case you'd like to know what one looks like.'

'But didn't you want to persuade me not to report Glazier?' He was too busy to more than glance at the drawing on the wall.

'Oh, no. If he's stolen the thing, that's exactly what you should do. Rather a special little Tiepolo too, if you're interested.'

'Then if you don't want to protect Glazier, why did you ask me here? The truth now!' Hector added making it clear he wasn't going to be mucked about.

Maggie smiled, raised her hand shyly, and just touched his jacket. 'I suppose,' she almost whispered, 'I've been thinking about you rather a lot.'

'I've been thinking about *you* quite a lot too,' he was delighted to tell her.

'I mean, we seemed to get on quite well together . . .'

'Absolutely! We hit it off,' he agreed.

'I always think there's something so glamorous about an MP. I suppose it's power.'

'And I do think you're an absolutely super girl!' He made a quick lunge at her but she stepped smartly away.

'No, Hector. Not here. Couldn't you take me out to dinner? Somewhere exciting? Not the Reform Club.'

'Somewhere really exciting?' The light of battle was in his eyes. 'I bet you've never been to the Conundrum?'

The Conundrum Club, somewhere behind Jermyn Street, wasn't very full nor did it seem to Maggie particularly clean. There was a small dance floor, pink spotlights and waitresses (they, she thought, had been the appeal of the place for the eternal schoolboy MP), not-so-young blondes, bursting out of gym slips, with school ties and boaters, and suspenders straining across white thighs to grab their black stockings.

Hector and Maggie had been eating prawn cocktails and *coq au vin* by candlelight. He was holding her hand at all opportunities and looking at her with enormous interest, while she tried hard to remain charming and, on the whole, succeeded. Then the time came for him to explain his tastes in women. 'I do like girls who are smallish, but . . .'

'Sort of perfect,' she helped him out.

'The elfin quality! Now my wife Mousekin is hardly elfin.'

'I'm sorry.' Maggie sounded genuinely sympathetic.

'She's larger, actually, than I expected when I took her on. We don't sleep together now, you know. Never share a bedroom. Even when we're staying at Ma's.'

'How fantastically interesting! But I did say that I thought I could help you.'

'You are helping me!' Hector assured her. 'You're helping me put up with, well, all the things I have to put up with. All the bloody worries. The European biscuit regulations and having to face years of school fees for Malcolm – and, well, Mousekin. I don't mean to treat her badly. It's just when I actually catch sight of her, looking like some clueless junior who's letting down the house, I lose my temper! Now, when I catch sight of you, it's something entirely different. Any chance of a kiss?'

'Before we start on all that' – Maggie was firm – 'could we discuss a bit of business?'

'What sort of business?' Hector became cautious.

'That manuscript. You know, there's no need to sell it through Klinsky's.'

'No?'

'We could find an eccentric millionaire. Someone with a secret collection, who'd just like to feel he owns the thing and doesn't want to show it around. That way we'd save Klinsky's commission.'

'Very interesting.' Hector was still guarded.

'And another advantage . . .?'

'What?'

'Your family need never know it's been recovered. You wouldn't have to share out the dosh. It could be yours, Hector, all yours. And you could take me out to this wonderful, glamorous club again . . .'

'Wouldn't you want a little more than that?' He was becoming businesslike.

'Oh, Hector! What a mind-reader you are. And so sensitive. I suppose that's why you've had such a brilliant career in politics.'

'Probably. So the deal is, you arrange a private sale. Not a word to Ma. I get the proceeds and you get . . .?'

'Oh, a little something.' Maggie smiled modestly. 'So I'll always think of you with astonishing gratitude.'

He looked at her and he smiled back. 'Well,' he said, 'I don't see why not.'

'All right, we'll drink to it.' She raised her glass.

'Why not dance to it?' Maggie thought about this and decided to be brave. She said, without enthusiasm, 'Lovely.'

So Hector got up to dance round with zeal, prancing as he had at college balls ten years before. Maggie danced minimally, doing her best to avoid physical contact.

'You'll hand over the article in question,' she told him as he gyrated.

'You mean, you'll get it from your friend, Glazier. He's got it, of course.'

'No, he hasn't!'

'What?'

'Of course he hasn't.'

'Who has, then?'

'You have.'

'What?' Hector's fists were clenched, his arms waving and he seemed to be squatting into a sort of twist.

'You took it off Ben's bedside table.'

'As a matter of fact, I didn't.'

'Pull the other one! Tell us where it is and we're in business.'

'I can't.'

'Why?'

'Because, I promise you, I didn't take it.'

Maggie stopped any attempt at dancing and looked at him in deep disappointment. She said, 'You're telling the truth!'

'As a matter of fact I am.' Hector also juddered to a stop. 'Glazier's got it. It's perfectly obvious.'

'It *wasn't* you.' By now she was furious with him.

'Of course not. Weren't we dancing?'

'Good-night, Hector.' There was absolutely no point in her spending a moment longer with this ghastly man. She made for the door.

'Maggie. Maggie darling! Where're you going?'

'Home!' And she was gone. He ran after her into the street and saw her slam the door of a small white car. She had started the engine as he called out angrily, 'But aren't we going on somewhere? Your flat, for instance?' But she had escaped him.

He had never thought it would happen but Ben found himself missing Klinsky's. He didn't bother to dress but stood in the kitchen and cooked himself a kipper. Well, surely, after all that had happened, he deserved some sort of a treat. After breakfast he could, he supposed, shave. He could get the Harley-Davidson out and go up to Hampstead Heath. He could speed down to Brighton and sit on the pier in a high wind, with a row of lonely men looking at the grey sea and facing eventual old age. He could plan his departure to Florence. He could write letters. Instead he put on a tape of *Porgy and Bess*, listened to 'It Ain't Necessarily So', and ate as slowly as possible. Then the doorbell rang and he did his best to conceal his delight as he let in Maggie.

'Kippers and a morning roll. What our Glasgow Granny always gave us on Saturdays. Something we keenly looked forward to after a week of porridge. Now, I suppose, I could have kippers every day. Nothing much else to do.'

'He hasn't got it.'

'What did you say?'

'Hector hasn't got the manuscript.'

'Who says he hasn't?'

'He does.'

'Then he's lying through his horrible upper-class teeth.'

'No!' Maggie was sure of it.

'What?'

'I know he wasn't lying. He'd swallowed my story hook, line and sinker. We were going to do a deal, avoiding Klinsky's, finding a mad collector, cheating the family. We'd shaken hands on it. So I asked him about producing the goods and he said he hadn't stolen anything. He sounded quite apologetic about not being the thief.'

'Who does he reckon was?'

'You, of course. He thought I'd get it off you and then we could do a deal. You *haven't* got it, by any chance?'

Ben looked at her and shook his head.

'So who else is there?' Maggie asked.

'Mother?'

'Gone mad and pinched her own property?'

'A burglar?'

'A cat bibliophile, shinning up the drainpipe after nothing but a Dickens story? Henry Quarles in a stocking mask? Don't you find that rather improbable?'

'The other son – Mike?'

Ben thought it over carefully and said, 'A man who hates Dickens is capable of any enormity.'

When Maggie passed the Klinsky's reception desk on her way back to work, a fair-haired woman called out to her, peeled herself away from Lucy Starr, and crossed the marble floor, reminding her that she was Lucky, 'Mike Bovington's Lucky', and that she needed an urgent meeting with Mr Glazier, 'on this ghastly subject of the Dickens manuscript. Is he available right now?'

'He's at home,' Maggie told her. 'I don't think he'll be in here today. Can you tell me about it?'

'Well, I guess not. No, it should be Mr Glazier. You got his home number? Do you think he'll see me?'

The tall, blonde woman seemed nervous, yet excited. Maggie came to the conclusion that Ben would rather talk to Lucky than sit alone with a skeleton kipper, and so passed on the address.

Lucky Bovington wasn't the only woman with troubles at Klinsky's that morning. Maggie had hardly got to the Old Masters office, when she was received with a cold smile and a meaningful glance at the clock by Annabelle Straddling-Smith who said, 'Traffic awful was it, Maggie? It's a good thing one of us got in early. Camilla's been on the phone pretty well since dawn. She says she's got bad news for you.'

The news was so bad, it seemed, that it couldn't be spoken of in Klinsky's, so they had to go out to the Italian café ('Are you going out *again*? What shall I tell people?' Annabelle asked). There Camilla fell on a Danish pastry as though it were a stiff brandy and poured out her troubles. 'It's that horrific girl in your department,' she confided between mouthfuls.

'Annabelle Straddling-Smith?'

'I don't know about Smith but she's certainly straddling Bernard Holloway!'

Maggie remembered the glimpses they had had, before being sent off on a mission to Moscow, of Miss Straddling-Smith joining the Lord Chairman for breakfast in the Epicure Hotel, and wondered, not for the first time, whatever hidden quality Bernard Holloway possessed which made girls seek him out in hotels and wolf Danish pastries out of despair when he was unfaithful.

'Bernard's got no *standards*!' Camilla was complaining. 'Can he be true to a woman? No. He's like a bloody butterfly.'

Maggie tried to imagine the Lord Chairman fluttering about, pollinating things, failed, and asked, 'I thought you quite liked that?'

'What?'

'Bernard being unfaithful to his wife. With you.'

'The ghastly thing is he's being unfaithful to both of us. The ingratitude. After all I've done for that marriage!'

'Which marriage exactly?' Maggie was puzzled.

'Bernard's marriage, of course. Do you think he'd stay with Muriel if he hadn't got me to cheer him up occasionally? They owe it all to me and now he's ditching both of us for the sake of a Miss Straddling-Smith – who looks like a horse, if you want my honest opinion. So he can indulge in a bit of dressage behind our backs. Look, you're really the only person I've got to talk to. Should I tell Muriel?'

Maggie looked at Camilla and was surprised to see that the Danish pastry had been abandoned half-way through and that Lord Holloway's slighted lover was drinking coffee with a sudden and dangerous look of triumph.

'Mike took it.' Lucky Bovington was sitting beside Ben on his sofa. He had received her in his dressing-gown and her shiny hair and fingernails, her sanitized beauty and clear decision made him feel scruffy and confused.

'You don't mean that?'

'Oh, yes, I do. I'm sure of it. My husband took the manuscript that night you were at the Moat House.'

'Did he tell you that?'

'No, of course not. There are a lot of things he hasn't told me. He's a very proud man. He's ashamed about doing so little for me and that we have to live here in the cold, on not much money. And he can't get tenure in a proper university in the States. That's why he took it, of course. To get the money to write.'

'You've seen it?' Ben asked.

'He wouldn't show it to me. He wouldn't say anything. The English are like that, aren't they?'

'Are they?'

'Scared of their mothers and that horrible old nurse-maid they keep on years after the kids grew up. The English are all scared of their nannies.'

'So I believe.'

'OK, I'll tell you how I know about Mike. I took a couple of sleepers that night when you were down at the Moat House. The cold keeps me awake, you see. Well, I'd gone right off but something woke me. It was Mike getting out of bed. I know what you're going to say but he didn't go up to the john because that's another door. Think of it! An *en suite* bathroom in the ice-house. He went out of the door that leads into the corridor. He must have been gone quite a while. I guess I was asleep before he got back. But I knew damn well he'd got it.'

'Then I ought to tell you to go straight to the police.'

'But you're not going to, are you?' Lucky smiled.

'No.'

'You're too much of a businessman.'

'Or tell the rest of the family.'

'They must never get to know. Look, I need your help. As someone who knows the inside-out of the art world.'

'You mean as a crook?' Ben translated.

'I didn't say that. But Mike's got it and he can't have a clue what to do with it. I figured you would know how to sell it off quietly and no one hears a word about it.'

Ben looked at her, stood up and said, 'I'll have to go and see someone.'

'Someone who might help us?' Lucky was eager.

'I very much hope so.'

After he had bathed, shaved and zipped himself into a leather jacket, got the bike out and set off for the grey and damp Cotswolds, Ben felt considerably better. He found Hester Bovington digging out some overblown dahlias with a fork and preparing to plant wallflowers in the bed beside the kitchen garden. She looked up and smiled at him, an odd way, he thought for her to treat the man her son had accused of theft.

'I'm sorry,' he apologized, 'I'm back again. Like the spectre at the feast.'

'Everything's going rather wrong here, I'm afraid.'

'I'm sorry to hear that.'

'Nanny's not been well. Not at all well. How on earth are we going to manage without Nanny Tucker? If we lose our tower of strength?'

'Mrs Bovington' – Ben started off briskly – 'about the manuscript . . .'

'You've come about that again, of course. Bringing trouble.'

'No one's gone to the police?'

'The police? Good heavens, no! We wouldn't want that, would we? Not the police. You haven't found it back in your office or anything? Of course, you haven't. It's lost and that's all about it.'

'I'm afraid it disappeared down here. Everyone seems to be accusing everyone else of stealing it.'

'Everyone?'

'Lucky thinks her husband did it.'

'Has she said that to anyone?'

'To me.'

'Ridiculous woman! She ought to go and live in a greenhouse. She must have a rotten circulation.'

'And Hector thinks I did it.'

'You, Mr Glazier?' Hester seemed astonished by the suggestion.

'Well, I had it down here and it vanished from my bedroom. He's complained to Klinsky's.'

'Oh, dear. Poor you! You're not in any sort of trouble, are you?'

'Not much. I think I managed to resign before they sacked me.'

'Nothing like that was meant to happen, I'm sure.' She looked at him, deeply concerned.

'Don't worry too much. I've always rather wanted to live in Florence. Only one person I'll miss . . .'

'You're in trouble, Mr Glazier' – Hester was sure of it – 'and I'm sorry. I'm sure Nanny Tucker will be quite distressed to hear that. I don't think that was the intention at all.'

'I don't see why Nanny Tucker should care about my problems.'

'All the same, I do think she'll want a visit from you. As soon as she knows you're in trouble.'

Nanny Tucker's bedroom was small, one of the old servants rooms at the top of the house. It was cold and filled with the sweet smell of illness and old age. There were dozens of knick-knacks, photographs of the two boys at all ages and of young Malcolm, shells, presents from the seaside, and a lot of pictures of the Royal Family. Nanny lay in bed, down but not entirely out, wearing her glasses and cardigan as Hester put a tray of supper on her lap. Ben sat in an upright chair at the bedside, talking in the slightly too loud a voice he used for invalids. Hester was worried when Nanny Tucker showed no interest in the food she had been brought. 'Have some of that nice soup, Nanny,' she said.

'Nice soup? *You* didn't make it, did you?' Nanny Tucker examined it closely.

'No, Nanny. Out of a tin,' Hester admitted.

'Well, thank God for that. She was never a cook,' Nanny confided in Ben. 'Not even when she was a child. When others would be making gingerbread men in the oven, she was always out in the garden. Or it was her rabbits.' She lifted a spoonful of soup, sniffed it doubtfully and forced it down. 'Later on, when she married Mr Bovington, we always dreaded the girl's night off. Hester's Castle Pudding! Lay on the stomach like lead, it did. I reckon that's what carried poor Mr Bovington off in the end, although he was never that strong, God knows. What carried him off was indigestion, what he got on the girl's night off.'

'Nanny, you say the most terrible things.' Hester smiled.

'It's the truth, Hester. Nasty medicine, the truth is, I know, but it gets you cleared out in the end. I shan't be eating any more of this, that's for certain. You can take the tray away.'

'Thank you, Nanny. You won't tire Nanny out, will you, Mr Glazier?'

'Oh, it would take more than him to tire me out. That I can tell you!' When Hester had gone with the tray, Nanny Tucker started her inquisition, 'She had you out in the garden, did she?'

'Oh, yes.'

'I hope you wrapped up warm.'

'It wasn't very cold.'

'That's what you all say, "It wasn't very cold, Nanny". And the next day you're sneezing your heads off and using up handkerchiefs. Hester said as you were losing your job. You're not to do that!'

'I'm not quite sure how I can help it.' And then he asked her, 'Have you got something to tell me?'

'That was never intended, not that you should lose your job.'

'What *was* intended, actually?'

The old woman leaned back on her pillows and sighed heavily, remembering the past. 'They was always a difficult pair of boys. All right on their own sometimes, but always quarrelling. Well, they hated each other, wanted to score off each other in nasty ways. I reckon that's why Master Mike's behaving like he is with Mrs Hector.'

'With Mousekin?' Ben was astonished.

'She's not such a Mousekin as all that, I can tell you. I expect she led him on. And now she doesn't sleep with Master Hector. Well, I've caught Master Mike creeping along the corridor, in his jim-jams. A "corridor creeper", that's what Mr Bovington used to call his like.'

'So that's what he was up to!' But nothing was clear, nothing was solved.

'Always a dirty little boy, he was. In the holidays from his first school I'd catch him, hands in his pockets! If you know what that means.'

'Yes, Nanny, I'm afraid I do. He and Hector always quarrelled?'

'The whole time. There was a row about a train set their father bought for Christmas. They fought over it, of course. Endless. And their mother cried over it. And their father couldn't stop it. So I did what I had to.'

'What was that?' Strangely, Ben felt he knew the answer.

'Packed it up in its box and put it all out for the dustman. Nasty medicine, but it cleared up the trouble in the end.'

'And the Dickens manuscript?' he asked her gently.

'You should never have found that thing in the first place. Soon as Hester told me, I told her what it would bring. Trouble!' Her voice was tired after a lifetime of children quarrelling. 'You should have heard them. Whose is it? Who's having the money? How soon are we going to get our hands on the cash for it? I'm the eldest. Well, I'm the cleverest. No, you're not. Yes, I am. Arguing their silly little heads off until it was long past their bedtime, just like they did over a packet of Smarties. Only one thing to do.'

'So *you* took it from my bedroom?' Ben understood.

'Little Mr Know-It-All, aren't you? Well, you're going to know all about it in a moment. I wouldn't want you to suffer for it.'

'So?'

'Tell them it's lost,' I said to Hester, 'tell them it's gone. So they can shut up arguing and finish their tea. "Oh no," she said, "they'll find it, wherever I put it!" So I said, "You get rid of it entirely, there's a good girl,

Hester. Nasty medicine," I said, "but it'll put things right in the end." I will say one thing for Hester, she was always obedient.'

'Thank you for telling me.'

'That's all right. Nanny's tired now, dear. Time for my forty winks.' She took off her glasses, folded them and put them on her bedside table. Then she closed her eyes.

When Ben went to say goodbye to Hester she had the bonfire going again, smouldering under a pile of hedge clippings with occasional little spurts of flame. He told her that Nanny Tucker was sleeping and he was going to ride back to London. She put on some more clippings with her fork and told him she loved bonfires, so good for the soil, which was much enriched by burning things on it.

'I suppose,' he said, 'it depends on what sort of things.' He noticed, among the ashes and blackened twigs, a charred scrap of paper covered with words, crossed out and rewritten. 'I think that's yours.' He stooped, picked it up and handed it to her.

'It *was* mine, wasn't it? I could do what I liked with it.' So she found a flame to consume it completely.

'She burnt it? Isn't that arson or something?' Lord Holloway was appalled.

'Bad luck on Dickens,' Maggie agreed.

'Bad luck on all of us?' Ben said. 'We've lost a Dickens story.'

'Rather hard luck on Hector Bovington,' Holloway thought. 'A most distinguished Member of Parliament.'

'Yes, let's look on the bright side.' Ben cheered up.

'Things aren't altogether bad,' Maggie agreed.

The good cheer was broken by a telephone call to the

Lord Chairman. They heard him say, as brightly as he could manage, 'Ah, Muriel. You're coming in? Yes, of course, I'm free. Absolutely.' And then they learned the full horror of the situation. 'You're coming in with Camilla Mounsey? You *both* have something to say to me?' He put the telephone down then and sat looking, Maggie said afterwards, like a man about to shrink to half his size. He muttered, 'Business meeting,' and so they got up and left him to his fate.

Ben had something to show Maggie, another object of his desire of which she had every right to be jealous. In half the Chairman's parking place, gleaming, glimmering and, no doubt, ready to go, was Ben's new BMW K1100LT, on which he offered Maggie a lift home, confident that no girl could resist it. She didn't and they went for a long drink before they parted.

And the unhappy Holloway, confronted by his formidable wife and dauntless mistress, found himself completely at the mercy of this unholy alliance. When he asked Muriel, in a strangled sort of way, if she had found out, she looked only faintly amused and said, 'Of course, I found out! How could I help finding out? You made it so obvious, ducking into improbable restaurants, hiding in doorways, making ridiculous telephone calls on the extension at home.'

'He can't be discreet about anything,' Camilla agreed. 'I think he *wants* people to know.'

'It's his past, in supermarket advertising,' Muriel suggested.

'Yes, I suppose it's that.'

'I'm so very sorry.' The Chairman was looking pathetic and puzzled by his wife's faintly pitying smile. 'Oh, don't bother to apologize,' she told him. 'You don't imagine I minded about Camilla, surely. She's a nice woman really, and old enough not to do anything stupid. Also, she gave me time to get on with my own life, which I don't intend to tell you about. But we've talked it over, Camilla and I, and we've come to a clear decision.'

It was Camilla who delivered the joint verdict which the Lord Chairman received with his head bowed, 'You've got to give up Annabelle Straddling-Smith!'

Discover more about our forthcoming books through Penguin's FREE newspaper...

Penguin
Quarterly

It's packed with:

- exciting features
- author interviews
- previews & reviews
- books from your favourite films & TV series
- exclusive competitions & much, much more...

Write off for your free copy today to:
Dept JC
Penguin Books Ltd
FREEPOST
West Drayton
Middlesex
UB7 0BR
NO STAMP REQUIRED

READ MORE IN PENGUIN

In every corner of the world, on every subject under the sun, Penguin represents quality and variety – the very best in publishing today.

For complete information about books available from Penguin – including Puffins, Penguin Classics and Arkana – and how to order them, write to us at the appropriate address below. Please note that for copyright reasons the selection of books varies from country to country.

In the United Kingdom: Please write to *Dept. JC, Penguin Books Ltd, FREEPOST, West Drayton, Middlesex UB7 OBR*

If you have any difficulty in obtaining a title, please send your order with the correct money, plus ten per cent for postage and packaging, to *PO Box No. 11, West Drayton, Middlesex UB7 OBR*

In the United States: Please write to *Penguin USA Inc., 375 Hudson Street, New York, NY 10014*

In Canada: Please write to *Penguin Books Canada Ltd, 10 Alcorn Avenue, Suite 300, Toronto, Ontario M4V 3B2*

In Australia: Please write to *Penguin Books Australia Ltd, 487 Maroondah Highway, Ringwood, Victoria 3134*

In New Zealand: Please write to *Penguin Books (NZ) Ltd, 182–190 Wairau Road, Private Bag, Takapuna, Auckland 9*

In India: Please write to *Penguin Books India Pvt Ltd, 706 Eros Apartments, 56 Nehru Place, New Delhi 110 019*

In the Netherlands: Please write to *Penguin Books Netherlands B.V., Keizersgracht 231 NL–1016 DV Amsterdam*

In Germany: Please write to *Penguin Books Deutschland GmbH, Friedrichstrasse 10–12, W–6000 Frankfurt/Main 1*

In Spain: Please write to *Penguin Books S. A., C. San Bernardo 117–6° E–28015 Madrid*

In Italy: Please write to *Penguin Italia s.r.l., Via Felice Casati 20, I–20124 Milano*

In France: Please write to *Penguin France S. A., 17 rue Lejeune, F–31000 Toulouse*

In Japan: Please write to *Penguin Books Japan, Ishikiribashi Building, 2–5–4, Suido, Bunkyo-ku, Tokyo 112*

In Greece: Please write to *Penguin Hellas Ltd, Dimocritou 3, GR–106 71 Athens*

In South Africa: Please write to *Longman Penguin Southern Africa (Pty) Ltd, Private Bag X08, Bertsham 2013*

READ MORE IN PENGUIN

A CHOICE OF BESTSELLERS

The Darling Buds of May H. E. Bates

Here come the Larkins, in the first of their hilarious rural adventures, crashing their way through the English countryside in the wake of Pop, the quick-eyed, golden-hearted junk-dealer, and Ma, with a mouthful of crisps and a laugh like a jelly.

Down with Superwoman Shirley Conran

This cheerful, friendly reference book is filled with sensible and practical advice. Shirley Conran tells you everything you need to know about all aspects of running a home using minimum effort and achieving the best results. Completely updated and expanded from her internationally bestselling *Superwoman*, it is now twice the size of the original.

Eva Fraser's Face and Body Programme Eva Fraser

Following the huge success of her facial workout, Eva Fraser now brings you her complete health and beauty programme, which reverses the signs of ageing – naturally. In her new book she shares with us her daily fitness programme as well as her philosophy for youthfulness of mind and body.

Better Than Life Grant Naylor

The sequel to the internationally bestselling *Red Dwarf* finds Lister, Rimmer, Cat and Kryten trapped in the ultimate computer game: Better than Life. BTL transports you directly to a perfect world of your imagination, a world where you can enjoy fabulous wealth and unmitigated success. It's the ideal game with only one drawback – it's so good, it will kill you . . .

Keith Richards: The Biography Victor Bockris

'The year's best book about rock music . . . The Rolling Stone was a dream topic, being both the rocker who took drugs until his teeth needed replacing, and the faintly aristocratic type who could still talk about it in complete sentences. Bockris sat back and let the story tell itself' – Giles Smith in the *Independent*, Books of the Year

READ MORE IN PENGUIN

A CHOICE OF BESTSELLERS

The Happy Isles of Oceania   Paul Theroux

'He voyaged from the Solomons to Fiji, Tonga, Samoa, Tahiti, the Marquesas and Easter Island, stepping stones in an odyssey of courage and toughness ... Not since Jack London has a writer described the Pacific islands so eloquently and informatively. This is Paul Theroux's finest, most personal and heartfelt travel book' – *Observer*

Floyd on Spain   Keith Floyd

'The recipes in *Floyd on Spain* are wonderful. The smells of herbs and onions, tomato sauce and grilled fish rise from the page and you want to get out, buy a hunk of hake and cook it with potatoes and garlic' – Prue Leith in the *Sunday Express*

Dylan: Behind the Shades   Clinton Heylin
The Biography

'The most accurately researched and competently written account of Dylan's life yet ... Heylin allots equal space to each of the three decades of Dylan's career, and offers a particularly judicious assessment of his achievements in the post-conversion Eighties' – Mark Ford in the *London Review of Books*

I Dreamed of Africa   Kuki Gallmann

'Written from the heart, without restraints – generous to the reader as few writers are ... It will add a memorable and vivid and at times most moving volume to the literature of Kenya, to that part of it which will last' – Elspeth Huxley

More Please   Barry Humphries

'A marvellous, funny, distressing and vivid autobiography' – Alec Guinness in the *Sunday Times* Books of the Year. 'One of the best self-exposures I have ever read, funny, painful and original ... gives a rare insight into how, and at what cost, a comic genius develops' – Anne Chisholm in the *Spectator* Books of the Year

BY THE SAME AUTHOR

Titmuss Regained

The Right Honourable Leslie Titmuss, the abrasive high-flyer who rose from poverty to power in *Paradise Postponed*, is now Secretary of State at H.E.A.P., the Ministry of Housing, Ecological Affairs and Planning, and in pursuit of the beautiful Jenny Sidonia, widow of a socialist Oxford don.

Paradise Postponed

Why does Simeon Simcox, the CND-marching rector of Rapstone Fanner, leave his fortune not to his two sons but to an odious Tory Minister? John Mortimer's brilliant and hilarious novel unveils the follies and passions of an astonishing array of characters, and creates a vivid portrait of English life from 1945 to the present.

also published together in one volume as

The Rapstone Chronicles

BY THE SAME AUTHOR

The Narrowing Stream

Each morning Julia drives her husband Swinton to the station and waves goodbye, conscious that he has already gone from her. Then her son sees a strange face in the boathouse. She hears about a beautiful dead girl who lived further down the river and was somehow connected with her husband. A young man enters her house and asks her questions which threaten to crumble her carefully created defences ... and the hot, endless day becomes a nightmare from which she is desperate to awake.

Summer's Lease

'It's high summer, high comedy too, when Molly drags her amiably bickering family to a rented Tuscan villa for the hols ... She is saddled (and we are delighted) with her randy old tease of a father, a lawyer husband suspected of feeble infidelity and three daughters ... with a cosy fluency of wit, Mortimer charms us into his urbane tangle of clues ...' – *Mail on Sunday*

Like Men Betrayed

Set in London *Like Men Betrayed* is the sinister tale of a middle-aged solicitor and his hopeless attempt both spiritual and real to find his son, and that son's search for his father.

and

Charade
Dunster

BY THE SAME AUTHOR

His acclaimed autobiography

Clinging to the Wreckage

'Enchantingly witty ... should be held as the model for all autobiographies of our times. England would be a poor place without Mr Mortimer' – Auberon Waugh

The creator of Rumpole, the best playwright ever to appear for a murderer at the Central Criminal Court, the son who immortalized a parent in *A Voyage Round My Father*, John Mortimer now gives us his funny, stringent and tender autobiography.

'Exhilarating ... hilarious ... repays reading for its wisdom and depth ... His evocation of his parents is one of the most remarkable things in modern writing' – *Sunday Times*

and two collections of interviews

In Character
Character Parts

BY THE SAME AUTHOR

Rumpole on Trial

In this sparkling collection of Rumpole stories, Horace Rumpole, that stalwart defender of criminals high and low, tormentor of fools and judges, goes fractionally too far and finds himself threatened with the sweet simplicity of home life ...

'Verdict is all in favour of Rumpole ... the old boy is addictive' – Peter Grosvenor in the *Daily Express*

The Rumpole Books

Rumpole of the Bailey
The Trials of Rumpole
Rumpole's Return
Rumpole for the Defence
Rumpole and the Golden Thread
Rumpole's Last Case
Rumpole and the Age of Miracles
Rumpole à la Carte
The First Rumpole Omnibus
The Second Rumpole Omnibus
The Best of Rumpole